True Tales of the Dai-Uy

An adventure novel that observes modern America's most defining late 20th Century events: Vietnam, Nixon's comeback, Watergate, and the Reagan Revolution

By Chuck Winn

Copyright © 2019 Charles J. Winn
All rights reserved
ISBN: 9781076501219

"Using the life of a young soldier returning to college after Vietnam as his backdrop, Chuck Winn provides a detailed, objective look at Watergate and many other aspects of the Nixon Administration. He captures the suspense of the 1976 race between Ford and Reagan for the GOP nomination along with the layers of behind-the-curtain politics involved in the campaign. Winn provides a good picture of the complex, yet carefree life in the 70's through the stories of his main character, Jack Wilson."

- Lisa Marie Macci, Attorney and Host of The Justice Hour radio show, Boca Raton, Florida

"Chuck Winn artfully enables the reader to live the crucial mid-1960s through late-1970s, by effectively recounting political events and policy decisions which adversely impacted our nation, using a Cold War backdrop. Winn also weaves in anti-war and other domestic movements, which other accounts too often intentionally allow to overshadow our intentions and operations in Viet Nam, and understate our nation's enduring quality. Jack, the main character, uses the "establishment" as student and soldier to his selfish advantage, although "doing his bit," clearly contrasting those who simply served honorably without further options. The grey ethical choices made, from those who never came back to the flag burners, can be felt by the readers. Colonel Winn provides an excellent insight to this period and even more so for those without a military background."

-Colonel Walter Riedle, Jr., USA (Ret), Former Foreign Area Officer and Security Assistance Chief

"In an age when many young people may not exhibit much political knowledge prior to the advent of social media, this book acts as a guide post in helping to bridge the history gap. Winn colorfully highlights a time that is very pivotal in order for Americans to better understand our national politics today. His work may very well capture the imagination of not only millennials, but future generations, sparking interest in further research of various topics, political events, and decision-makers like Tricky Dick and Watergate, through Gerald Ford and Ronald Reagan, the likes of which have left an indelible mark on how politics has been engaged for decades now, not to mention such influence on new eras in the ongoing American political saga."

T.J. Harrington, MA, PhD Candidate, Educator, & Former Campaign Professional/Lobbyist

DEDICATION

To Dr. Raymond W. Houghton, PhD; Dr. Herbert Winter, PhD, Dr. Milburn Stone, PhD, Dr. Camella Santoro, PhD; and the Honorable Francis H. Sherman for their mentoring and my academic development.

To Lieutenant General (then-Second Lieutenant) Johnny Mack Riggs, USA (Ret); Major General John R. D'Araujo, USA (Ret); Major General Stewart W. Wallace, USA (Ret); Colonel Arthur L. Holmes, USA (Ret); Colonel Donald Lavimoniere, USA (Ret); Colonel Paul R. Shields, USA (Ret); Colonel John A. Stockhaus, USA (Ret); Colonel Eric W. Braman, USA (Ret); Lieutenant Colonel Robert Swartz, USA (Ret); Lieutenant Colonel George H. Ferris, USA (Ret); Major Kenneth P. Short, USA (Ret); former Captain Michael J. Hayes, USA; former Captain Thomas D. Todd, USA, Sergeant Major Tom Pitts, USA (Ret); Sergeant Major Ronald L. Stull, USA (Ret); First Sergeant Roosevelt Greer, USA (Ret); Platoon Sergeant LeRoy Hawkins, USA (Ret); Staff Sergeant Otis Boor, USA; Sergeant Lew Kelleher, USA, and Sergeant John Verbonitz, USA; for showing me how to lead and soldier.

To General (then Major General) Eric K. Shinseki, USA (Ret), for inculcating a modicum of professional writing ability within me.

To Private First Class Daniel Nelson, USMC, my high school classmate, and all our other great American young warriors who did not return from what President Ronald Reagan described as a noble cause.

TABLE OF CONTENTS

ACKNOWLEDGEMENTS	i
AUTHOR'S FORWARD	ii
1. FORMATIVE YEARS THAT SAVED A PRESIDENCY	1
2. DECISIONS AND CONSEQUENCES	14
3. GRINGO POSSE	29
4. SEARCHING AND AVOIDING SNAKE PITS	39
5. DIVINE PAYBACK	54
6. GETTING SHORT	67
7. BACK HOME	75
8. TO THE PLAINS OF ABRAHAM	84
9. PIPE DREAMS	94
10. A BLOWOUT YEAR	102
11. ELUSIVE VICTORY	118
12. OUT OF OPTIONS	131
13. LAST MAN STANDING	146
14. LEAVING ON A HIGH NOTE	156
15. THE LONG COUNT	172
16. HOLLOW FORCES AND LUSTING HEARTS	194
ABOUT THE AUTHOR	214

ACKNOWLEDGEMENTS

My loving wife Lynn Carol Scott; Jill Shaffer; Colonel Charles J. Coates, USA (Ret); John McGhee; Former Army Captain Tracy Darrow; Honorable Art Argenio; Elizabeth Kates, Esq.; Lisa Marie Macci, Esq.; David Levine, Esq.; Colonel Paul Loschiavo, USMC (Ret); Colonel Ronald Nemeth, USA (Ret); Major Emilio Sanz, USAF (Ret); Former U.S. Senator Bob Smith (R-NH); Eric D. Miller; Command Sergeant Major Bill Hicks, USA (Ret); Colonel Walter Riedle, Jr. USA (Ret); Dr. Michael Carelli, O.D.; Major George W. Davey, USA (Ret); David E. Dupree; Robert Bullwinkle; Robert Blaisdell; Lieutenant Colonel William Gessner, USA (Ret); Honorable Troy McDonald, former Mayor of Stuart, Florida; First Sergeant Ray Carmona, USA (Ret); Deena Messinger; Michele Schirru; Sergeant Major Ronald L. Stull, USA (Ret); Major General Jack D'Araujo, USA (Ret); Ron and Sandy Gagne LeCuivre; Lisa Marino-Atherholt; T. James Harrington; George Andreassi; Honorable James Campo, Mayor of Sewalls Point, FL; Gerald Wysoczynski, Sr.; Michele Schirru; Nola (Stachurski) Zanelli; Robert Vandevender; Colonel David Wellington, USA (Ret): and Marianna (Riordan) Bellizzi

Special thanks to my good friend photo journalist Sevin Bullwinkle for working her magic with the author's photo; and to Cheryl Rosenzweig for her professional assistance in developing the concept for the cover.

AUTHOR'S FORWARD

True Tales of the Dai-Uy is a tool for teaching basic concepts of America's contemporary political system against the backdrop of major events that transpired during that critical window of U.S. History from 1965 through 1977. To keep the reader's attention, I have juxtaposed fictional, often times humorous adventures, and characters who are growing up during that period. Jack Wilson and supporting characters view major national and world events unfold as they actually happened. These include Lyndon Johnson, the Cold War, the Great Society, the impact of increased draft calls and the gradual U.S. escalation in Vietnam; the comeback of Richard Nixon and his demise; a personal Vietnam experience; the 1972 takeover of the Democratic Party by the progressive left; Watergate and Nixon's demise; Jerry Ford's commendable stewardship; the fall of South Vietnam; Reagan's 1976 challenge to Ford; and the election of Jimmy Carter.

Although I do address the tragic impact of the Vietnam War on people's lives, this book is not about the horrors of war. Neither is it a justification of our involvement in that conflict. It does however dispel many myths of revisionist historians that have been accepted by far too many as true. First, America was not engulfed by a nationwide wave of protests during that era. In fact, a majority consensus supported the war until the January 1968 Tet offensive. However, that event only caused a demand for a change in leadership and direction of the war, not a unilateral withdrawal. There were several regions that were hot-beds of anti-war protest, mainly the Northeast and the West Coast. By the time of the April 1970 Cambodian invasion, these had spread onto many campuses in Middle America. Even after the tragedy of Kent State however, a majority never supported a unilateral unconditional withdrawal, as evidenced by Nixon's landslide reelection over George McGovern in 1972. Second, the North Vietnamese communists never defeated the U.S. militarily by driving our forces into the sea. In fact, they had taken such a military beating that they were forced back to the conference table and accepted the Paris Peace accords in January, 1973. The former Republic of Vietnam in the south, lasted two years after U.S. forces withdrew. Our allies had even kept the communists at bay without U.S. ground forces or air power until 1974. Watergate however, emboldened Congress, controlled by Nixon's political opposition, to enact the War Powers Act. This essentially nullified key assurances given by the U.S. Government to the Republic of Vietnam when the Paris Peace Accords were signed.

Vietnam unquestionably shaped America as we know it today, if for no other reason than its direct or indirect impact on every Presidential election from 1964 through 1976. Bad decisions the characters make and the consequences during their entertaining personal misadventures, parallel the major national events that unfold along with the fateful decisions made by America's national leaders during that period. The satirical attitude of the lead character during his time in Vietnam is in no way intended to minimize the great sacrifices made by the gallant young Americans who fought there. Neither is Jack Wilson intended as a role model for encouraging anti-social, rebellious behavior or subverting the system. There is no subtle message that you can beat the system. On the contrary, characters do indeed pay the consequences for their bad choices. What ultimately happens to them will be revealed in the sequel, *True Tales of the Trung-Ta*.

CHAPTER 1

1. FORMATIVE YEARS THAT SAVED A PRESIDENCY

Jack Wilson learned the doctrine of states' rights as a sophomore in high school at a 1964-65 New Years Eve party in Coventry, Rhode Island. That was when he met his friend, mentor and later "business partner" Dan Debre, who lived on an estate that straddled the state line. It was in the western part of town, where his father was the long time care taker. The party was in the summer house on the Connecticut side where the Coventry and Rhode Island State police had no jurisdiction. Jack and Dan knew this because they had read about the Door Rebellion of the 1840s. Thomas Door had fled to the Commonwealth of Massachusetts to escape retribution, after his rebellion had failed against Rhode Island's corrupt government. They also knew that the Connecticut police were not going to drive a meandering 25 mile route that included a five mile slice through Rhode Island, to break up high school beer parties. Dan's folks were the antithesis of disciplinarians, so word spread to every out-of-control teen in Kent County that the best place for a party was at Dan Debre's summer house where "anything goes."

The country had been at peace since the Korean War ended in an uneasy armed truce almost 12 years earlier. Internationally however, a tense Cold War standoff existed between the two post World War II super powers, U.S. and the old Soviet Union. The "peaceful coexistence" policy of Stalin's successor, Soviet Premier Nikita Khrushchev, never renounced developing opportunities to expand communist influence. Fidel Castro had established a communist regime in Cuba as a Soviet client just 90 miles from Miami. In August, 1961, after East Germany erected the Berlin Wall, President Kennedy demonstrated U.S. resolve by reinforcing NATO.

FORMATIVE YEARS THAT SAVED A PRESIDENCY

The world even came to the brink of a nuclear exchange in October, 1962, when Kennedy forced the Soviets to withdraw the ballistic missiles they had installed in Cuba. An attempted communist insurgency was contained in Laos, but a much larger one was growing in South Vietnam. Peaceful coexistence seemed to be continuing under Leonid Brezhnev and Alexi Kosygin, who the Kremlin's ruling Politburo had unexpectedly replaced Khrushchev with in October, 1964. Brezhnev became the Communist Party Secretary and Kosygin the Soviet Premier.

By November, 1963, the U.S. military presence in Vietnam had grown to over 22,000 advisors, who were becoming increasingly involved in combat. President Lyndon Johnson continued the Kennedy domestic and foreign policies. During his 1964 election campaign against hawkish Senator Barry Goldwater, Johnson had pledged that "no American boys would die in a war that Asian boys must fight."

That August however, after an incident involving two U.S. warships and North Vietnamese patrol boats, Johnson responded with overwhelming force. Congress, with little debate, gave this an overwhelming bi-partisan endorsement by enacting "The Gulf of Tonkin Resolution." Nobody from Jack and his high school cohorts to the highest levels of corporate America ever dreamed that this vaguely worded document would become the sole legal basis for an undeclared land war, that stationed over a half million U.S. troops in South Vietnam, with over 58,000 of them being killed.

Dan was articulate, well read, charming, superficially sophisticated in the arts, and quite conversant in international affairs. He could have passed as a cousin of a reigning European royal family. Dan would have to repeat his senior year because he had missed several months of school recovering from an auto accident. Partying with his first

FORMATIVE YEARS THAT SAVED A PRESIDENCY

The climactic 1954 Viet Minh victory over the French at Dien Bien Phu had occurred right after the bloody Korean War. After Truman dropped the first atomic bomb on Hiroshima in August of 1945, Stalin finally honored his Tehran and Yalta commitments by declaring war on Japan. The Soviets fought the Japanese in Manchuria for the month before their surrender. This left Stalin well-postured to "liberate" the Northern half of Korea above the 38th parallel. A "democratic peoples' republic" under Kim IL Sung was subsequently installed. American forces liberated the South and a pro-western government was established. The U.S. soon withdrew leaving only a residual military presence to train a lightly armed South Korean constabulary force.

In June, 1950, the heavily armored, Soviet-trained North Korean Army launched an unprovoked invasion of the South. President Truman went before the United Nations. At the time the Soviets were boycotting it over the seating of the Chinese Communists, who had taken control of the mainland that January. Without the Soviets present to exercise their Security Council veto, the U.S. sponsored resolution easily passed. A U.N. command was established, under U.S. executive agency, with the mission of repelling the invasion. Under General Douglas MacArthur's command, it had virtually annihilated North Korea's army by that November. The Chinese then intervened with hundreds of thousands of "volunteers." Three years of bloody fighting, and the loss of over 38,000 Americans, restored the status quo of the "two Koreas" with an armistice.

The 1954 Geneva Accords withdrew all French forces from Vietnam, and temporarily divided the northern and southern sections of the country at the 17th parallel. Ho Chi Minh established a "peoples' republic" in the North. In the South a pro-western regime was formed under Ngo Dinh Diem, who had been the French puppet Emperor Bao Dai's prime minister. The Accords also provided for free elections to decide the reunification issue by the end of 1956.

CHAPTER 1

Jack articulated current events well enough to easily pass for a college freshman or sophomore with an undecided major. He frequently pontificated about how Earl Warren's Supreme Court's had doomed the Republic to destruction by unleashing the forces of cosmopolitan decadence in its recent "Reynolds v Sims" decision. Thomas Jefferson's statement *"I view great cities as pestilential to the morals, the health, and the liberties of man"* was the basis of Jack's prognosis. "Reynolds v Sims" forced states to apportion both houses of their legislatures strictly on a population basis. State constitutions had previously provided for mini-federal systems that gave sparsely populated counties representation, but additional seats to those containing metropolitan areas.

Jack could also expound intelligently about foreign affairs. He was well read into the history of America's Vietnam involvement. It began in 1946, when President Truman made the decision to support France in reestablishing a neo-colonial government there. Truman's motives were heavily influenced by the need for French support in highly unstable post-war Europe. Because Stalin left Red Army formations in place after they had defeated Nazi forces from the East, the early Cold War years saw every East European country fall into the Soviet orbit. This shaped the not unrealistic perception of communism as not only a brutal threat to freedom, but also a monolithic global one directed by Moscow.

During the fifties however, in countries like Yugoslavia and China that had not been occupied by the Red Army, communism taken on a national flavor. The Viet Minh, Ho Chi Minh's home grown brand, evolved as a guerilla movement against the Japanese occupiers who had displaced the French during World War II. Ho and his guerillas had even been an American ally and aided downed U.S. airmen.

FORMATIVE YEARS THAT SAVED A PRESIDENCY

"rum-running" trips by seniors to and from New York where the drinking age was 18.

What Jack liked most about this business though, was that it brought him into contact with girls who were a year or two older. "They're more anatomically mature," as he put it. Bright, but a selective underachiever, it took the Vice Principal reading him Rhode Island's minimum statutory attendance requirement for advancement in the middle of his Junior year to break his streak of excessive truancy. Although bored with, and not challenged by school, Jack was, none the less, very status conscious. He would have rather died than to have not graduated on time.

Jack was already a chain smoker, but did isometrics and lifted weights to give the impression of being in great physical shape. A believer in the phrase "bare minimum," after playing the required number of quarters to earn a letter, he abruptly quit the football team. He resented the coach constantly holding up as standards to emulate, his team mates who were 19 pushing 20, but still playing high school football as sophomores and juniors. The coach, at least, learned a lesson about managing his players better. He ensured that no other mediocre player ever again got enough quarters in to earn a letter until very late in the season.

Jack lied about his age to the older girls he dated, and had even purchased a 1965 class ring directly from Balfour rather than order one with his own class of 1967. He much preferred taking dates to rustic western Rhode Island dives on weekends, over high school hang outs. He even had a cosmopolitan dive called "The Crystal Tap" in a blighted district on the fringes of the East Side of Providence where Brown and Rhode Island School of Design undergrads, or at least those claiming to be, frequented. To impress really special dates with his culture and sophistication, Jack would take them there for "after dinner drinks" following a movie at the Avon and hamburgers at the restaurant across the street.

CHAPTER 1

senior class trumped the drudgery of make-up work in the Trig and Chemistry that Dan brushed off as "trade school for technicians with shirts and ties." Yet Dan still received a national current events honors award that year. "Triple-play Dan" had other bad luck. He had recently been caught by two girls he'd been dating simultaneously, because he was pursuing a third one who was "better looking and drove a better car." By the end of his first senior year, Dan's reputation had even filtered down to the freshmen, forever ending the aura of his well-earned varsity letters. Although at 18 he was toast in his mid-sized school, in little Rhode Island, especially in Kent County, there were plenty of other close-by high schools to find dates.

Jack had always looked several years older than his age, even though he was one of the youngest in his class. At 15 he could easily pass for 18 or 19. In the days before photo ID's, Dan showed Jack how easy it was to forge the few documents that facilitated him getting served and established in several area package stores. Under the laws of the State of Rhode Island and Providence Plantations, an establishment protected its liquor license by maintaining a "minor book". The book contained forms filled out by individuals of questionable age, that documented they had produced valid identification when challenged.

No fools, Dan and Jack patronized establishments in Coventry where they actually lived. Liquor stores were easily accessible in neighboring West Warwick, West Greenwich, Warwick and East Greenwich. Soon they became "business partners", founding what they called "Kent County Beverage Distributors." They were popular on the high school weekend party circuit, and especially around holidays, prom and graduation time. By not hitting the same store twice, multiple runs to liquor stores could easily be made during an evening without arousing suspicion. Parents and police all thought the beer and alcohol for these parties came from

CHAPTER 1

A number of factors influenced and reinforced President Eisenhower's decision to support South Vietnam's boycott of those elections, and to provide Diem military aid. Following their takeover of China, Mao Tse Dung's communists had ruthlessly exterminated millions of small land owners. In East Germany in 1953, and again Hungary in 1956, the Soviet Union had brutally suppressed popular anti-communist uprisings. In Vietnam itself, millions had fled to the South as the French withdrew. If a communist takeover of South Vietnam wasn't challenged, very soon one country after another would fall like dominoes. Eisenhower's troop commitment however, never exceeded 700 training advisors.

Jack's flair for the written word came in helpful during an experience with the juvenile justice system. After being caught shoplifting a sports jacket on a dare from a mill outlet, he found himself in family court before a judge, who had reviewed his school record. Shocked at being abruptly silenced by the judge, Jack was put on indefinite probation, had his license suspended and was ordered to write reports on college level books every week. Failure to comply would immediately land him at the notorious Rhode Island Training School for Boys. Jack was shaken but knew what the judge wanted. He submitted his first book report accompanied by an eloquent and contrite letter that so impressed the judge that within two weeks Jack's probation was lifted and his license was restored.

Jack's solution on school attendance was to show up just late enough to be recorded absent rather than tardy on the daily attendance report from the Principal's office. This still gave him credit for the day. If he kept a low profile, Jack could skip out of classes he found boring without his teachers reporting him because they would assume from the report he was absent. Jack's real motivation was his discovery that if he lied about his age and worked a second shift job in a textile plant, he could make three times the minimum wage that his class mates who worked flipping hamburgers or as sales clerks did. The classes he skipped were usually the two at the end of the day, one of which was phys ed. Since he worked 30 hours a week, he was driven more by a desire for rest than rebellion. Years later, after the Freedom of Information Act was passed, Jack was amazed to see himself categorized as a "severe disciplinary problem" in his records.

Ryan was Jack's friend who lived in the same neighborhood. Ryan wasn't quite in the same intellectual class as Jack, but had the looks and television-inspired savoir faire to eventually charm his way into the sectarian college in Providence that had been the Irish and Italian immigrants' answer to Brown University. Ryan was the archetypical baby boomer whose parents bought him everything, including the new 1965 Mustang he liked to drive at excessive rates of speed. Ryan also always seemed to have incredible luck.

In early November, Jack rode shotgun as Ryan successfully fled from the Providence Police while speeding though fashionable East Side neighborhoods, often times flooring it through narrow residential streets, without a scratch. Overreacting to a police cruiser he spotted, assuming that they had "staked out" the liquor store Jack had just exited with three six packs, Ryan impulsively decided to "out run the cops." He drew their attention when he floored the Mustang about a block from the liquor store on Gano Street.

Ryan continued down Elmgrove to Blackstone Boulevard, sometimes reaching 75 to 80 miles an hour. When the police were out of sight, Jack hurled the three, unopened six packs of Budweiser out the passenger window, littering several well kept lawns. He had his phony I.D.s out, ready for burning, just in case the police reappeared. When they were in Pawtucket, Jack told Ryan to cross into the town of South Attleboro, in the Commonwealth of Massachusetts, to get on Interstate 95 for about 10 miles and then head west. In case the Providence Police had radioed in a description of the

CHAPTER 1

Mustang, they could avoid detection by crossing back into Rhode Island near Pascoag.

Enjoying how it made Jack flinch, Ryan buried the needle after they were back in Rhode Island along the rural Route 102, before stopping in Foster. The $1.75 they had left was enough for Jack to pick up a six pack of Krueger and a pack of Marlboros at one of the "re-fill stores", used for the parties at Debre's summer house, and where they ended up. Since everyone there was with a date, they left after a beer, gave away the rest and drove back to their houses in a new development off Route 117, arriving shortly after midnight. After telling his parents what a dull night it had been, Jack spent about a half hour watching TV in the family room with them before going to bed.

About two weeks after getting his driver's license on his sixteenth birthday, Jack totaled his parents' 1963 Falcon Sprint convertible. Earlier that December afternoon, Jack, Dan and Ryan had made plans to meet some girls at their high school basketball game. The girls were from the neighboring town of West Warwick, whose team would be playing theirs. After deciding to first drive out to Dan's place in western Coventry to eat, they meandered into Foster on the way to pick up some hamburgers from a diner. Jack then bought a couple of 16 ounce six-packs and a pint of blackberry brandy from an adjacent liquor store to "wash them down" while they ate them at Dan's.

Since Dan's parents were out somewhere, they finished the burgers and beverages in the living room. This avoided having to freeze while waiting for the kerosene space heater to warm up the summer house. When Dan's parents returned, he decided to pass on the basketball game. Jack then headed out with Ryan to drive the 15 mile rural highway to the Town's high school.

FORMATIVE YEARS THAT SAVED A PRESIDENCY

As he was regaining consciousness, the last thing Jack remembered was driving 80 miles per hour with the AM radio blaring "I'm a Man" by the Yardbirds. Sensing the smell of an electrical fire he rolled over on the asphalt onto his back and looked up at the sparks and flame from a transformer at the top of a utility pole. About 50 yards away the Falcon was turned over on the pan-caked convertible top. Jack staggered up to his feet, his shoulder broken and blood oozing from the top of his foot that had been sliced off as he flew through the windshield. Brushing off little cubes of safety glass and immediately realizing what had happened, he pulled his wallet with the fake IDs out of his back pocket and threw it into the woods with his good arm.

Jack was relieved to see his friend Ryan out of the car, but alarmed by his moaning and laying semi-conscious on a shoulder of the road with blood all over his face. He pulled him away from the live utility wire lying on the road from one of the poles he had snapped. Besides breaking his jaw, Ryan's chin had received a deep gash when he flew through his side of the windshield. This accounted for all the excessive blood, which made it appear that Ryan had a severe brain injury.

The subsequent accident investigation revealed that the car had hit two trees, a brick wall and a telephone pole before flipping over and skidding 100 feet on the convertible top. Jack always assumed he and Ryan ejected through the windshield after it hit the first tree. This was a decade before mandatory seat belt laws, which in this case had been a blessing for both of them.

Jack and Ryan spent about a week in separate hospitals and fully recovered. About 8 months later however, Ryan's folks saw an opportunity for financial security by suing the Wilson family's insurance company for "loss of their son's continued services in their old age due to the permanent disabilities he had sustained from John Paul Wilson's reckless

CHAPTER 1

driving." A real joke, since other than the 4 weeks that Ryan had worked with Jack on a summer construction job spreading gravel onto a tar road from the back of a truck, Ryan had never worked a day in his life. Neither did he do any household chores.

Jack's parents' insurance company requested him to go to Ryan's parents' lawyer's office in Providence for a deposition. Surprisingly Jack's parents didn't insist on being present with him. All Jack's father told him before he drove up to Providence was "Tell the truth but be brief. Only give information that directly answers the questions they ask. Don't volunteer any additional information. Whatever you do, don't ask them any questions like "What do you mean?" Just say "I don't understand."

Here is a summary of Jack's testimony.

ATTORNEY: Where were you coming from?

JACK: "From my friend Dan's house. We had dinner and watched some TV after dropping him off after school."

ATTORNEY: "Did you have anything alcoholic to drink?"

JACK: "Yes, a few cans of beer." *(Jack's rationale was that a partial answer wasn't a lie, and it was better than risking detailed follow-up questions that might require him to reveal the exact quantity he had had to drink.)*

ATTORNEY: "Where did you get the beer?"

JACK: "It was there when we got there." *(Again, a technically factual and therefore a truthful answer. The beer had arrived at Dan's house when they did so it was indeed "there when they got there".)*

ATTORNEY: "Where were you heading?"

JACK: "To a basketball game at the high school."

ATTORNEY: "Were you speeding?"

JACK: "I was generally observing the speed limit but on the straight section I did get up to over 65 and didn't see the curve soon enough to slow down." *(A truthful answer since he was not specifically asked how fast he was going at the time of the accident.)*

The rest of the questions were focused on what had happened at the scene during the aftermath and the injuries he and Ryan had sustained Even Ryan said that Jack had probably saved his life by pulling him away from that live transmission wire. Jack had also insisted that the first ambulance that arrived treat Ryan. So Jack had finished his deposition in less than a half hour. He never heard another word about the law suit which the attorneys apparently settled with his folks' insurance company.

Now in his senior year, Jack had transitioned into a pattern of a model student and spent most of his free time with his steady girlfriend Suzanne, a beautiful but somewhat naive girl about a year and a half older, who "most indubitably" met his "anatomically mature" standard. He decided to pay a visit to his old buddy Dan, who he hadn't seen for a few months. Dan was now living in a dive apartment in Providence where he attended the new public Junior College located in an old manufacturing plant. Now 19, in the spring of 1966 as troop levels in Vietnam were escalating, Dan was playing it double safe. He not only had a student deferment, but also a part time job in a screw machine shop with defense contracts, for a fall back.

Jack's only concern with the draft at 16 was to obtain a draft card with an alias to use as back up identification for

CHAPTER 1

buying booze. That day, both he and Dan were short of cash, with just barely enough for some hotdogs from the New York System on Smith Street. Luckily for Jack, it was early on a Saturday afternoon, so there was plenty of beer in the refrigerator because Dan's college roommates would not be returning for the weekly party until hours later. As he popped open a Budweiser, Jack began his account of the morning in the lawyer's office. "You'll be impressed by this truly splendid and magnificent account of the accident I gave them." "What marvelous bullshit!" replied Dan. After going through two six packs it was early evening. A friend of Dan's arrived at the apartment and took Jack to get Suzanne so she could drive his car home in case he couldn't sleep if off at Dan's apartment by the end of the evening.

Nobody knows for certain, but decades later Jack claimed his deposition probably "saved a Presidency." Surely such legal reasoning must have ended up in an ambulance chaser's case law textbook that William Jefferson Clinton studied in law school. Jack's legal reasoning sure seemed like it could have been the basis for Clinton crafting that memorable response in his civil deposition as the President of the United States, forever immortalized on video *"It depends upon what is, is!"*

2. DECISIONS AND CONSEQUENCES

As Jack's junior year was concluding, his high school vice principal felt that an example had to be made to keep the "Jack Wilson system" from spreading. His grades, although not spectacular, weren't nearly bad enough to make him repeat the year. The solution therefore, was to expel him after finals to deny him the privileges of basking in the status of being in the new senior class during the week that remained after the Class of 1966 graduation ceremony.

The principal assured Jack "You're welcome to return in September as a senior in good standing, but under no circumstances will you return for the remainder of this school year." Appeals by Jack's parents were to no avail. That was fine with Jack because the post-prom and graduation parties were very demanding on his Kent County Beverages responsibilities. He also loved the acceptance by the recent graduates at the parties he procured the beer for. It was at one of these the previous year that Jack met Suzanne, who had invited him to her senior prom.

Late in the summer before his senior year, Jack met Fred Shannon, a local politician running for the legislature. Jack's business partner Dan introduced him while the two were drinking in a dive just over the town line. They both were interested in politics, but also realized that having a friend who was an elected state official could be very helpful in situations that involved the authorities. Shannon had known Dan as a hockey coach. Fred was very conservative for a Democrat, but went on to dispatch the local Democratic establishment's primary candidate.

CHAPTER 2

When Dan started at the junior college in the fall, Jack began his senior year and continued volunteering on Shannon's campaign. He assisted with writing radio ads and press releases. Fred Shannon won decisively by bucking the Republican wave of November, 1966. All of the local Democrats were wiped out, except for the state senator and the other state representative who squeaked by on the absentee ballot count.

Since 1965, the U.S. troop buildup in Vietnam had continued in gradual increments. When 1967 began, over 450,000 were stationed there. President Johnson reassured the public that this was "only temporary until our South Vietnamese allies were organized and trained up sufficiently to take the lead." American casualties had also begun to reach 150 per week, but the U.S. Command in Saigon reported that enemy body counts were 10 times that many. The communists could not sustain these losses and would soon abandon their aggression. A free Vietnam would justify the American sacrifice. Administration spokesmen cited the fall of 1965, when the Indonesians demonstrated how unpopular the communists were in Asia. A countercoup overthrew the Maoists who had heavily infiltrated President Sukarno's government. The new regime, led by pro-U.S. General Suharto, abruptly reversed that country's drift towards Beijing.

Jack's high school class of 1967 had experienced the tragedy of President John F. Kennedy's assassination as freshmen, but the Country seemed to have returned to normal. The post war expansion of the manufacturing economy continued providing well paying blue collar jobs, not only for high school graduates, but even those with GEDs. Jack and his classmates were heavily influenced by their fathers who had served in World War II, and accepted the possibility of being drafted for Vietnam. The draft could be deferred, or even avoided entirely, by going to college. Several from the Class of 1965, after discovering that high school deferments

DECISIONS AND CONSEQUENCES

were good until age 20, did two senior years. Two even did three senior years. After dropping out just before the end of the previous two Mays, they finally graduated with Jack.

Employment in defense industries like General Dynamics's Electric Boat in nearby Groton Connecticut also provided deferments. Many of Jack's friends enlisted shortly after graduating. The star athlete from the Class of 1966, who joined the Marines with a dozen fellow classmates the summer after graduation, lost both legs. Dan Debre's boyhood friend, Bob Gerhard, enlisted for four years in the Navy for guaranteed duty as a corpsman at the nearby Newport Naval Hospital. After 18 months however, Bob found himself attached to a Marine Corps rifle company as a combat medic in Vietnam, where he routinely went on combat patrols with his platoon. In addition to experiencing enemy ambushes on combat patrols, Bob also withstood the six month siege of Khe Sanh. Danny Nelson, a member of Jack's class, was killed in Vietnam within two years after he had enlisted in the Marines after graduating.

On June 14, 1967, Governor Ronald Reagan signed a "therapeutic abortion act" that legalized abortions in California under certain circumstances, the second state after Colorado to do so. Jack's respectable finish of his last year of high school with a 3.2 GPA was not enough to make up for his abysmal academic record during the previous two. Especially problematic were the principal's comments about him being truant for almost as many days as he had attended as a sophomore and junior. His finish in the "upper part of the bottom half" of his class was not even close to being competitive for acceptance at one of Rhode Island's two public universities.

Jack's parents however, saw an opportunity to give him the benefit of structure and discipline at a military junior college in Georgia. Since Jack was still 17, he saw no alternative to complying. After duly reporting that

CHAPTER 2

September, on the heels of the "Summer of Love," Jack went AWOL after 3 days. He didn't have a problem with serving in the military, but college was for partying and preparing for the business world, not marching around in white pants every day, followed by playing good housekeeping in dorms organized like barracks each night. The college declined his parents' request to "lock him in a room until he saw the light," so Jack returned home.

His dad, Jack senior, and his mother, Lynnette, had worked hard to achieve solid middle class success. Both had come from Polish ethnic upbringings in Grand Rapids, Michigan. Jack senior had served in both World War II and Korea. He recently had started a second career after retiring from the Army as a major. Lynnette was an R.N. During the Korean War, Jack senior had been captured and held by the Chinese Communist Forces as a prisoner of war for nearly three years. The Korean War had a more evident impact on Lynnette, who frequently drank heavily in the evenings, and especially on holidays.

After a good snoot full, Lynnette could easily have given the Joan Crawford character played by Faye Dunaway in the movie "Mommy Dearest" a very competitive run for the money. Jack senior, was quiet and reserved but had a very subtle sarcastic wit, and was a master at head games he must have mastered with his communist Chinese captors. Lynnette was exceptionally well read, a good money manager and very generous. Her insecurities however, abnormally manifested themselves in putting others down. Neither Jack senior, nor Lynnette, could ever admit their own personal shortcomings.

When it came to Jackie, as they called Jack junior, any trouble he got into was always because of the bad influence of others. Naturally, Jack's closest friends were always targets. Dan Debre was second in Lynnette's eyes only to Charles Manson, especially on those several late evenings when they had to pick up Jack in a blacked out drunken state.

DECISIONS AND CONSEQUENCES

Jack however, would have made his decision that a glorified military prep school was not for him regardless of who his friends were. Unfortunately, the second night after his return from the military school while he was staying at Suzanne's parent's house, Lynette called in a drunken rage. "No whore that Debre pimped out to my son is going to ruin his life" were the last words that poor Suzanne ever heard from Lynette when she abruptly hung up. Since Lynnette and Jack senior never admitted mistakes, reconciling with Suzanne would take a near miracle.

General Westmoreland's reports from Saigon indicated the war would certainly end within the next 16 months, before Jack turned 19. So Jack's biggest concern remained making enough money to take Suzanne out, and for the six packs and sacks of New York System hotdogs to bring to the next party. His former Kent County Beverages partner, Dan Debre, was entering his second year at the Rhode Island Junior College. Kent County Beverages dissolved at the end of Jack's junior year when he began seeing Suzanne almost daily.

Under parental pressure Jack then enrolled in Roger Williams College, a private diploma mill that had recently expanded into a four year college. It was temporarily housed in the Providence YMCA so he saw it as a joke, and spent much of the semester hanging around at the nearby apartment that Dan Debre and his roommates rented. Jack was also cross enrolled in the ROTC program at Providence College where he pledged and was accepted into the Pershing Rifles fraternity, just prior to dropping out that December.

The following month, the North Vietnamese Tet Offensive and the possibility of the draft however, prompted Jack to enroll at the University of Rhode Island's extension for the spring semester. While carrying a full course load, he continued working part time as a screen printer in a textile plant. The owners apparently liked Jack. Whenever he called in with "car problems" after a night of partying, they would

CHAPTER 2

send their son to pick him up. Jack enrolled in more courses at the University's summer school, but fishing, the beach and local politics distracted him. That summer President Johnson signed Senator Ted Kennedy's Selective Service reform that had the major feature of - DRAFTING 19 YEAR OLDS FIRST!

Richard Nixon had been Eisenhower's Vice President before narrowly losing the Presidency to John F. Kennedy in 1960. In 1962 he had been written off after his famous "you won't have Nixon to kick around anymore" press conference after losing the California governor's race. He then became a successful corporate attorney, and loyally campaigned for the doomed 1964 Goldwater Campaign that many GOP establishment leaders abandoned. Nixon's leading role in the 1966 mid-term elections, where Republicans made a major recovery from their catastrophic 1964 losses, reestablished him as a leading contender.

The GOP eastern establishment, led by New York Governor Nelson Rockefeller, organized behind Michigan Governor George Romney. A former American Motors President, Romney had survived the 1964 Johnson landslide in Democratic Michigan. He led a generally successful administration, although he had to request federal troops to restore control during the 1967 Detroit riots. Romney fatally damaged his campaign during a press conference that fall. Attempting to explain his previous support of Johnson's Vietnam policy he stated that during his visit to that country "I allowed the generals to brainwash me."

On January 30, 1968, Vietnamese communist forces launched their nationwide Tet Offensive, blatantly violating a Vietnamese Lunar New Year holiday truce. Their objective of a spontaneous nationwide uprising to topple the South Vietnamese government failed. Tet was an equally disastrous military defeat, from which the communists took years to recover. Strategically however, Tet caused a seismic shift in

DECISIONS AND CONSEQUENCES

U.S. public opinion away from supporting the Administration's conduct of the war.

The "credibility gap" between years of Defense Secretary Robert McNamara's rosy projections of victory within sight, and the true situation on the ground was patently obvious. President Johnson had announced McNamara's departure in December, ostensibly to head The World Bank. This was shortly after Senator Eugene McCarthy announced his challenge to Johnson as a peace candidate. Tet however, proved decisive in propelling McCarthy to embarrassing Johnson with a near upset in the New Hampshire primary. Always the opportunist, Senator Robert Kennedy finally entered the race.

On March 1st, Clark M. Clifford had been sworn in as Secretary of Defense, succeeding Robert McNamara, the Administration's manager and chief salesman of the war. In his memoirs, Clifford gave the following account of his initial days in office, during what would be America's most deadly year in Vietnam. *"I wanted to know, what is the military plan for victory in Vietnam? There was no military plan," Clifford said. "The Joint Chiefs said, 'What we must do is just continue to carry on as we are, and we believe that the attrition ultimately will become unbearable from the enemy's standpoint.' So, I say, 'How long?' 'We don't know.' 'Six months?' 'Oh, no, it can't be done in that period.' 'A year?' 'Well, no.' 'Two years, three years, four years?' Well, nobody knows. Here's this kind of bottomless pit. We could just be there year after year after year, sacrificing 10,000 American boys a year, and it just didn't add up."*

Robert S. McNamara, the chief "whiz kid" of JFK's "best and brightest" had for six years forced Harvard MBA-based systems on the Defense Department. Whether deliberate or self-delusional, he manipulated the statistics from those systems to paint a false picture of the situation in Vietnam to Congress and the American people. This ultimately resulted

CHAPTER 2

in 525,000 U.S. troops being engaged in combat. When McNamara left the Pentagon, 25,000 Americans had already died in that war for which he never even had a military plan for victory. This alone earned him the justifiable scorn of generations of historians to come.

In a March 31st address to the nation, President Johnson signaled a major shift in Vietnam strategy by announcing a halt in the bombing of North Vietnam, except for the area immediately north of the demilitarized zone. The major surprise however, came at the end of the address when he unequivocally withdrew as a candidate for reelection. Vice President Hubert Humphrey soon entered the race, with a slight edge as the establishment favorite. Only about half of the states had Presidential primaries, and most of those didn't bind their delegates to the winners.

Bobby Kennedy's strategy was to decisively beat McCarthy in the remaining primaries. He could then make a strong case to the bosses, who heavily influenced the caucuses that chose most of the delegates, that he was the strongest Democrat. On April 4th, tragedy struck when Dr. Martin Luther King, the era's leading Civil Rights leader, was assassinated in Memphis. Rioting soon erupted throughout major cities, including the Nation's capital.

The "New Nixon" reinforced his link in public memories to the peace and prosperity of the Eisenhower years. His experience and intelligence made Nixon one of the best prepared Presidential candidates in history. He had performed superbly on the international stage, by bravely staring down a violent mob in Caracas, and later by besting Khrushchev at the 1959 Moscow International Exhibition's "kitchen debates." However, Nixon still had difficulty shaking his take-no-prisoners ultra-partisan aggressive image from previous campaigns that had earned his "Tricky Dick" moniker. Liberals had never forgiven him for the tactics he used to take down Alger Hiss for giving State Department

DECISIONS AND CONSEQUENCES

secrets to the Soviets. Some even compared him to the late Senator Joseph McCarthy.

Many Democratic centrists, hawkish union members, as well as liberals, viewed Senator Kennedy as the most electable, especially with Wallace's third party threat. Kennedy had broken with Johnson over Vietnam, but had impeccable anti-communist credentials, as the top advisor to his brother on Berlin and Cuba. Eight years earlier he had also served as counsel to Senator Joseph McCarthy's investigating Committee on Government Operations.

George Corley Wallace had been a racial moderate. In 1962 however, he reinvented himself as an arch segregationist to win the Alabama governorship. Shortly after taking office in 1963, he forced a confrontation with the Kennedy Administration by attempting to block desegregation at the University of Alabama. His surprisingly strong run against Lyndon Johnson in several northern Democratic primaries in 1964 had revealed an emerging white backlash in the suburbs. Unable to succeed himself in 1966, Wallace successfully ran his wife Lurleen as a surrogate.

Toward the end of 1967, Wallace launched his anticipated third party bid. After pausing to mourn Lurleen's death from cancer in May, 1968, he resumed his campaign. Wallace could easily win electoral votes in a few southern states like Strom Thurman did in 1948, but could also spoil it for the Democrats and Republicans in many "must win" northern ones. His hawkish Vice Presidential choice, retired Air Force General Curtis Le May, had even advocated bombing Hanoi "back to the stone age."

McCarthy upset Kennedy in Oregon, who came back in California with a 53 to 47% win. This regained enough momentum to at least force him onto the ticket's second spot, if he could not beat Humphrey outright. Tragedy struck again

CHAPTER 2

however, right after Kennedy gave his June 5th victory speech when he was fatally shot by Sirhan Sirhan, a Palestinian immigrant. Late that July, Nixon prevailed on the first ballot at the Republican convention in Miami. He defeated a last minute movement to stop him, fueled by the late entries of Governors Nelson Rockefeller and Ronald Reagan of California, aided by favorite sons. Maryland Governor Spiro Agnew was Nixon's surprise pick for the number two spot.

Concurrent with all the national political activity was a local primary campaign, into which Jack and Dan had injected themselves. Their friend State Rep. Fred Shannon, an upset winner two years earlier, remained at odds with the Democratic regulars with his outspokenness. Fred now was not only challenging the local state senator who had barely won the last time, but also running an entire slate of primary challengers. Dan joined it as a Town Council candidate with Jack managing his "front porch" campaign. The two enjoyed scheming about leveraging Dan's Council seat in the event that the two local parties evenly split the other four. Dan was too infatuated with a new girlfriend to do much campaigning. Both proved themselves adept manipulators of the local media however, with a press release endorsing GOP Governor John Chafee. Another one, that took a slap at the National Guard, was so controversial even Rep. Shannon disavowed it.

Events that had been unfolding in Czechoslovakia during the year were being interpreted as signs of a thaw in the Cold War. After students had protested against the Stalinist Czech leader Anton Novotny the previous December, Brezhnev refused to send in Soviet troops. In January, Alexander Dubcek replaced Novotny as Communist Party First Secretary. In April Dubcek unveiled his new program of "Communism with a human face". It instituted significant economic reforms, but also far reaching political reforms, including the rehabilitation of dissidents, increased freedom

DECISIONS AND CONSEQUENCES

of speech and the press; and even allowed non-communist political parties.

Even though Czechoslovakia remained in the Warsaw Pact, Brezhnev soon announced that the Soviet Union would not allow Eastern European countries to abandon their communist systems, even if it meant another World War! On August 20, 1968, the "Brezhnev Doctrine" was inaugurated with an invasion of 500,000 Soviet-led Warsaw Pact troops into Czechoslovakia. Dubcek, was soon replaced by hard liner Gustav Husac. As in the Hungarian uprising of 1956, the U.S. and its Western allies did nothing but protest. Stripped of his seat in parliament and expelled from the Communist Party, Dubcek was shunted into a Forestry Service position, but not executed like his 1956 Hungarian counterpart, Imre Nagy, had been.

In late August, Humphrey, who had not entered a single primary, was the favorite going into a chaotic Democratic convention in Chicago. Senator George McGovern, attempting to keep Kennedy's delegates together, joined McCarthy as another Humphrey opposition candidate. Thousands of their youthful supporters had converged upon Chicago hoping to influence the delegates. McCarthy and McGovern however, were both too far left for the Democratic establishment.

Extreme leftists had infiltrated the mostly peaceful demonstrators and provoked a severe police crackdown. Images of the Chicago "rioters" played well into the law and order themes of both Nixon and Wallace. Humphrey seemed doomed as he addressed the delegates as the Democratic nominee. Two years later, seven of the most extreme agitators would dominate headlines for months with their courtroom antics as "The Chicago Seven" during their federal conspiracy trial. Back, in Coventry Rhode Island, the organization regulars routed Fred Shannon and his insurgent Democrats in the primary.

CHAPTER 2

Jack had blown his first year of college, but he had a decent "Plan B" when his Draft Board reclassified him as immediately available for military service. By volunteering to be drafted, and then for a lot of long service schools, he could run out the clock as the war wound down. When Private Wilson reported to Fort Dix that September, the Paris Peace talks had been going on for months. Jack kept up with current events during basic training by listening to radio news and reading newspapers. Humphrey was eroding Wallace's union support and closing on Nixon. Then, Johnson's "Halloween Surprise" of a bombing halt made it too close to call.

Jack's platoon had guard duty election night, but he was able to watch some returns on TV. Nixon led the popular vote all night, but Wallace had won five states. At 7:00 A.M. on November 5th, as his platoon left mess hall for the rifle range, a constitutional crisis from an Electoral College deadlock looked possible. Shortly after 10:00 A.M. however, the company commander interrupted a class on the M-16 rifle being given to the unit in the bleachers on a rifle range to announce that Richard M. Nixon was now the President-elect. He had barely edged Humphrey in the popular vote, with each polling 43 percent, but Nixon's decisive electoral vote majority was widely accepted. The framers of the Constitution had known what they were doing.

True to plan, Jack volunteered for a leadership school that extended his radio telegraph operator's course at Fort Huachuca, Arizona. Then he applied for officer candidate school, knowing that accepted OCS applicants could not be reassigned anywhere while awaiting class dates. That same policy also put them in leadership positions while awaiting orders. After finishing his course in January, Jack became an acting platoon sergeant with an open pass. His evenings were now his own. As long as he was standing tall in front of his

25

DECISIONS AND CONSEQUENCES

platoon at 0530, Jack was free to roam Sierra Vista, Tucson or even Nogales, Mexico.

Several nights each month, Jack was required to perform a tour as Charge-of-Quarters. This duty required monitoring the phone as the first sergeant's representative in the company orderly room after duty hours, and supervising trainees on details. Jack was far too busy to take any college courses. His "great responsibilities serving the Nation defending the Country" entitled him to have some fun. That line obviously still worked with Suzanne since she had loaned him part of the money to fly home for Christmas. At least Jack's travel allowances paid for his second leave before starting Infantry OCS at Fort Benning, Georgia. Having just turned 19, he could settle down with Suzanne later in the year after he graduated.

Wartime requirements for combat arms lieutenants far exceeded what the sources of college ROTC programs and West Point could produce. The OCS program, which trained enlisted men to become officers, was expanded to make up the difference. Huge numbers of those ideally suited to be officers by virtue of education and maturity were riding deferments in graduate schools, opting for the other Services, or joining the National Guard and Reserves. As an expedient, the Army relaxed admission requirements to high school graduates who could pass an exam that was equivalent of scoring a combined 1100 on a SAT.

A typical OCS class was comprised of recent college grads, career sergeants and an assortment of draftees and enlistees ranging from ditch diggers, to college drop outs, to PhDs. Infantry OCS was a six month, physically and mentally demanding course. Commanding a 40-man platoon in combat required the ability to operate under pressure, and a mastery of tactics and weapons. Deliberate intense pressure designed to break the candidates caused an attrition rate of nearly 50 percent. A new OCS officer was usually more

CHAPTER 2

technically proficient than his ROTC or even West Point counterpart in a tactical environment. However, the ones who were 19 and 20 occasionally had to overcome maturity issues in garrison.

In August, Dan had finished a year at Willimantic State Teacher's College in Connecticut and was transferring to Rhode Island College (RIC) in the fall. He had driven up to Woodstock with a couple from his "ReJec-tech" days. The found themselves sitting 200 yards from the stage as joints passed from blanket to blanket. A month earlier, Jack had been able to watch Neil Armstrong walk on the moon on live TV while on a detail cleaning the pool table in his company's day room. Non-appropriated funds paid for these facilities intended for use by the enlisted members of a unit. The officer candidates were the enlisted troops who justified the funding, but only the TAC officers ever used them. The TV was probably kept on during cleaning details so that the time could be counted as "troop usage."

Just prior to OCS graduation, a disturbing incident was discussed in a military justice class. A Lieutenant named Calley had just been held beyond his separation date at Fort Benning for a General Courts Martial. During an offensive operation on March 16, 1968, Calley had allegedly ordered his platoon to kill dozens of unarmed noncombatants in a Vietnamese village called MyLai. An officer's fundamental duty was preventing those types of incidents, and failing to do so would bring major consequences.

On September 19, 1969, Jack graduated at "the top half of the bottom third of his class". Even finishing last was no shame, since half of those who started didn't even make it. "At least I came close to setting a record for total demerits" bragged Jack to his parents' chagrin. All of the graduates were highly proficient in small unit tactics; and the employment of every tactical weapons system in the U.S. inventory.

DECISIONS AND CONSEQUENCES

What saved Jack from washing out, were his tactical, organizational and planning skills that he articulated in operations orders quite well. He could also write these tactical operations directives for units up to even battalion level. The Infantry School tactics instructor who ran the live fire platoon attack problem, cited Jack's field order as the best he had ever seen. This frustrated Jack's first TAC officer's attempt to eliminate him on technical proficiency grounds. However, the "sissy college frat boy," which was Jack's epithet for him, continued to give him excessive demerits for dust on his furniture and other housekeeping violations. However, that only got Jack set back three weeks behind his starting class.

Jack's commission issued under the Presidential seal didn't necessarily confer mature thinking. He didn't even consider applying for opportunities for advanced schooling followed by an 18-month stabilized assignment. All this required was committing to one more year of service, which would have been ideal for someone planning to get married. A few hundred dollars in temporary duty allowances would also have been paid each month during that schooling. Jack's ego was eager to take charge. He opted instead for a two year obligated volunteer contract with a first assignment as the second-in-command of a basic training unit at Fort Gordon, Georgia. Orders to Vietnam would likely follow six months later.

3. GRINGO POSSE

The old U.S. Canal Zone roughly bisected Panama for a distance of 50 miles from the Atlantic to the Pacific. In 1903, shortly after Columbia had rejected a U.S. proposal to resume a failed French canal project, a "spontaneous Panamanian independence uprising" erupted. President Theodore Roosevelt dispatched U.S. warships "to closely observe" the situation off the Panamanian coast. Soon after, a newly-independent Panamanian government granted the U.S. a perpetual lease, along with the authority to build the canal across the isthmus. The Hay-Bunau-Varilla Treaty even granted the U.S. sovereignty within the five miles parallel to each side of the canal. The massive ten year construction project came at a large cost in dollars and lives. Army Surgeon Walter Reed however, implemented measures that eventually eliminated the threat of malaria which had been fatal to as many as 10,000.

During the late sixties, the Army had a bootstrap program for sending officers like Jack to civilian colleges to complete their undergraduate degrees. Selection only required demonstrating a modest degree of motivation by completing 12 hours of actual classroom study. Jack did take some CLEP exams and salvaged some credits from his year of college partying to get a two-year equivalency letter, but he preferred the Augusta, Georgia night life to a classroom. When bored with the upscale Augusta clubs, Jack took the low roads which led to the more earthy establishments like the Hayloft in Thompson.

One night Jack's grand-standing at the Hayloft, while attempting to defend a sergeant while out drinking with his company's softball team, produced a most diplomatic apology as he suddenly was staring at the barrel .25 caliber revolver. Jack had volunteered to take over the coaching job from his company commander. The team was in the running for the post championship, and if they made it to the Third Army playoffs that fall, how could an indispensable winning coach be sent to the Nam?

Meanwhile, back home, the eyes of Suzanne, who had been loyally waiting for two years, began to open. Although Jack was making roughly a school teacher's salary, he was living pay check to pay check. He had only been home on leave once since OCS, but Suzanne had visited him twice at her expense. Excuses about his "demanding and arduous duties defending our Republic" were wearing thin.

The Canal Zone's triple canopy rain forest is among the densest in the world, definitely equal to the jungles of Vietnam that our units operated in. That was why the Army sent infantry lieutenants and captains to the jungle warfare school there as the last stop en route. Slogging up and down the seemingly endless, wet, steep, slimy hills for that three week course counted towards completion of the 12-month tour in Vietnam. Although the malaria threat was eliminated a half century earlier, the jungle was still inundated with insects, and boundless opportunities remained for experiencing the exotic native species of reptiles and mammals.

A couple of hundred lieutenants en route to their final Army year in Vietnam filled Jack's jungle school class. Also mixed in were a few dozen junior enlisted men assigned to units in the Zone, who needed the Jungle Expert designation for promotion. This sufficiently stimulated enough fake enthusiasm from the officers to pull for their enlisted cohorts. This also preempted attitude problems caused by resentments due to half the lieutenants in their 1969-70 year group receiving orders for Korea rather than Vietnam.

CHAPTER 3

Jungle school wore off most of the pudginess that Jack put on during the previous 6 months. His second Fort Gordon assignment as an executive officer of a student company in the Signal School was an unusual job for an infantry lieutenant. It resulted from the drawdown that Nixon started the previous year that caused the inactivation of the infantry training center where he was initially assigned, and at several other posts. Jack easily adapted to the 7:30 A.M. to 5:00 P.M. work days and weekends off. This beat the 70-plus hour weeks he had put in overseeing basic combat training of new recruits, and all the physical activity associated with field duty. Administrative duties came easy. Jack's writing ability made his boss look good, which is why he never received more than verbal reprimands for the many times he reported hung over for duty at mid-morning.

Knowing this assignment might not last more than 8 weeks, Jack volunteered for airborne and Special Forces training which required extending his service obligation. He submitted paperwork for voluntary indefinite. This would change him to a career status, but for all practical purposes he could leave the Army one year later than his original obligation.

The Paris Peace Talks were now in their third year and Nixon's Vietnamization program was on track, so it reinforced Jack's Plan B. By the time he would complete the Special Forces Course around late spring of '71, the war would have wound down. He'd probably end up at another training center somewhere in the States and finish that final year as Captain. He might even marry Suzanne, and perhaps hang around on active duty a few more years finishing his degree on a campus somewhere.

On April 10, 1970, pop culture was shocked to learn that the Beatles, the vanguard of the 1960s "British Invasion," and who had dominated popular music charts since 1963, were breaking up. One night towards the end of that month, while heading back from an unfruitful "night patrol" of Augusta gin joints, Jack plowed his Triumph TR-4 convertible into the back of a Corvair. The rear engine prevented any serious injuries to the passengers, so he was only charged with a technical misdemeanor. Jack was battered enough to spend several days in the post hospital, where he cheered while watching President Nixon announce on TV that our troops were in Cambodia going after the main Viet Cong command infrastructure. A simultaneous coup quickly installed General Lon Nol, replacing Cambodia's neutralist Prince Norodom Sihanouk. When he wasn't producing, directing and starring in his own movies, Sihanouk had turned a blind eye to years of communists staging operations into South Vietnam from his country's border regions.

The Cambodian "incursion" provoked the expected liberal reaction. This time however, the campus protests spread beyond the usual bastions of Berkley and Cambridge into Middle America. Demonstrations in the college town of Kent, Ohio had grown violent and culminated in burning down the ROTC building at Kent State University. Governor James Rhodes called out National Guard to restore order.

During the Vietnam escalation, Johnson had decided not to activate the Guard or Reserve for Vietnam. Therefore, those units had received the lowest levels of resources and were only marginally trained. These low priority forces also became another avenue out of Vietnam. Units had waiting lists for enlistments, but they could be bypassed by the well-connected. The Guard had performed admirably in their state militia roles when called up by their governors in response to urban riots. However, the Guard only had a level of training appropriate for a support force, not for direct law enforcement. Tragically, on the morning of May 4, 1970, an inept commander decided to issue live ammunition to the units at Kent State. After several demonstrators threw bricks

CHAPTER 3

and other objects, a few Guardsmen overreacted by opening fire.

The resulting Kent State press photos showed dying and injured students lying on the ground with armed troops wearing U.S. Army uniforms in the background. To Jack and his peers, and especially their professional superiors, those damned draft dodgers in the rag tag Ohio National Guard, acting as that state's militia, had indelibly stained the honor of the uniform by recklessly killing 4 students and severely wounding 6 others. A sympathy strike immediately spread, shutting down colleges across the country. Dan Debre was near the end of his fourth year but barely a junior. He hadn't been attending classes for months, but the decision of Dan's college making finals optional, gave credit for all courses he was enrolled in and another year of deferments.

The misdemeanor charge from Jack's auto accident caused his records to be flagged. Because the paperwork for Special Forces training and VOL INDEF status had not reached Headquarters, Department of the Army for final approval, it was returned without action. Jack's mentor and drinking buddy was Gus Melton, an older, but barely more mature captain who had recently returned from Vietnam. "Nothing can happen to you when your records are flagged, including orders to Nam" Gus informed him. The wheels in Jack's head began turning, "Then I just keep attention away from myself for the next two months till I make first lieutenant, then I'm home free, right?" "You got it Ace!" replied Gus.

Jack's personnel office notified him about two weeks later that he could not be promoted with the flag, which could only be lifted after he had cleared the civil charge. Separating as a second lieutenant was totally unacceptable to Jack's status consciousness so he paid a $20 fine to the Richmond County Courthouse. A week later, Jack's Infantry Branch manager called him from the Pentagon. The major cheerfully greeted him on the phone. "Hi Jack. Glad you're out of the hospital.

GRINGO POSSE

VOL INDEF is no longer an option, but you can still extend for a year and we'll schedule you a Special Forces class date." Jack replied "I've decided to just stay here at Fort Gordon and get out next year. "Well Jack", said the major, "the extension will give you some good training before we send you to Vietnam." "But I'm getting promoted in September and won't have enough time left" said Jack. The Major replied "That's OK, we'll just send you for a short tour in October." Realizing that the jig was up, Jack negotiated jungle school en route to Vietnam.

At daybreak on an early 1970 November morning in the Panama jungle, Jack came to a rude awakening. He sat bewildered on his hammock attempting to pull a black palm needle out of his thigh. About 3 weeks shy of 21, and a recently promoted first lieutenant, his evaluator had just "bayoneted" him out of the prestigious Jungle Expert designation with the stinging remark, "How many people's lives would your mistake have cost, LT Wilson?"

The evaluator conceded that Jack's operations order contained a an outstanding plan. However, in the dark unforgiving jungle he had led an attack up the wrong hill, right next to the one where the objective, a radio tower, sat. "The next time," he thought, "I'll delegate the navigation rather than doing it myself. I'll have too much to oversee controlling a 40 man gaggle through this type of mess over there."

Until that moment of truth, Jack had still been half in denial about where he was headed. The course was a tough tactical school, but it stood down for the weekends. Jack even enjoyed the first week which focused on jungle survival skills. These included adventure tasks associated with crossing the half-mile-wide Chagres River. One entailed swimming across with an individual raft fabricated from a tied-off poncho, stuffed with vegetation, clothing, weapons and equipment that gave it buoyancy. The other crossing

CHAPTER 3

required climbing 30 feet up a tree, then jumping off to begin a slide underneath a taught rope to the other side of the Chagres, suspended from a U-shaped rope looped underneath both arms, and attached to a fabricated pulley.

Tensions with the Panamanian locals that had erupted into rioting on the Canal Zone's boundaries five years earlier had subsided. This gave student officers the opportunity to do some sight-seeing in the Republic. Jack and three of his cohorts took the trans-isthmus railroad along the canal from Fort Sherman on the Atlantic side, to Panama City on the Pacific. After spending an afternoon in a casino at their high-end hotel along the main drag, Jack and his friends organized themselves into "a gringo patrol" for some nighttime activities.

An obliging taxi driver had no difficulty understanding where his gringo patrons wanted to go and cruised along the low road. Dressed in their hideous bell bottoms and wide collared paisley shirts they had purchased earlier that day in the PX, and wearing their military low quarters, Jack and his cohorts made their grand entry into "the Blue Goose." This was one of the premiere bordellos of the Republic, with an ambiance rivaling any south-of the-border saloon in a wild-west movie.

The gringo posse basked in the attention of the ladies, drawn by the charisma of their obvious bankrolls. They were great actresses who excelled at appearing interested in their every spurious utterance. A two-man U.S. Military Police patrol approached the quartet, and abruptly demanded identification. "What are you doing in an off limits establishment?" demanded an M.P. sergeant. Ted, the group's elder with a Masters from Yale no less, explained that they were on temporary duty and unaware of the restrictions. Upon determining that they were registered at a reputable hotel, the M.P. directed them to take a cab back there.

Ted instructed the taxi driver to circle the area for nearly a half hour. After the M.P. vehicle was gone, the taxi re-deposited them at the Blue Goose. The gringos were cheered like conquering heroes upon their grand re-entry and quickly reengaged with a different quartet of ladies. A Guardia National patrol entered and initially showed no interest in them. Suddenly the Guardias approached the gringos motioning them to follow. The ladies smiled and reassuringly took them by their hands, leading the way into a back room. One of them explained in broken English "Americano M.P.s back, but they no come in here." Jack, thus had the opportunity to blow through the remainder of the three-month advanced pay he had taken five weeks earlier, before starting a 30-day leave from Fort Gordon.

When Jack showed up at Suzanne's house at the start of his leave, they went out but it wasn't like old times. She wasn't going to drop everything and spend the entire month with Jack. Months earlier Suzanne had made it clear that she was going to start seeing other people when she discovered some girls' phone numbers while searching for a pen in the desk of Jack's Augusta apartment while he was at work. After a nasty break up fight with Suzanne, Jack flew back down to Augusta to get his motorcycle and spent the rest of his leave, and most of his money riding up the east coast.

That fall the mid-term elections had heated up. Jack enjoyed listening to Vice President Spiro Agnew, a master of alliteration, tear into the anti-war protesters and the liberal establishment leaders in academia, the press and the politicians who encouraged them. While Jack was on Long Island, Agnew even referred to New York's appointed Republican U.S. Senator as "the Christine Jorgensen of the GOP" making it unequivocally clear that President Nixon backed Conservative third party candidate James Buckley, brother of columnist William F. Buckley, Jr., a Young Americans for Freedom icon. Jack was always impressed by

CHAPTER 3

the way that Buckley spoke on "Firing Line". He frequently would trip himself up using polysyllabic words without knowing their actual meaning, typically when trying to impress college-educated women.

During the last day of the final stint in the jungle warfare course, Jack faced the reality that he would be doing this for real in Vietnam in less than a week! Not only that, but now that he and Suzanne were on the outs, the life he had known might never be the same again. Drifting back into denial, Jack pondered who he could borrow money from for a final night out in seedy port city of Colon on the Atlantic side.

The "gringo posse, took pity on their Comandante and loaned Jack the money, enabling him to go along on their final night of reveling at the Hotel Sibone in Colon. His Comandante status was due to having completed his twelve months time in grade for the automatic promotion to first lieutenant four to six weeks before the others did. They had their fill of the most delicious meat ever skewed on a grill outside on the street in front of the hotel, but never did determine if it was rodent, alligator, boa constrictor or even cat.

Jack paid them all back in full after leaving the finance office, and then bought a round of drinks at the Howard Air Force Base officers club while they watched the news waiting for their aircraft. Nixon claimed a moral victory in the 1970 mid-terms. Although the Democrats retained control of Congress, several vocal anti-war critics like Maryland's Senator Joseph Tidings, and New York's Congressman Allard Lowenstein both lost. In Tennessee hawkish Republican Bill Brock beat Democratic Senator Albert Gore, Sr. who had attempted to play both sides on Vietnam. Conservative Jim Buckley had also won Goddel's New York Senate seat, in spite of Governor Nelson Rockefeller's comfortable reelection over Arthur Goldberg heading the GOP ticket. Congressman George H.W. Bush lost the Texas

U.S. Senate seat to Lloyd Benson. That loss was mitigated however, since Benson was ideologically similar to John Connelly. Hubert Humphrey had won retiring U.S. Senator Eugene McCarthy's seat.

Jack was 10 days shy of his 21st birthday. Like hundreds of thousands of troops, and many officers who were under 21 while serving in Vietnam, he did not have the right to vote for the decision makers who sent them there. The nationwide 18-year-old voting age would not take effect until a year and a half after the November 3, 1970, mid-term elections.

Suzanne had finally answered one of Jack's letters positively, so his morale was fairly high. He even had several hundred dollars left in travel pay in case there were recreation opportunities when the flight reached its final destination.

CHAPTER 4

4. SEARCHING AND AVOIDING SNAKE PITS

The jungle school graduates were on their own during three days of travel time from Panama to catch the flight out of Travis Air Force Base, near Oakland. About eight hours after a mid-flight stop in Fairbanks, the chartered Alaska Airlines Boeing 727 began its final approach towards Bien Hoa Air Base. They gazed though the clear sky at the cratered countryside. Years of artillery and aerial bombardment had pock-marked the terrain which gradually cleared at the outskirts of the heavily urbanized region. Smaller cities like Bien Hoa and Long Binh formed the greater Saigon area known as Military Region III.

It was sundown on Armistice Day when the new replacements disembarked. All 200 lieutenants had orders assigning them to the U.S. Army Vietnam (USARV), which was the major headquarters for the combat divisions, where all anticipated being rifle platoon leaders. After waiting around in the hot terminal they boarded Army buses, modified with fencing installed over the windows for protection against grenades, for the ride to the 90th Replacement Battalion in Long Binh. After a couple hours of in-processing and receiving a clothing issue, the group went to the local officers club for a few beers. Then they turned in for the evening in the BOQ, another transient barracks segregated from the enlisted men.

Heading to breakfast the next morning, Jack grabbed for the Pacific "Stars and Stripes". The front page story was about the opening of the Courts Martial of Lieutenant William Calley. This sensational murder trial at Fort Benning would dominate the headlines for the next four months. The group however, was more focused on whether the preference

SEARCHING AND AVOIDING SNAKE PITS

sheets they filled out the previous night would actually influence their unit assignments. Since Nixon's Vietnamization announcement in his "Silent Majority" speech the previous November, U.S. troop levels in Vietnam had fallen about 25 percent to just over 300 thousand, and were continuing. In typical bureaucratic fashion, the Army's right hand had not clearly communicated its manpower requirements to its left hand. Consequently, Jack unexpectedly found himself on a bus bound for the Military Assistance Command, Vietnam (MACV) compound at Ton San Nhut. He and about a hundred lieutenants had been cross-leveled for advisory duty with units of the Army of the Republic of Vietnam (ARVN).

The sprawling MACV headquarters on the Ton San Nhut complex was known as Pentagon East. The group spent three more days of in-processing, with plenty of free in the late afternoons and evenings. Official U.S. currency was illegal and had to be converted into military payment certificates, or MPCs. As an anti-black market measure, MPCs could not be used on the Vietnamese economy. On their first night, after converting about hundred dollars of MPCs into piasters, Jack and his cohorts checked out the Vietnamese Air Force Officers Club, the notorious V-NAF Club.

Upon entering, not one Vietnamese officer, or even an airman could be seen. The establishment was divided into an upscale dining area, and a darkly lit lounge located in a sunken area that one entered by separating long, beaded hanging fly curtains. Immediately upon descending the three steps, Jack and his cohorts were grabbed and dragged to a booth by four elegantly dressed bar girls. "You buy me drink, Trung Uy (Vietnamese for first lieutenant)?"

After spending over $100 on infamous "Saigon Teas" in less than a half hour, they recognized the hustle. The VNAF Club's "Snake Pit" was far different than the laid back Blue Goose of Panama City. Jack and the Gringo Posse decided to

CHAPTER 4

spend the remaining two evenings at the bars and restaurants located in the Brinks and Massachusetts. These were upscale contracted hotels where U.S. military officers assigned to units in Saigon stayed. U.S. contractors, businessmen and reporters also frequented them. Jack met and dined with a pleasant girl named Rosie, an ethnic Chinese minority who worked as a secretary for one of the local U.S. headquarters. They met for dinner again the next evening. Jack and his cohorts however, were being sent north to Di An in the morning, for a recently established Advisors' School.

Traditionally, U.S. advisors to ARVN divisional tactical units were reassigned to MACV after they had been with American units for six to twelve months. Jack's group however, was not going to ARVN units but was being trained for duty with Regional Forces and Popular Forces (the RFs and PFs known as Ruff-Puffs). President Nixon's concept of Vietnamization provided for the regular ARVN to assume the overall combat role from the U.S. throughout the entire country.

Within the provinces, the Government of Vietnam (GVN) equivalent of states, the RF were assuming the former role of the ARVN. At the District (i.e. county) level, the PF and Popular Self Defense Forces, or PSDF, were taking over the former RF role of securing villages and hamlets. The USARV Advisor School was located at Di An, a large base camp where the 11th Armored Cavalry Regiment, and the 3rd Squadron of the 17th Cav, an aviation unit, were also stationed. Jack turned 21 there on November 17th.

Officers, mostly lieutenants and captains, comprised half of the three week course. Senior NCOs, mostly sergeants first class and master sergeants, comprised the other half. About a dozen Australians were also in the course. Classes ran for about 10 hours each day with a half day off on Sunday. About a third of the day was spent listening to spoken Vietnamese language tapes over headphones in hot trailers with overhead fans. Other classes were conducted by combat experienced advisors on counter guerilla operations, Vietnamese history and culture, and the organization of the Vietnamese government and armed forces. Jack enjoyed the time on the ranges firing the old family of weapons like the 30 caliber and Thompson sub-machine guns, and Browning automatic rifles that the village and hamlet militias known as Popular Self Defense Forces (PSDF) and some PFs still used; and familiarizing on the communist favorites like the AK47 and SKS. There were several field trips to nearby villages and hamlets for students to see the Mobile Advisory, or MAT teams, they would shortly be assigned to, operate.

    The "Red Horse" was the local officers club run by great hell raising combat aviators of the 3rd of the 17th Cav. It had a great atmosphere and employed some cute local girls as waitresses. Jack spent most of his nights there with a couple of the Australian advisors engaged in the lively crap game. One night he even won back the Seiko wrist watch he had lost thanks to the $20 one of the Australians had loaned him to get back into the game. On a ride back from a field trip one day, Jack was discussing a Time magazine article about Australia's immigration policies that discriminated against non-Europeans. An Australian Warrant Officer responded "Did you get a good look at the village we just visited? We don't want to live like the Vietnamese, that's why!"

    The students also socialized with several ex-advisors on the school's support staff. The more unvarnished accounts of their experiences and the situation in the field made it obvious why they weren't instructors. They candidly shared that the GVN counterparts valued American advisors as an immediate source of aerial fire support, medivac and resupply, not because they wanted to emulate "the American way" of doing things. Far too many were also more concerned about having access to sundry items from the PX system, and pilfered stocks from American-resourced ARVN supplies with which they could enrich themselves on the black market.

CHAPTER 4

Civil Operations and Rural Development, or COORDS, was the division of MACV the MAT teams came under. It had been established a few years earlier by "Wild Bill" Colby, who later became CIA Director. The COORDS command structure was staffed with Senior State Department and military officers. The geographical boundaries paralleled those of the GVN's four Corps or Military Regions. In theory the GVN was a civil government with an elected President and National Assembly.

Both the President, Nguyen Van Thieu, and Vice President, Nguyen Cao Ky, were generals who had retired upon their election in 1966, and all regional, provincial and district top officials were military officers appointed by the Saigon government. The wartime situation necessitated this, but the students were assured that elected local governments would soon be introduced in the more secure provinces.

A COORDS Military Region Senior Advisor was either a lieutenant general or career State Department foreign service officer (FSO) equivalent. A Province Senior Advisor, (PSA) was either a colonel or civilian FSO, who advised the Province Chief, a military governor. At the regional and provincial levels, whenever the senior advisor was military, a FSO was the deputy, and vice versa. District Senior Advisors, DSAs, were always Army majors. Each MAT Team was authorized a captain, first lieutenant, two infantry platoon sergeants E7s, and a sergeant first class E7 medic, and an ARVN sergeant as an interpreter.

Graduation came a week before Christmas. General Fred Weyand, the four-star Deputy Commander of USARV and MACV who gave the graduation address, presented the diplomas. This demonstrated the high level of command interest in their mission which was to "work themselves out of a job." The days of the pitched battles involving U.S. company-sized and larger units in force-on-force engagements with the North Vietnamese Army (NVA) regulars and main force VC were over. This meant that Jack would be working with his RF and PF counterparts to improve the security situation so that they could take it over without any U.S. presence.

A snapshot of the nation-wide military situation briefings indicated that Region I in the north still had significant enemy activity. Region II comprising the Central Highlands was mostly stable as was Region III surrounding Saigon. The exceptions in those two Regions were the western districts bordering Laos and Cambodia. These experienced heavy infiltration of material from the Ho Chi Minh trail.

Region 4, consisting of the Mekong Delta provinces in the South, was the role model used for instruction. Those were considered pacified after two years under that Region's Senior Advisor John Paul Vann's tutelage. By the end of 1970, ground combat operations by the remaining U.S. divisional units, were limited to securing the areas surrounding the large U.S. installations where combat aviation, artillery, and logistical support units were still based. Throughout the entire country, reports of even U.S. platoon size units taking casualties were becoming rare.

Jack found himself heading north to Region II headquarters in Nha Trang. After a couple more days of in-processing, Jack received his assignment as an assistant MAT Senior Advisor in Tuyen Duc Province. The security situation there was stable enough for a civilian Province Senior Advisor, so Jack saw that as drawing a lucky straw. After flying into Cam Ly airfield, Jack was greeted and driven to the province headquarters in the City of Dalat. After a brief orientation meeting with the military Deputy, a light colonel, he headed to his assigned MAT team command post, or CP, that another MAT team shared on the outskirts of the City.

CHAPTER 4

The CP was located within a small enclave of the National Police Field Force (NPFF) training center. It was an old converted concrete storage building surrounded by layers of sand bags up to about chest level. Outside were four well-constructed bunkers that tied into an inner perimeter of tangle-foot barbed wire extending for approximately 50 yards. The bunkers had solid timber overhead cover reinforced by a double layer of sandbags. Each had chain link fencing solidly emplaced 10 yards forward to pre-detonate enemy RPG rockets. Each day, the disconnected Claymore wire safety caps and their firing devices had to be inspected for tampering.

Located in the southern Central Highlands, Dalat was an autonomous city in the center of Tuyen Duc Province, comprised of three districts. The City had been a mountain resort under the French and was now a show place of the GVN. The ARVN Command and General Staff College, other senior level schools, and National Military Academy, the West Point of South Vietnam, which even had a nuclear reactor, were all located there. An international university also graced the city. Expectations from Panama of triple canopy jungles were pleasantly not met. Unlike most forested areas in Vietnam, the vegetation covering the steep terrain surrounding the city was not tropical. It somewhat resembled the pine studded training areas of Fort Benning, but with much steeper hills and ridgelines.

The outlying three districts of the province had been the Emperor Bao Dai's hunting grounds. Unfortunately, the tigers, once quite common, had been hunted to near-extinction. Duc Trong District was heavily populated by Montanyards, the original indigenous people. Ethnically closer to Polynesians than Vietnamese, they had settled centuries before them. The last major enemy engagement had occurred six months before Jack's arrival when a U.S. engineer unit was caught in a NVA ambush.

SEARCHING AND AVOIDING SNAKE PITS

    The following afternoon, Bo, Jack's senior MAT Team sergeant, took him on a brief tour of the City and to the local U.S. installation occupied by a signal unit. It had a small PX and club, but the main attraction was Madame Thai's restaurant just outside the gate, where Bo knew every bar girl personally. He took Jack there for dinner and introduced a pretty girl named Mai to him, inviting her to join them for dinner. Bo left them alone while he exchanged pleasantries with the girls at the bar, working them like a politician.

    Jack noticed that these girls weren't like those at Ton San Nhut's V-NAF Club, who uttered clichés in pigeon English while rapidly hustling troops for "Saigon Tea". Although an occasional "Dalat Tea" was expected, Mai and the other girls were quite fluent in English and capable of providing pleasant companionship. By the end of dinner it finally dawned on Jack why Bo brought him there. Mai's American boyfriend had just rotated and she was looking for a newly assigned officer or senior sergeant to support her. When it became obvious Jack was not going to commit however, Mai began pressing him for more frequent Dalat Teas.

    The typical arrangement was a monogamous relationship that lasted for the duration of the American's tour. The GI paid the monthly rent of about $100 for a one room flat, and kept it furnished with furniture, appliances and sundry items from the local PX. Most of the Americans were from the local compound and actually lived in the flats every night. The MAT advisors like Jack spent most of their days in the field, and could only get into the City several evenings a month.

    Support arrangements permitted the girlfriends to earn a living by providing companionship to American's willing to spend $15 per hour buying "Dalat Teas." Dinner at Madame Thais, or even at another higher end restaurant in the City was also within bounds. However, any outside sex on the part of the girl terminated the arrangement. Some officers on the

CHAPTER 4

Province Staff would even proudly arrive at social functions at the Province Senior Advisor's villa with girlfriend on the arm.

On the way back to the team hooch, Bo encouraged Jack to take up with Mai. Now 21, Jack was still immature and full of personal vices that included binge drinking, chain smoking, womanizing, and gambling. His "devout Catholicism" had involved attending Mass to evade Sunday morning details while he was in OCS, but faded when he became eligible for weekend passes. Jack was therefore not averse to occasionally patronizing a hooker, and wouldn't think twice about giving a girl rationed items like a carton of cigarettes or a fifth of top shelf booze. He did however, have a sense of duty and professional ethics. Jack knew very well that the thriving black market financially and logistically benefited the enemy. He also realized from several illegal petty currency transactions he had just observed, that a flat with a steady girlfriend would likely put him too close to that sort of thing. There were other establishments that Bo could introduce Jack to, but that would be another day.

On the afternoon of Christmas Eve the advisors stationed near the city attended a party hosted by the military mayor of the City, ARVN lieutenant colonel. Later, Jack and his fellow advisors spent a quiet, uneventful evening in their shared hootch. Occasional Christmas greetings could be heard from the radio room over the U.S. Advisory Command NET.

Jack's initial experiences quickly verified the official classroom instruction from the Advisors course, and the candid accounts from the ex-advisors at the Di An officers' club. American advisors could try to persuade their counterparts to take certain actions, but final command and control decisions rested exclusively with the Vietnamese. The most common tactical missions of patrols were conducted in villages adjacent to the City with the objective of interdicting cells of VC couriers, or conducting ambushes. Typically comprised of three to five VC irregulars, these cells frequently infiltrated into the City and back to the remote areas of the districts where their parent units were based, with supplies, information or currency.

Shortly before New Years, Jack went on his first tactical operation as an advisor with a PF unit. The mission was to set up a night ambush along a dirt road leading into a village just outside the City. Jack, his boss Mike, who was a more senior first lieutenant, and Bo arrived at the link up point. It was obvious that their Vietnamese counterpart had done little, if any, prior coordination. There was not even a basic patrol plan designating the assault, fire support and security elements. Neither were there any details about the ambush mission and objectives, or commands and signals for opening and ceasing firing. They had not even brought a claymore mine with them. Detonating a claymore normally triggered the ambush followed a heavy volume of fire into a kill zone, which the PF platoon leaders also had not delineated. The three American "covans" watched the PF platoon leader awkwardly trying to emplace his people along the road. About an hour after Mike radioed in to the Province tactical operations center (TOC), the mission was aborted. This sound decision more likely preempted the potential of inflicting casualties on friendly personnel operating in the vicinity than harming any enemies.

Official MACV press briefings attributed the exponentially lower U.S. casualty rates and reduced levels of enemy activity to the phenomenal success of Vietnamization. There were several outstanding regular ARVN divisions, and Military Region 4 was exceptionally stable. However, the NVA and VC had outstanding intelligence. No NVA regular divisions operated within Tuyen Duc Province. However, several main force VC battalions, estimated at regimental strength, operated base camps with sophisticated heavy weapons caches and logistical supplies in remote parts of the

CHAPTER 4

districts. Intelligence indicated that they were mostly manned by part time VC, but with significant numbers full time main force VC and a few NVA cadres.

Most of the VC troops came from South Vietnam. The heavy casualties they took during Tet 68 had diminished their capability to quickly mass from their small clandestine cells, into well organized and trained combat formations up the level of a battalion of over 500 troops. These battalions also could no longer combine with others to form regiments. However, even platoon sized VC formations still posed a lethal threat. Their trademark capability of almost instantaneously disbanding and blending back into the local population remained undiminished.

Friendly units from the regular 53rd ARVN Regiment frequently made contact with these main force VC units, but usually outside of Tuyen Duc Province. This confirmed the intelligence indicating that these VC units conducted their major combat operations in neighboring provinces. Regional Force units would occasionally engage company sized VC elements in remote districts, but rarely when U.S. advisors were with them. These were all strategic indicators of a shift in communist strategy of avoiding the risk of disrupting the rapid pace by U.S. withdrawals by inflicting heavy American casualties that might give Nixon second thoughts.

By New Years Day, 1971, American troop levels were down to 280,000. The daytime operations Jack went on revealed serious RF and PF coordination problems with other GVN units. The unit leaders frequently did not rehearse their plans with the troops prior to missions. If their higher headquarters had even coordinated to determine what other friendly forces would be operating in their areas, they often failed to inform their subordinate units.

On one daytime patrol, Jack was moving along a ridge when a PF platoon spotted a unit moving in the valley

SEARCHING AND AVOIDING SNAKE PITS

approximately a half mile away. The platoon leader immediately deployed his unit and prepared to engage with small arms fire. Fortunately he accepted the tactful advice to "Wait to see if I can get you supporting fire so we won't have to risk accurate return fire on our position." The U.S. Advisory TOC then confirmed the unit in the valley was from the 53rd ARVN Regiment while initiating the request for artillery support.

The most likely enemy contact in the area that Jack's MAT operated in would be lightly armed cells attempting to infiltrate supplies away from the City into the remote areas. Several MAT teams in the outlying districts however, did operate with RF units that occasionally engaged more heavily armed platoon-sized VC units. Most Vietnamese cared about their country, but far too many leaders were more focused on their commercial enterprises. Most were also in denial that the Americans were leaving. Senior level ARVN commanders never ordered aggressive combat patrols into the areas where main force VC were located, always claiming "Too many VC down there."

The MAT teams spent only about ten days a month going out with and advising RF and PF units on actual tactical operations. Most other days were spent making routine visits to their Vietnamese military counterparts at outposts, other advisory elements and to the handful of supporting U.S. units in the Province. One was B Battery, a field artillery unit that was prepared to rapidly deliver heavy fire support on pre-plotted targets should the MATs find themselves in a jam.

Since all MAT members were either junior officers or senior sergeants, they all shared in the routine maintenance and housekeeping duties. Jack enjoyed weekly evening dinners with the Korean Advisors from the Vietnamese Military Academy that were followed by Tai Kwon Do classes. About every three weeks there was an opportunity to ride shotgun on an ad hoc scrounging convoy that some U.S.

CHAPTER 4

advisory unit in the Province had organized. The destination was normally Cam Ranh Bay, or other major installations on the coast, located approximately 60 to 80 miles to the east.

By mid-February, Lam Song 719, the major ARVN offensive against NVA divisions in Laos was underway. This was the largest ARVN ground combat operation with no U.S. advisors present, and all nearby U.S. combat units held in reserve. However, tactical operations in the vicinity of the City had stopped altogether, and Jack's MAT and several other teams were alerted to prepare to deactivate.

Shortly before the MAT teams received orders to stand down, several ARVN MAT interpreters had been reassigned to ARVN divisions that had been alerted for Lam Song 719 because they needed fluent English speakers on the ground to call for U.S. tactical air and long range artillery support. Now Jack and his fellow MAT advisors understood why their interpreter had "accidentally" shot himself in the hand the previous month.

Jack spent his final two weeks on the MAT team preparing equipment for turn in. Most items that were not on the official property books had been acquired over a year before he was assigned, and could be used for bartering to make up shortages. However, disposing of a major weapon, like their 4.2 inch mortar, a high angle medium artillery piece, required documentation through the U.S. logistical system. Jack was angry and frustrated by the Province logistical section repeatedly refusing to accept the weapon until he had spent several hours re-writing a creative justification statement explaining why the Team had this heavy weapon they were not authorized to have. Didn't these logistical advisors have more important things to do?

It was no secret that American-resourced material was being pilfered from ARVN Depots This didn't just involve petty amounts of fuel, or an occasional refrigerator or stove,

SEARCHING AND AVOIDING SNAKE PITS

but large quantities of rations, medical supplies construction material, and even major end items like vehicles. It was OK with Jack if the loggies wanted to show off their girlfriends from Madame Thai's at the PSA's parties. However, couldn't they at least pump the girls for information they picked up about the major ARVN black market players were as reciprocity for their flats?

By the end of the week Jack and his fellow excess advisors would be cross leveled to the remaining advisory elements. Jack's final MAT mission was to ride shotgun on a convoy to Cam Ranh that would include several jeep trailers full of excess MAT items. Most of these like butane powered refrigerators and stoves were great barter items. Upon his return Jack would be going to the District Team that worked with the Montanyards in Duc Trong District.

Convoys first involved driving on stretches of winding roads through the mountains in standard U.S. tactical vehicles that were painted in the distinctive lighter shade of ARVN green with their tactical markings. Outside of the City passengers riding shotgun in the vehicles stayed alert and tense with their M16 locked and loaded, while moving slowly along 15 miles of the winding narrow mountain roadway. The advisors began seeing bamboo and feeling the tropical heat as they approached the town of Dong Doung, the seat of the province's eastern district. Once clear of the pass at Song Pha, the troops breathed a sigh of relief as the vehicles moved at a high rate of speed along the flat open terrain of Ninh Tuan Province.

The primary scrounging mission was to beg, borrow or steal items from the U.S. units at the major bases for the various Province Team elements. This was where the NCOs proved their weight in gold. Ours seemed to know every alcoholic mess sergeant in the Army, who would gladly trade a case of frozen mess hall steaks for a fifth of Seagrams or Johnny Walker Red. It was highly desirable to have contacts

CHAPTER 4

on the Air Force side of Cam Ranh or at Phan Rang Air Base, 20 miles south.

The Air Force had traditionally placed a top priority on resourcing quality of life programs. A transit BOQ on the Army side was always a drab, primitive, flimsy barracks-like building with crudely fashioned rooms, torn screening, and perhaps a few ceiling fans. Typically, Army clubs had either Vietnamese or Filipino rock bands, but that carried a good tune, none the less. Visiting the Air Force side of Cam Ranh or Phan Rang further south, was like being transported to the States. Cinder block or attractive solid frame buildings were always painted in pastel colors, and air conditioned.

The convoy spent the first night on the Army side of Cam Ranh where there was some officer and NCO socializing. A master sergeant who kept a girl in a Dalat flat, was desperately trying to borrow money "to meet my family on R&R in Hawaii". Jack gave him five dollars. They spent the next day in air conditioned transit billets at Phan Rang, where the officer's club even had an Australian female rock band performing.

Prior planning standards for these convoys barely exceeded those of their Vietnamese counterparts. Girlfriends in the Dalat flats passed the word to their friends so that they could prepare shopping lists for their boyfriends to buy major goods at the big PX in Cam Ranh. It was not unusual to hear planning details broadcast in the clear over the command radio network. It would have been impossible for the VC not to have been aware of them. Fortunately, no U.S. advisor scrounging convoys were ever ambushed during Jack's 5 months in Tuyen Duc, or after he left. This was another indicator that the communists' strategy was to patiently wait out the American withdrawal.

5. DIVINE PAYBACK

On his return to Dalat, Jack stayed overnight at the Province Team villa before reporting to Duc Trong. He had taken up gambling for excitement as an alternative to risking the clap at the brothels in the province capital. At one point Jack went into the hole for over $1,000 to some slick NCOs who taught him the game of black jack under rules where the dealer rotates, and dealer pays a $5 fine to each player whenever a dealing error is made. That all changed on March 8, 1971.

Jack not only wiped out his gambling debts, but actually pulled ahead after betting double or nothing on Joe Frasier in his heavyweight title fight against convicted draft evader Mohamed Ali. After that he limited his gambling to poker where the highest chips were worth no more than $5. That evening Jack got into a game with several province staff officers, and a CIA operative and a couple of contractors who lived in nearby villas. They all took turns telling war stories as the cards were dealt into the early morning hours. Jack now took his turn expounding on his "aerial combat" adventure.

Most of the province staff officers and Jack's older contemporaries had at least a bachelor's degree. Several even had a masters. They loved to catch him using polysyllabic words for which he was clueless as to their actual meaning. "I most indubitably and catigorizingly earned an Air Medal with a V" uttered the Trung-Uy. He had started a second six pack during that marathon game. How could that be when the RFs and PFs, who were like GVN mobilized reservists, never conducted air mobile operations? Or at least the ones he advised. Racking up hours riding in Hueys during insertions into landing zones for combat assaults was the only way non-aviators usually qualified for that award. Well Jack

CHAPTER 5

was immature, tactless, and quite the budding raging alcoholic, but nobody had ever accused him of being a liar.

The Trung-Uy's war story stemmed from a three-day trip he had taken to Cam Ranh Bay two months earlier. Jack had hitched a ride on a Huey that was going to Dong Ba Tinh, the base camp of an aviation unit close to Cam Ranh. From there he would catch another bird to his final destination in the morning. About midway, while flying over a heavily canopied area, his Huey took some small arms fire. The door gunner and crew chief immediately manned the 7.62 door-mounted machineguns and opened up.

The pilots made a few passes over the suspected enemy location. It apparently was no more than one or two Viet Cong delivering a little harassing fire. As the only passenger, Jack just waited for instructions. Suddenly the crew chief patted him on the shoulder gesturing for him to fire his weapon out the door. Jack immediately locked and loaded a magazine into his M16, put the selector switch on automatic and fired up the magazine in the direction where the crew chief had pointed.

After they landed at Dong Ba Tinh the seasoned pilot, a Chief Warrant Officer about Jack's age, said "Congratulations L.T. You just won the Air Medal for participation in aerial combat". "I guess the paperwork must have got lost" said Jack, as he ended the story. It was now after four in the morning and Jack, who had been down over $250, was now only $20 light. Jack wanted to get a good night's sleep so he would be alert the next afternoon, when he reported to his new boss, the new Duc Trong District Senior Advisor. He cashed out and said good night.

Jack's account of the aircraft taking and returning fire was accurate, but he knew better than to tell the rest of the story. It had been early evening when the Huey landed at Dong Ba Tinh. The pilot told Jack where to find the battalion

DIVINE PAYBACK

headquarters in the morning to fill out the air medal paperwork for them to forward to his own command channels for final processing. The pilot and co-pilot then took Jack to their BOQ and found him a vacant room to stay in for the night. After dropping off his duffle bag and securing his M16, Jack, with a nose like a blood hound for any type of beverage alcohol, needed no help finding their officers club.

The club was full of Cobra gun ship pilots, who were renowned for getting rip roaring drunk. Naturally Jack viewed it incumbent upon himself to demonstrate that they were no match for this power drinking infantryman. After about five hours of rounds, he was falling down drunk, but did eventually make it back to his BOQ. It was a wooden barracks-like building with individual rooms crudely configured. In Vietnam, combat aviators got to sleep on mattresses with sheets as compensation for the perilous missions they routinely flew during a 12-month tour.

Suddenly, shouting and an alarm rudely awoke Jack from his alcohol induced coma. Mortar attack! That meant the enemy was either delivering harassing and interdicting fires, or possibly even preparation fires for a major ground attack. Jack got dressed, still drunk but somewhat coherent. A pilot from a nearby room pointed him towards a bunker. Since Jack was virtually incapacitated, he went the wrong way and stumbled into a sand-bagged Tactical Operations Center (TOC). Jack was drunk but recognized what he had stumbled into before he was bodily thrown out by one of the duty officers.

Jack, found himself disoriented again but was sober enough to know that big-time trouble awaited him if he stumbled into that TOC again. That would prompt the unit commander to send a nasty report to his own commander. Jack spotted a ditch, where hours later he found himself waking up, squinting as the brilliant light of day-break hit his eyes.

CHAPTER 5

The mortar attack turned out to have only been harassing fire. As Jack entered the BOQ to gather his gear and weapon, he ran into a pilot he was drinking with the night before. He alerted Jack that Major Burns, their unit XO and "a real hard ass," had been asking "who was the MACV asshole staggering around last night?" "There's a bird going to Cam Ranh at 0800 from the helipad next to the water tower so you had better get on it."

Jack was still in the hole for a thousand bucks to the nice sergeants who had taught him Black Jack. He already had received one "hate letter from a duplicious little man with a big rank who couldn't take a joke." His math was good enough to quickly calculate the amount of a fine from a general officer's Article 15 that "hate mail" from that aviation commander could generate. Deciding discretion was the better part of valor, the Trung Uy wisely chose not to follow up on the air medal paperwork at the headquarters. After slithering through the rain to a building with an overhanging roof a short dash from the helipad, Jack waited for the Huey that would get him out of Dodge. No "hate mail" ever followed.

Waking up rested and alert the morning after the poker game, Jack made sure to look the part for his first impression with the District Senior Advisor (DSA). He put on a pair of ironed starched jungle fatigues that the maids who worked in the province team villa did regularly. Jack even had shined the brass GVN eagle and two blossoms denoting his ARVN Trung Uy rank on his black RF beret that all the American advisors wore. A captain and staff sergeant, who formed the District Team's intelligence element, picked Jack up in their jeep that had a trailer attached to it.

Their ride on surfaced roads ended after about 25 minutes out of the City. Under the best conditions it took another half hour over narrow dirt roads through small rural villages to reach the District Team headquarters. It could only be safely traveled at night with heavily armed escort vehicles. The Duc Trong District Chief's headquarters was located within an outpost on a high ridge secured by a RF light infantry company. It was organized with interlocking, fortified dug-in positions. The imposing ridge at the base of a mountain dominated the valley, where wreckage of a Chinook helicopter, that had crashed two years earlier, now sat. Approximately a mile up near the peak was a small U.S. compound hosting a transmitter site, operated by a reinforced signal platoon.

The District Advisory Team had its own internal perimeter. Major Jim Bennett, the DSA, greeted Jack with a hearty hand shake. Bennett, a seasoned combat experienced airborne infantryman from Texas, who resembled the actor Frank Sutton, was a real soldier. He left no doubt that this terrain was far more dangerous than the City where Jack had been operating. Although there were no main force VC battalions nearby, Charlie was very active and capable of forming into small unit combat patrols for ambushes, and delivering harassing 82 millimeter mortar fire. A thought immediately entered Jack's mind. "Why had the two deactivated MAT teams been operating so close to Dalat when there were none stationed out here?"

The Team headquarters was a concrete building foundation that had been modified into a bunker. It had double walls of sandbags layered like bricks against the exterior of sunken concrete walls resembling the basement of a raised ranch. Double sandbags also covered a reinforced timber roof. The interior was sectioned off with walls constructed with ammunition crate lumber that separated the TOC from the kitchen and living area. Each of the 7 advisors had a room. Like the MAT team house at the NPFF training center, sleeping bags and space blankets rested on the thin mattresses of army cots.

CHAPTER 5

Outside the entrance stood a water tower constructed with two by fours. The Team mascot, a monkey named Henry, usually sat on a high horizontal beam. Henry had previously lived inside, but had tormented their dog Blackie so badly that he had to be moved outside for his own safety. Whenever Blackie was let out, Henry still taunted him. The team members fed Henry finger-sized bananas and put other items on the ledge around the roof that was level with the tower. He had to be tied to a long 20 foot cord, because if he escaped, monkey brains were a delicacy of the locals.

The District Chief, Major Tanh, was an ARVN major who coordinated the activities of the civilian village and hamlet chiefs, and also commanded all the RF and PF units in the district. Tanh and most of his officers were ethnically Vietnamese in this Montanyard area. The one exception was his outstanding RF company commander, Dai Uy Knom, a Montanyard. Captain Knom frequently visited the Team headquarters to plan support for his operations. He was one of less than a dozen Montanyard ARVN officers in the entire country above the rank of first lieutenant.

The Montanyards despised all Vietnamese, but especially loathed the communists. They trusted the Americans however, and had established a great reputation as their loyal warrior-allies. Discriminatory GVN policies towards the Montanyards made a mid-century state government in the U.S. South seem progressive. One evening, after discussing a nationwide Montanyard uprising of the late sixties that he had played a major role in negotiating to an end, Dai Uy Knom said, "Next time, I might not do."

Major Bennett was eager to get out to the different RF outposts and units in the district. Major Tanh however, insisted that he accompany Bennett on all visits. Bennett was becoming increasingly frustrated because Tanh always found excuses for not going with him, and routinely cancelled those that they had planned. Was this guy chicken, or hiding ghost

DIVINE PAYBACK

units that only existed on paper whose payrolls he was pocketing?

Letters still came to Jack from Suzanne with each mail delivery that the Team received with copies of the Stars and Stripes about four days a week. It was either dropped off by a visiting province staff member, or picked up during runs to the City. In the evenings the advisors discussed the latest news stories.

Lam Son 719 ended on March 24th with the ARVN withdrawing from Laos. Severely compromised intelligence blew the element of surprise, so the NVA divisions were prepared. The GVN objective of destroying them in Laos was not achieved. However, the ARVN fought well. They not only held their own, but also had disrupted the NVA so badly, that it took the enemy another two years to rebuild their capability to launch another major offensive.

On March 29th, Lieutenant Calley was found guilty of 22 counts of murder. Major Bennett's assessment was that Calley could not have picked a worse defense attorney. No eye witnesses testified they had actually seen him shoot anyone. However, Calley's defense strategy was not to deny the charges, but to put the system on trail. Another interesting Courts Martial of an Air Force colonel was in progress at Tan Son Nhut. He was defending the charges that he had regularly smoked marijuana with his troops on the grounds that it had raised unit morale.

A left-leaning veterans' group, that was led by a decorated former Navy Lieutenant named John F. Kerry, the Vietnam Veterans Against the War, now regularly made the front pages. The team's consensus, shared by virtually all who were still serving in Vietnam, was that the VVAW had every right to demonstrate, but the grossly exaggerated tales of widespread atrocities were demoralizing as hell.

CHAPTER 5

Major Bennett knew what he was doing. He insisted that all Team members review the fire support plan with its precisely plotted coordinates of potential targets. In the event of an ambush during a trip to Dalat, or even a remotely possible major ground attack on their compound, deadly accurate U.S. artillery or helicopter rocket fire could be quickly delivered. That would enable them to hold out until a Huey could arrive to extract them. It was a major morale boost knowing they were not totally at the mercy of their RF counterparts.

Bennett also encouraged Jack and Chuck, the team's medic, in their fire power demonstrations a couple days a week. As a deterrent to nighttime VC penetration attempts, and for their own recreation, the two would display their marksmanship prowess by firing the team's M60 machine gun and M203 grenade launchers; and their individual M16s at small items located next to the wreckage of the Chinook, now an artillery reference point, located 300 meters down in the valley.

Bennett finally went over Kahn's head to the Deputy PSA who persuaded the Province Chief to direct Kahn to permit Tieu-ta Bennett to visit any of his units unaccompanied, as long as he informed Khan in advance. One afternoon Jack was in the Team's TOC monitoring the progress of Barnett and two team members as they radioed in the checkpoints they had cleared heading to a remote outpost. Major Tanh suddenly burst in. Extremely agitated, he claimed that he had just received a report of "beaucoup VC" along the route. Jack's gut told him it was bullshit, but he radioed the report to Barnett who aborted the mission.

The rapid pace of American unit withdrawals had reached Dalat when the signal unit at Kraus compound pulled out. The Province Team would be taking it over, so in early April, Jack, to his dismay, was pulled back into the City to work logistical aspects of setting it up. He had grown to utterly despise most of the field grade officers and many captains on the Province Team. Jack was impressed by a couple of majors though. One was the Phoenix Advisor, who his peers harassed mercilessly and relentlessly in front of the junior officers.

With several noteworthy exceptions, however Jack saw the PSA and his senior staff as corrupt or incompetent trough-swilling careerist swine. "Archetypical political butt-holes with teeth." One of the prima donnas, a captain, had even deliberately sabotaged his rotation date so that he could spend a couple more weeks with his shack job waiting for a new port call. What disgusted Jack the most however, were the grossly exaggerated reports submitted under the unit and hamlet evaluation systems that all lauded how great the Regional Forces were doing assuming their combat and security roles.

Jack was still on his original post-OCS contract that would end in September. After being reassigned back to the City, he learned that he had been given an OER (officer evaluation report) a month earlier. It had been written by people who observed him for less than two months in his previous MAT assignment. However, it covered the 6 month period that included Panama and Di An! The system was inflated, so an "above average" report was technically favorable, and therefore nearly impossible to appeal.

Jack's OER contained a lot of faint praise with several critical comments about his maturity. By no means adverse under the regulations, it was a likely career killer just the same. The major who wrote the senior rating, wasn't even in Jack's chain of command! Not one of the four, who had signed off on that report, including Mr. Whoosh, the PSA, or his pious West Point military deputy, even had the guts to show it to him. The Army had recently announced an early out policy reducing the term of every obligated volunteer officer by two months. For Jack, this meant he could return

CHAPTER 5

home in mid-July, so his response to the OER was "Screw it, I'm out of here."

One day, Jack's mail contained an invitation to one of Mr. Whoosh's mandatory social events the upcoming Sunday afternoon. In a master stroke of passive aggression, Jack picked up a hooker from the bar at the Hotel Dalat, paid her the "long time" rate, and then showed up with her on his arm at the garden party at the PSA Mr. Whoosh's villa. It was only fair. If the other advisors in all their Regular Army purity could bring their girlfriends from Madame Thai's, why couldn't he bring a date? Jack made sure to make the rounds and exchange pleasantries with everyone. He later returned his girl to the Hotel Dalat without even getting a "short time."

Jack shared a large attic room in the villa with two lieutenants. One named Bobby, was another former MAT team advisor. The other one was temporarily filling the province intelligence advisor position. Jack got along well with those guys, who were made of "very solid stuff." A fourth bed was kept open for advisors visiting overnight from the districts. There was plenty of time to read the newspaper reports about the April anti-war demonstrations back home. Some crowds had reached 200 thousand, and more were planned for May. In response to an invitation from the Peoples Republic of China, on April 10, 1971 a U.S. Table Tennis Team became the first officially sanctioned visit for any Americans to the Chinese mainland since 1949.

Closer to Dalat, a totally unexpected early May event shook the entire Province Advisory Team command group that delighted Jack. John Paul Vann had just been reassigned from Military Region IV to become the Senior Advisor for Southern Military Region II. He was also bringing a new two-star military deputy with him. Even U.S. media critics of the war agreed that Vann had pacified the Delta Region. However, this "pacification" looked a lot like martial law by a competent but benevolent militia. The PSA, Mr. Whoosh,

DIVINE PAYBACK

and his newly assigned military deputy had the entire province jumping through hoops for the command briefing they would be giving him. "I can't wait to see that," thought Jack. He would not be disappointed.

John Vann arrived in Dalat early in the evening, only four days after he had assumed his new duties. Vann was accompanied by his military deputy, and the II Corps ARVN Commanding General, Lt. General Ngo Dzu. Jack had a prime seat among the American military and civilian advisors. Only a handful of senior GVN counterparts from the Province were present. As a light colonel early in the War, Vann had destroyed his career with his brutally truthful after action reports, citing the marginal to poor combat performance of ARVN units he had advised. President Johnson was later so impressed by Vann's articles in Esquire magazine, that by 1965, Vann was back in Vietnam as a two-star level Foreign Service Officer in the new COORDS program.

After a brief introduction by the PSA, Mr. Vann took less than a half hour to deliver his remarks that undoubtedly burned into the memories of those present for a lifetime. Vann articulated details about both friendly and enemy unit operations throughout the Province. He knew not only the names of GVN leaders down to the company and village levels, but also the names of their Viet Cong counterparts! Vann firmly and clearly stated his expectations for all military advisors to participate in weekly operations with their counterparts. He then turned it over to the PSA for his military staff principals, mostly majors, to brief him.

The newly assigned light colonel Deputy PSA was fortunate that he only had to introduce each staff principal. The Phoenix Advisor, whose do-nothing peers harassed relentlessly, gave the singularly outstanding briefing on enemy activity. The young first lieutenant acting as the province intelligence advisor was also impressive. Next up

CHAPTER 5

was the major who was concluding his 18 month tour with advisory responsibilities for all RF and PF activities. His five minute briefing, like those of the rest of the principals who followed, would have been barely acceptable for newly assigned lieutenants filling in for absent bosses.

At the conclusion of the last presentation, Mr. Vann requested all the Vietnamese present to excuse themselves. Lieutenant General Dzu, who a Time investigative report had recently fingered as one of Southeast Asia's top drug lords, remained seated and smiling. After two polite requests, Mr. Vann raised the inflection of his voice and said "General Dzu, you're excused. Colonel, please escort the general to the social where we will soon be joining him."

Mr. Vann then laid down the law to the Tuyen Duc PSA and his staff making it clear he would be back within six weeks expecting major progress. Jack sat through the entire briefing without even a smirk. Perhaps the Lord had rewarded him with a "Divine payback" for riding shotgun with the Chaplain on his Easter rounds, even though Jack's motives had been just to get away from the City.

For days after Vann had read the command group the riot act, Jack's discussions with his roommates speculated on where they would all end up. Reestablishing MAT teams didn't seem feasible. Augmenting the District teams for going out on increased RF missions seemed a more likely course of action. On a late May Sunday morning Jack was sleeping after pulling a shift as the province TOC duty officer. Bobby woke him up. A major calling from the province headquarters told Jack over the land line "You need to be at the lake helipad ready to move out in an hour and a half. This is a permanent move so bring all your gear."

Jack was given a copy of the message from Vann's headquarters while he packed. It directed each province to designate one of their combat arms officers for duty with the

DIVINE PAYBACK

17th CAG. The designated officer was to report to Tuy Hoa that day. The command group had assumed the officer would soon accompany an ARVN "combined arms group" that was being assembled for a major operation in the highlands. That was fine with Jack, who quickly packed up two duffle bags and his ruck sack before throwing them into Bobby's jeep. The new Deputy PSA was waiting at the helipad to see Jack off. As Jack turn to approach the Huey for boarding, the lieutenant colonel shook his hand saying "Do a good job."

CHAPTER 6

6. GETTING SHORT

Within two minutes after it touched down on the lakeside helipad in Dalat, Jack boarded and was strapped into the Huey by the crew chief. He kept both hands on the M16 between his knees while looking down at the two figures waving good bye as the chopper lifted off. He then put on the head phones and asked the pilot over the intercom, "Where are we headed?" "Tuy Hoa", replied the pilot, "but first we need to stop at Dong Ba Tinh."

Jack suddenly tensed up, but relaxed as the pilot continued "to pick up another passenger and refuel". He breathed a sigh of relief since that was where he had ended up passed out drunk during that mortar attack the night of his "aerial combat". During the 15 minute stop, a lieutenant named Bill Romano, another ex-MAT advisor, who Jack knew from Panama and Di-an, joined the last leg of their flight. The pilots informed Jack and Bill that Tuy Hoa was a former U.S. Air Force base that had just been taken over by the Army's 17th Combat Aviation Group, or CAG.

Upon their late afternoon arrival, a jeep and driver were waiting to take the two lieutenants to Aviation Group headquarters. Bill and Jack were quickly ushered in to the office of the Group Commander, a full colonel, who warmly greeted them. After quickly seating and putting them at ease, the Colonel gave a 10 minute in-briefing while they finished the cold beverage an orderly had brought them. "Mr. Vann wants to free up more rated aviators holding jobs that involve a lot of ground duties so they can spend more time flying. You two will be assigned here, with the 268th Combat Aviation Battalion (CAB) for airfield security duties." The two were then driven to the 268th CAB headquarters.

A duty NCO quickly signed them into the unit and said "the battalion commander wants you to get settled in now. He's looking forward to meeting you after in-processing tomorrow morning". After Jack and Bill checked their weapons into the unit arms room, they were driven to their BOQ. The sun was just setting, so they noticed that all the buildings were still painted in nice Air Force pastel colors. They were delighted to find the BOQ air conditioned. Each was assigned his own room with sheets, bedding, a wall locker and dresser. Maid service cost $5 per week. Jack remarked to Bill "This is great. The Army must be too busy to start screwing with the Air Force influence".

The next morning, Jack and Bill received a friendly greeting from their new battalion commander, Lt. Colonel Day. He was with his S2 Intelligence and Security Officer, Captain Bob Stolz, who would be their boss. After exchanging pleasantries, Stolz took the two into his own office where he briefed them on their general duties. Aircraft on every base where the Group's units were stationed had recently been experiencing increasing sabotage.

Each lieutenant would have three sergeants permanently assigned to them, to organize and operate two ad hoc security detachments. They would perform internal security from six in the evening until six in the morning. The two leadership elements would rotate, giving them the next day and evening off. No funds were available for flight pay, but the lieutenants could fly aerial surveillance missions with Captain Stolz during the days if they were interested.

Jack was assigned the first tour and then introduced to his three NCOs. Otis Boor was a staff sergeant in his late twenties. John Verbonitz and Lew Kelleher were buck sergeants in their early twenties. All three were exceptionally sharp seasoned combat veterans. Otis and John were on their second combat tours. The troops would be detailed to them from duty rosters of the Group's units that were stationed at Tuy Hoa. Making a unit work, that was comprised of troops who they did not formally command, would require a lot of teamwork, coordination and leadership. That afternoon they

CHAPTER 6

established the organization and system. The troops reported at 1730 with their weapons and prescribed combat gear. After they were issued ammunition, Jack conducted the initial inspection and briefing. Afterwards, he and one of the sergeants drove them to their assigned posts and gave them individual orders and instructions.

The mission of securing the outer perimeter of the sprawling Tuy Hoa installation belonged to one of the infantry battalions that was preparing for redeployment stateside. Jack was responsible for a dozen guard stations in areas adjacent to unit hangars or sandbagged revetments where the aircraft were parked. Jack replaced and rotated the troops back to the security building to rest every two hours. Since this was an internal security mission, the policy was for each sentry to lock a full magazine into his M-16 while on post, but to only load a round into the chamber if he was in personal danger.

Jack required the sentries to wear their pistol belts with canteens and ammunition pouches attached. He also authorized them to wear soft hats, but required them to place their flak jackets, steel pots and other combat gear at a location they could get to within 60 seconds. Most sentries pulled this duty after a day of flying or pulling maintenance. Jack and the sergeants visited each post hourly, not just to keep them alert, but also to reassure them that help would quickly arrive in an emergency. In the morning Jack wrote down names of any troops who had performed exceptionally or several repeat tours.

The Tuy Hoa officers' club was located on the beach across the street from his BOQ. Jack quickly established his routine for days off by spending an hour or two in the club writing to Suzanne. He also drafted up atta-boy notes to the unit commanders of the troops whose names he had written down. On his second day off, Jack was sitting at the bar in a bathing suit and t-shirt drinking a gin and tonic when two senior staff officers from his former province team walked in. When they saw Jack, both grinned widely and with spontaneous insincerity rushed over to him with outstretched hands. "We all thought that by now you'd be stomping around with some ARVN combined arms group north of Ban Me Thut." Jack just smiled and responded "Yup, they sure showed me." "Tell them I want a copy of my report card." Both abruptly finished their drinks before sheepishly begging off "to catch their flight back to Dalat."

Jack resumed drafting some "atta-boy notes" from the previous night. These short, routine letters of appreciation to unit commanders of sentries paid off. During Jack's six weeks of running the security operation there was only one disciplinary problem. He then answered Suzanne's recent letters that she continued to faithfully send. In spite of his gambling, the total from monthly allotments to his savings account now exceeded $5,000. That would be enough for Jack and Suzanne to get started on. His attitude and morale were quickly recovering.

Jack got along well with Captain Stolz. He had been a rifle platoon leader before briefly commanding a company on his previous Vietnam tour, before going to flight school. Taking Stolz up on his offer, Jack occasionally went with him on observation flights in a light observation helicopter. He observed a few B-52 strikes over heavily wooded areas, called in by American advisors with their ARVN units. One time he saw some sharks swimming about 500 yards off the coast.

Stolz regularly passed on to Jack the compliments he received about the improved security posture of the airfield to Jack and encouraged him to stay in the Army. By mid-June however, Jack had received orders to report to Ton San Nhut for out-processing on July 7th. He was shocked to see a MACV, not a USARV letterhead, and that he was still

CHAPTER 6

officially assigned to the MACV COORDS Second Military Region.

Jack regularly listened with great interest to the experiences that his NCOs shared with him. Otis Boor, the Staff Sergeant, had done a tour with an infantry battalion. Both Lew Kelleher and John Verbonitz were combat aviation NCOs. Both had flown hundreds of hours, first as helicopter door gunners, then as crew chiefs. One evening Otis and Jack shared their experiences working with our South Korean allies. "The ROKs" as they were referred to, loyally honored their Southeast Asia Treaty Organization commitment by sending two divisions to Vietnam. Highly respected by their American allies, they were equally feared by not only the VC, but even crack NVA regulars.

The ROK organization and tactical doctrine had a heavy American influence. However, they still employed the draconian disciplinary systems of most Asian armies. Jack's experience with them had been limited to the weekly dinners and Tai Kwon Do lessons with the ROK Advisors during his Dalat days. He did learn that trying to out-drink the ROKs with Souju posed a serious risk of alcohol poisoning. Otis Boor had recent operational experience with them during an assignment in Qui Nhon, that involved joint ROK-US sentry patrols. Otis recalled one night when the ROK and American duty officers came upon two sentries asleep next to a bridge they were supposed to be guarding. The American GI eventually received a fine and restriction under a non-judicial Article 15 punishment. The ROK duty officer summarily administered an "Article 45", short hand for shooting him on the spot with his .45 caliber side arm.

The mission-orientation of Jack's combat aviation battalion bred the professional bonding inherent in real soldiering. Every job was clearly related to keeping the helicopters combat ready so that they could provide rapidly responsive combat or logistical support to troops on the ground. There was indeed a problem with heroin however, and other drug use by as many as five percent of the troops. Marijuana use was far more prevalent, but no troops from units detailed to Jack's security operation ever reported stoned. Jack loathed the hard drug users, but didn't make any effort to find pot smokers. The overwhelming majority of troops who served in Vietnam were the best young men in America. Even draftees who hated the Army were willing to pull together for the sake of everyone making it home safely.

Jack was in good standing with his command which would normally get him at least a one-year extension. However those paragons of Regular Army virtue in Dalat would do the final processing and endorse it forward. Jack decided to take advantage of the GI Bill to go back to college and get his degree. After separating from active duty, he would still have a reserve commission. Jack's Tuy Hoa experience heavily influenced him to join the National Guard when he returned home.

On July 5th President Nixon formally certified the 26th Amendment giving 18 year olds the right to vote. Total U.S. troop strength was now almost under 200,000. By the 1972 election, when every U.S. soldier could finally vote, most of the 25,000 remaining in Vietnam were senior personnel over 21. Since mid-June, the New York Times had been publishing the "Pentagon Papers". Nixon had lost his court battle to block the release of these classified documents that one time CIA analyst Daniel Ellsberg had illegally obtained.

In Vietnam, a June 27th ABC "Issues and Answers" interview with Colonel David Hackworth shook the entire military U.S. military hierarchy. Hackworth, who had earned a battlefield commission during the Korean War at 19, was now, at 38, the Army's youngest full colonel. He was on his fourth combat tour in Vietnam, and currently serving as a province senior advisor. This Army role model, who had earned every combat award except for the Medal of Honor,

CHAPTER 6

was now airing all the dirty linen. Hackworth validated virtually all of Jack's conclusions about our Vietnamese allies, as well as the severe integrity shortfalls of many senior civilian and military officials running the war.

Jack spent his final evenings off at the officer's club playing nickel, dime and quarter poker, and drinking Johnny Walker Black. He ran into several of his OCS classmates who were assigned or in transit at Tuy Hoa. This included a friendly encounter with his last TAC officer from OCS, newly-promoted Captain Johnny Riggs, who was now an aviator in one of the Group's battalions. Jack had to report to Camp Alpha at Ton Son Nhut for out-processing on July 8th. On the morning of July 7th his last security shift ended. He said goodbye to his NCOs and gave them copies of commendations he had submitted to the unit. After a brief farewell office visits at the headquarters with Captain Stolz and Lt. Colonel Day, Jack caught a Huey to Tan Son Nhut.

By late 1970 the problem of troops addicted to heroin had become so severe, that everyone below the rank of full colonel was required to spend three days in quarantine for several urine tests, before being cleared for their flights home. During their stay at Camp Alpha they were free to explore the Ton Son Nhut complex, however. The first afternoon, Jack changed into his gringo posse civilian clothes from Panama, then caught a ride to Tudoc Street in the heart of Saigon.

Jack was accompanied by another ex-advisor with an attitude named Don, a highly decorated directly-commissioned former career Sergeant. They were only out for a last look, and perhaps a few final Saigon Teas. In less than an hour however, an American MP patrol approached and sternly informed them that Saigon was off limits. Jack politely explained that he had just arrived for out-processing and truthfully claimed ignorance. The MPs dropped them off at a U.S. contracted Brinks hotel, directing them to take the next shuttle back to Camp Alpha. After spending the next

GETTING SHORT

two days playing a lot of poker and drinking with fellow outbound officers, Jack boarded the freedom bird.

A loud cheer erupted as the chartered 747 took off. Jack and Don sat next to each other alternating turns at the window seat. As Jack gazed out at the pock marked countryside, he thought about the dead Regional Force soldiers and Vietnamese civilians he had seen. Divine intervention had spared Jack the anguish of seeing fellow U.S. soldiers getting killed, especially while carrying out orders he might have issued. He felt guilty about returning without a scratch, when over 55 thousand gallant Americans before him had made the ultimate sacrifice. What was it all for?

Jack and Don discussed the maverick Colonel David Hackworth's recent interviews as they engaged in a long philosophical discourse about what it had all about. One of Hackworth's statements that really stuck was *"I haven't seen the improvements that I read about in many papers and different magazines, and I hear leading statesmen of our nation say. I don't think the Vietnamese are that good. I don't think the whole Vietnamization thing is real."* When Don nodded off, Jack re-read his most recent letters from Suzanne, contemplating how their reunion would go.

7. BACK HOME

Jack first stepped on U.S. soil at Hickam Air Force Base in Honolulu, where the plane landed after sundown for a brief stopover. An old Air Force Master Sergeant admonished him to extinguish his cigarette while walking on the flight line to the terminal. It was midnight when the plane was airborne again, so he didn't even get a view of the scenery. The returning Vietnam vets reached Travis Air Base at mid-afternoon on July 10th. They had lost a day crossing the International Date Line.

A shuttle bus took Jack, Don and the others scheduled for separation out-processing to Oakland Army Terminal. The officers were put up in a shabby BOQ for the evening. Jack called Suzanne to arrange their reunion. Very out of character, Jack not only passed on the opportunity for a night on the town, but only drank a few beers as he and Don spent the evening continuing their philosophical discussion from the flight. The FM transistor radio Jack had purchased in the Tuy Hoa PX played a San Francisco Bay FM station. The avant garde dialogue about "Wilber Funk eating crotch cheese" was a far cry from the AFVN they had been listening to only two days earlier. Things were definitely changing on this side of the pond. Don's statement "I have more respect for the VC than the ARVN" said it all about their advisory experiences.

The assembly-line separation processing began after breakfast with a physical exam. The final step was a records review after a litany of mandatory out-briefings. Since officers were expected to read things, they received a separate accelerated version. That meant they would be free and clear by noon, unlike the enlisted group that would finish in the late afternoon. Their packets contained a letter permanently promoting them in the Army Reserve to the temporary active duty ranks they held on active duty, and a couple of certificates with President Nixon's and General Westmoreland's signatures on them.

An administrative specialist dutifully emphasized that "The most important document is the official report of separation from active military service – the DD Form 214. For VA benefits, all that really mattered was that the items accurately verified the character and length of service. Any omission or errors in the sections indicating home of record, military and civilian education, and awards and decoration can be corrected by coming back during the enlisted briefing that would continue after lunch." It's far easier when dealing with lower level clerks who process veterans' benefits, or reserve military personnel actions to use a single DD214, than trying to explain several other documents to verify omitted information. Many who decided to write a letter later on, requesting a DD215 for adding missing items, would regret not returning that afternoon.

Jack and Don shared a cab to San Francisco International wearing their Class A uniforms. During the anti-war years the most likely areas for demonstrations would have been in traditional hotbeds of the left like Northeast college campuses, the San Francisco Bay area and certain suburbs or districts of cities like New York, and Cambridge outside of Boston. Organized anti-war militants did indeed accost service members in public, but usually as part of an organized protest. It was never spontaneous. President Nixon had recently announced that an all volunteer military would end the draft. The absence of that threat must have dampened the zeal of the morally superior anti-war activists, since none were at the airport.

After having a drink in the lounge together, the two shook hands as Don left for his Nashville flight. Soon after, Jack boarded his flight to Boston. It was no different than any of his previous experiences flying military standby. There were

CHAPTER 7

no hostile approaches from anyone, or even disapproving looks. Jack sat next to a businessman who had served during the fifties, and engaged in conversation. Although Jack mentioned he was just returning from Vietnam, they mostly talked about cars, boxing, colleges, and feminism. On the last topic, they lamented more about their preferences for miniskirts over bellbottoms and pants suits, which had rapidly spread through women's fashion. They also discussed how the topping of New York City's World Trade Center, scheduled for the 19th, would make it the world's tallest building. Jack was encouraged to take advantage of his GI Bill because the economy was lousy.

Jack's parents, who now lived in a South Shore suburb of Boston, greeted him at the gate. Suzanne still lived more than an hour away in Rhode Island. Jack would not have expected her to participate in such a family affair and for good reason. Suzanne had not spoken to Jack's parents since Lynnette had vulgarly berated her following his four day stint at the military college four years earlier. After dinner with his folks at their house Jack drove down to Rhode Island to see Suzanne. Her parents, who had always treated Jack like a son, warmly welcomed him. After visiting for about an hour, Suzanne and Jack went out to an upscale restaurant and lounge for dinner, and spent the remainder of the evening talking and looking over the "Apartments for Rent" ads. Jack was staying at his parents' house, so he was motivated to move quickly.

Jack's parents immediately attempted to reassert control over him as if he was still in high school. They pressured him to enroll in Stonehill College, an overpriced Catholic liberal arts college up the road. This fueled Jack's resentment over their failing to call nearby state colleges to facilitate the application process as he had asked them to in several letters from Dalat and Tuy Hoa. May was the absolute latest application deadline for the fall semester at most state

BACK HOME

colleges and universities. Since he had missed it, Jack would have to wait until January.

Jack had already decided to attend Rhode Island College or possibly the University of Rhode Island. One rainy evening after a pointless discussion about Stonehill, Jack senior and Lynnette refused to let Jack use their car to see Suzanne, so he merely rode his motorcycle down. This was no big deal to Jack, since it paled in comparison to the Monsoons in which he had recently operated.

On his fifth morning back home, Jack moved into a one bedroom apartment in West Warwick, the town where Suzanne still lived with her parents. It was next to Coventry, where he graduated from high school. Jack and Suzanne discussed their future over several days of shopping for clothes and household items. After five years together, Suzanne was focused not only on the idyllic notions of marriage and a family, but on the practical aspects like the security of a home and a stable productive husband. She viewed Jack's apartment as a brief transitional step. There was no way Suzanne was going to play house without a ring and a mortgage.

Jack had a vaguely defined concept of pursuing a career as a lawyer. He had also structured an achievable plan for a comfortable income that combined his monthly GI Bill payments, with the pay he would receive from the National Guard. The new all volunteer force relied heavily on more robust reserve forces, so there were abundant opportunities for professional development active duty tours, and attending army schools during semester breaks. Suzanne immediately saw a red flag because this could require Jack to go away for up to 8 weeks in the summers.

Jack had demonstrated some financial responsibility by saving almost six thousand dollars while he was in Vietnam (thanks to Joe Frazier, unknown to Suzanne). Since they

CHAPTER 7

would need two incomes while Jack was going to school, she couldn't just take off with him in the summers. Suzanne also had flashbacks to Fort Gordon. Jack's philandering life style there had left him too insolvent to buy her an engagement ring, or to even pay for her trips to visit him.

Suzanne was now in her fourth year of a good job with benefits. As a first lieutenant, Jack had been making decent money, so her practical side encouraged him to file for unemployment, since he qualified for the maximum benefit. Following Suzanne's advice, Jack filed a veterans' unemployment claim the same day he moved into his apartment. He was amazed upon discovering that his weekly benefit exceeded the salary for an entry level job. Since he would be going back to college in January, and it was almost August, why waste time reading the want ads? Jack also rationalized that these weekly payments were emoluments to which he was entitled for his gallant service to the Republic.

After their two weeks of being back together, friction surfaced when Jack showed up one evening in her car that she had loaned him for the day. He had decided to "surprise her" by bringing their "old friend Dan Debre" with him. Dan had been coming off an all night binge when Jack had linked up with him earlier in the afternoon, and was now barely able to walk. Dan and Jack had finished off a couple of six packs and a sack of New York System hot dogs over the afternoon. When Dan started heaving the hot dogs, a quick decision was made to drop him off at his apartment. Suzanne, whose partying days were over, sat silently seething during the half hour drive to Providence. Living like an adult was long overdue for Jack!

After five consecutive years in college, Dan had failed to graduate the previous May. He had hit the skids and was now renting a flat in a condemned triple-decker tenement building. It was located in the same run-down Providence neighborhood off Smith Street, where his previous places had

BACK HOME

all been. The young owner, who lived on the first floor and was bringing it up to code, was charging Dan $50 a month for rent, with credit for any improvements he made. Dan's girl friend Dee Dee, a fellow student who sang in a local rock band, had just moved out. All he had going for him now was a second shift factory job.

Jack soon was spending the days waiting for Suzanne to get out of work hanging around with Dan and Jim Gromulka, another friend from his pre-draft Providence partying days. Jim had also recently gotten out of the Army, after serving with the Special Forces in Germany. Jim had made it up to sergeant but had been demoted to Specialist 4 just before he separated.

In the evenings Jack would drive his motorcycle over to Suzanne's. From there they would go over to Jack's apartment for dinner. Although the kitchen was now fully furnished with utensils and tableware, Suzanne found it odd that they were still eating off their laps on the floor because there still wasn't any furniture. Jack explained that they needed to save money if they were going to furnish a house. She retorted that the place could be furnished for a few hundred dollars using second hand stores and thrift shops.

Since Suzanne had picked out a decent wardrobe for Jack, she suggested that perhaps he should take a job until January. Jack responded that he had lined up a two week active duty tour in mid-October. This was partly true since he had researched dates for a service school through his new reserve unit. However, the bullshit sessions at Dan's apartment, where Jim liberally shared his pot with them, had preempted following up with the application paperwork.

During one of those afternoon bullshit sessions Jack accepted Dan's suggestion that he take in Jim as a roommate to share expenses. Suzanne was upset when Jack informed her, but calmed down after he explained that it would only be

CHAPTER 7

until January. Jack also rationalized that he could sell Jim his half of any furnishings that they would accumulate together when he moved out. It was now August, and there still was not a stick of furniture in Jack's apartment. He also hadn't done anything about applying for admission to college in January.

During a lobster dinner that Jack had fixed at the apartment, he assured Suzanne that he would check out the UPS part time driver's program she had told him about. The next day Jack decided to make the calls from Dan's apartment. By three o'clock in the afternoon, Jack was on the phone to Suzanne explaining that he was going up to Quebec with Dan for a couple of days. She responded that she wanted to spend some time with her girlfriends anyway. It was Tuesday. They would see each other when Jack returned Thursday evening.

Riding on the 175 Honda, Jack and Dan had made it to the northern suburbs of Boston on 128/I-9 when it began raining. The rain became heavier so they would stop for a break about every half hour. They looked up a high school friend who was now living in Portland, Maine around 11 that evening. It was 8 hours after they had started their trip. They were invited in out of the rain. After less than an hour and a half and a few drinks, their friend, who had to get up early for work, sent the two on their way. The weather had cleared up, but the two decided to head back to Providence. It was 5 A.M. and still dark when they reached Dan's apartment. Jack slept for a couple of hours on a mattress in one of the spare bedrooms and drove back to his place. When he arrived Jim came out of the bedroom with a girlfriend. "What happened to the trip to Quebec?" After Jack explained the comedy of errors, he crashed on the sofa in the living room that Jim had donated "for his share of the month's rent."

That evening Suzanne stopped by Jack's apartment. She had never been fond of Jim, so the couple quickly left for the upper-scale supper club where Suzanne wanted to see Sergio Franchi. Jack was completely sober but exhausted. The failed trip to Quebec on top of all the events of the past few weeks had finally caught up to him. After he began to doze off waiting at a railroad crossing, Suzanne took over the driving. Unable to hold them in any longer, she released all her frustrations that had been building up. In spite of his philandering in Georgia she had given him another chance, even loyally waiting during his Vietnam tour.

The last thing Suzanne said before dropping him off was: "People who make something of themselves don't sit around drinking with losers in dive apartments. You had better get away from them, or you'll be just like them!" Jim was sitting in the living room when Jack walked in to his apartment. "What happened?" Jack took several tokes from Jim's hash pipe as he explained the situation. "Who does she think she is treating you like that? Especially after you've just returned from "the Nam" responded Jim. He was totally clueless about the dynamics of Jack's relationship with Suzanne, since he had not had any contact with them for nearly four years. The lack of any direct experience or expertise never deterred Jim from sharing his expert opinions however. Barely able to remain awake, Jack went to bed.

Jim was not around when Jack woke up shortly after noon the next day, so he went out on his motorcycle to a diner for something to eat. When he returned to the apartment Jim was back. They began drinking the beer that Jim had just stocked the refrigerator, with. In no time they had gone through two six-packs and it was after six. When Jack tried calling Suzanne, her mother informed him that she had gone out with her girlfriend. Jack ended up riding up to Providence with Jim to pick up Dan. They spent that evening together at Armando's on the fringes of the East Side. It had formerly been the Crystal Tap, the dive where Jack used to take his dates in high school. They ran into Cindy, the girl Jim was dating, who was with her girlfriend. When Armando's closed

CHAPTER 7

the five went to an all night restaurant. After doing a joint at Dan's apartment, Jim left with Cindy and her girlfriend. The loser would have had to have gone with the girlfriend had Dan and Jack decided to fight over her.

Jack listened to the "Debre economic theory" until day break over a few joints they had rolled out of the ounce of grass that Jim had given him "in lieu of his share of the rent". Several days earlier on August 15th, Nixon had announced the end the Breton Woods system by declaring the U.S. would no longer convert dollars to gold at a fixed rate. Taking the dollar off the gold standard, had effectively made the U.S. dollar just one more fiat currency. The two reminisced back to 1965, when they had recognized the first step in this direction when Lyndon Johnson replaced silver coinage for copper-clad with nickel. Dan elaborated on his personal circular flow diagram. He had run up over fifteen thousand dollars in debt on revolving credit accounts and several Bank Americards and Mastercards. Dan had used these to purchase expensive gifts for his girlfriends like gold bracelets, and Dee Dee's apricot poodle. Unfortunately, he had failed to keep one of the cards open to maintain the other ones in good standing with minimum payments. Dan urged Jack to "leverage that six thousand from Nam" since the inflation that Nixon had just unleashed would whittle it down to nothing in no time.

8. TO THE PLAINS OF ABRAHAM

Jack's apartment building neighbors were leaving for work when he returned from his all-nighter in Providence. He barely woke up in time later that afternoon to pick up his weekly payment before the unemployment office closed for the weekend. What an indignity it was for these ingrate state bureaucrats to make a great American soldier like him stand in line for it! "She's just bluffing," Jack said to himself thinking about Suzanne's parting words to him. "What does she know? Unemployment has hit 6.1 percent. If she thinks I am going to take some nothing job until January she's crazy." Jack assumed this break-up would last about two weeks, so Suzanne could wait at least six days until after he returned from Quebec City.

That evening Jack picked up Dan, and then drove to Pawtucket to check out a 1963 Triumph TR3 convertible advertised in the paper for $550. It ran OK, but the body was in such rough shape that he was able to talk the seller down a hundred dollars. Riding his motorcycle, Jack followed Dan, who drove the TR3. Dan's condemned tenement building gave him access to its detached two car garage. Jack used it the next day to work on the TR3, readily accepted Dan's technical advice to use door hinges and metal screws for the hood problem. The two made the car road worthy and gave it a brush painting with forest green Rustoleum. Inclement weather would not abort this Quebec trip like the earlier one on the motorcycle.

Quebec City had a continental ambiance that made a visit there very much like a poor man's trip to Europe. The old walled city preserved the original colonial architecture from the French colonial period that began in 1608. France ceded the Province to Britain in 1763, after losing the Seven Year's

CHAPTER 8

War. In spite of mass resettlements by the British, a large residual presence of former French colonists remained. When French Canadian Clement Gosselin committed to the American Patriot's cause in 1775, the Continental Congress authorized two Canadian regiments. Major Gosselin's forces did indeed fight well at battles in the rebellious colonies, most notably Yorktown. However, the British had defeated the Patriots' threat to their control of Canada in the Battle of Quebec, where the Continental Army's Brigadier General Benedict Arnold and Major Aaron Burr had distinguished themselves. They then broke the subsequent Patriot siege by May, 1776. Following the 1783 Treaty of Paris, the newly independent American Confederation granted refuge to Canadians who had supported their cause.

Learning from their lost colonies, the King's visionary government under William Pitt, wrote the Constitutional Act of 1791. It divided the remaining British North American territory in half. Upper Canada (now Ontario) was where over 10,000 loyalists from the former 13 colonies had settled. In Lower Canada, the Quebecois were given sufficient autonomy. The protections afforded to the French language, customs, and Catholic religion in what is now the Province of Quebec, were major factors that ensured its loyalty during the British-American War of 1812.

During the American Civil War, Canada provided a friendly neutral haven to the Confederates. President Lincoln however, was far too engaged preventing Robert E. Lee's Army of Northern Virginia from threatening Washington City to aid a Quebecois insurgency; or to even morally support one. The British North America Act of 1867 reinforced the 1791 Act by creating an autonomous Canadian federal system. The 1931 Statute of Westminster finally ended the power of Parliament to unilaterally annul Canadian laws, but retained the British monarch as a figurehead.

TO THE PLAINS OF ABRAHAM

The lack of Quebecois enthusiasm for the alternative of becoming an American state did not mean they were satisfied with the status quo.

Generations of deeply rooted separatist sentiment still lingered in Quebec. In 1885, a Catholic Francophone rebellion in Saskatchewan was suppressed. Louis Riel, its leader, was subsequently tried and hung for treason. A French Canadian, Louis St Laurent, had served as Prime Minister from 1948 to 1957. In 1965, the Canadian government made another symbolic overture by replacing the old federal flag with the Union Jack banner with the red and white Maple Leaf standard. Separatist sentiment remained strong in Quebec however, with its nearly 80 percent ethnically French population. In 1967 however, a massive crowd went into a frenzy after President Charles De Gaulle ended his speech at Quebec City's Hotel de Ville with "Vive Le Quebec Libre."

The current Prime Minister Pierre Elliot Trudeau, a French Canadian, had held office since 1968. Trudeau had also become the darling of international liberals by his opposition to the U.S. military involvement in Vietnam. However, during the late sixties, the Quebec Liberation Front (FLQ), a violently extreme left wing separatist paramilitary group, had emerged. It was responsible for 160 violent incidents and eight people being killed. After the FLQ had kidnapped and murdered Quebec Labor Minister Pierre La Porte in October, 1970, the Canadian federal government finally invoked the War Powers Act and decimated it.

Dan Debre and Jack Wilson were rehearsing their act while passing several joints during the 8 hour drive to Quebec. Not only left-leaning separatists, but also main stream liberals loathed Nixon and supported Trudeau's Vietnam position. Draft dodgers and military deserters were hailed with open arms, especially in Quebec City. "I'll get tripped up trying to pose as a deserter, but they'll believe me

CHAPTER 8

if I tell them I'm a Vietnam Veterans Against the War organizer," said Jack, shortly after crossing the international border north of Jackman, Maine,

Upon reaching the small city of Ste Georges that night, Dan and Jack had finished off a six pack of La Bat, on top of two six packs of Budweiser they already had consumed before entering Canada. Upon entering the lounge of a three star hotel they dropped into around 11:00 PM, they immediately asked a couple of local young ladies to dance. Michelle, a very attractive brunette, hung on to every word Dan said. They were impressed with Debre's French surname, frequently chanting "Danny, Danny" in their heavy French accents.

Dan had suddenly snapped back into his old self. Unfortunately, Jack's "drunken charisma" as Dan called it, had turned off Michele's friend. She pressured Michelle to leave the hotel lobby soon after they had gathered there when the lounge closed. After the management finally gave them the bums rush around 3:00 A.M., Dan took the wheel. Jack was passed out in the passenger seat for most of the two hour drive to the ferry crossing at Levis. He finally began to sober up as the ferry crossed the St Lawrence River. A drunk driver hitting an iron siding caused a slight delay while the vehicles disembarked on the northern bank outside of Quebec's city limits.

Shortly after 7:00 A.M., Jack registered at the Chateau Frontenac, casually tearing off five hundred dollars in traveler's checks. The luxury hotel was a commanding edifice. Designed like a castle, it dominated the old walled city, overlooking the Plains of Abraham. Although Quebec had long been the epicenter of French separatists, very few would be found here. Debre evaluated their suite. Even though it lacked a view of the St Lawrence, he found it to be "suitable quarters" for the next three days. After receiving a $20 tip from Jack, the valet arranged for a rollaway bed so that Dan wouldn't have to sleep on the leather couch in the sitting room. After a late afternoon wake up, they left to eat and scout out the City. Returning to the Chateau, they filled the refrigerator with a case of LaBat. Shortly after 9PM, and several tumblers of Johnny Walker Black, they went out for the evening.

Jack's black beret, with the brass Vietnamese eagle and Trung-Uy blossoms, turned a few heads as they bar hopped that Monday evening. It was after eleven however, and they had gotten nowhere with the mademoiselles in "Le Circle Electrique". "Le Circle" was a night club in an old converted theater, but about the only place that evening with unaccompanied women. For that night's last stand they selected "Le Bistro", a packed café with standing room only. Both were still relatively sober and lucid as Jack removed his beret and stepped up to the bar.

Jack noticed a beautiful brunette standing next to him, but engaging in animated conversation with a waiter. She was soon joined by a girlfriend from a group at a nearby table. Jack smiled as their eyes met while Dan ordered a second round. She not only returned the smile but asked him in English with a pronounced accent where in the States he was from. "How did you know we were Americans?" "Because the few Anglais (a pejorative for an English Canadian) who come here never try speaking French" she responded. Jack introduced himself and Dan to Patrice and her friend Marie.

In his only unembellished comment of the evening, Jack responded that they were from Rhode Island. The girls agreed to join them at a recently vacated table. Both were nursing students at Laval University, and lived in the suburb of Ste Foy. Dan told Marie, who resembled Yvette Mimiuex, that he was a doctoral candidate at Brown University. Jack chimed in that they were taking a break from organizing students for Senator George McGovern's Presidential campaign the following year. This impressed Patrice who asked Jack the significance of the brass eagle and blossoms

CHAPTER 8

on the beret tucked in his belt. He responded truthfully that it was a memento from his days advising Montanyard tribesmen of Vietnam's central highlands.

Jack then shamelessly claimed that he had "earned a battlefield commission from the ranks, but had recently resigned in disgust, and was now attending the University of Rhode Island studying to be a lawyer." There was little chemistry between Dan and Marie, who interrupted the small talk flowing freely between Patrice and Jack with "we must to get to our clinicals early, Patrice". To his surprise, Patrice gave Jack her phone number as she got up to leave. The waiter, who had been talking to her earlier, responded very surly to Dan after he ordered last call, and threw the nickel on the table in response to Jack's "by all means keep the change".

The next day was spent exploring the City's historical landmarks, including the historic fort where an active ceremonial Canadian Army unit was garrisoned. By dinner time, Jack was disappointed that there had been no answer the three times he attempted calling Patrice. "Guess she was playing games with her bozo waiter boyfriend," thought Jack. Dan and Jack then spent most of the evening checking out the night spots that a pleasant waitress in Ste. Foy had suggested.

By eleven, Tuesday night seemed to be as dead as Monday. Dan suggested that they head to the Bistro. Jack agreed saying "Let's cut this trip short if I can convince the Chateau to refund the last night's charges with some hokum bullshit about a sudden emergency." As they walked up to the Bistro's bar Jack pretended not to notice Patrice seated with three girls at a far end table.

After ordering two La Bats, Jack noticed Patrice coming towards him out of the corner of his eye. She warmly greeted Jack and Dan. Jack grinned as he accepted Patrice's invitation to join her friends at the table. She introduced her

TO THE PLAINS OF ABRAHAM

friend Michelle to Dan as soon as they sat down. "A good omen" murmured Dan to Jack, "same name as the one you blew it for me with in Ste Georges". The two gringos basked in their glory as the four girls seemed to take in every one of their outrageous utterances. When the moment of truth arrived at last call, Patrice and Michelle accepted their invitation to get something to eat. Their friend, whose car they came in, then went home without them.

Michelle laughed uncontrollably as they approached the uniquely painted TR3, parked on a side street four blocks away. Patrice smiled at Jack's animated shoulder shrug that accompanied his remark "I never claimed to be rich." Dan removed the top and threw it in the trunk before they headed to a Chinese restaurant in Ste. Foy. Michelle copied Dan's rebel yells as both held on to the ridge underneath the ledge they were sitting on, with their feet in the well of the two-seater convertible.

It was almost 3:00 A.M. when they finished the mediocre pooh-pooh platter with sweet and sour sauce made with Maraschino cherries. Jack took the girls back to their apartment complex because both had to get up early. Patrice definitely would see Jack again Wednesday. She then passionately reciprocated his good night kiss. Dan was smiling as he returned from walking Michelle to her apartment.

The next morning Dan was watching the movie "Billy Budd" on TV in the living room drinking a La Bat, when Jack emerged from his bedroom. "Damn it Debre! It's only 10:30 in the morning. You want to blow it by showing up drunk this evening?" Dan just laughed. "Must you always be a petty-bourgeois asshole Wilson? Not everyone who drinks emits obnoxious toxic charisma like you do." Pushing Jack's buttons further, Dan continued. "I'll leave a note for room service to just leave the roll-away so I can get Michelle into the sack more quickly." With less than $300 remaining from

CHAPTER 8

over a thousand they had arrived with, they ate lunch at a Marie Antoinette chain restaurant on the City's outskirts.

After finding a decent, modestly priced restaurant in the City, Jack called Patrice, who told him they would be arriving in Michele's car. She then asked him to meet them at the Chateau's entrance ramp so Michelle could use the hotel's guest parking. Shortly before 5:00 P.M., Jack got into the passenger's seat of Michelle's 1970 Pontiac Firebird, and easily obtained a guest pass as they entered. Michelle, who had worn no make-up and a sweat shirt and jeans the night before, looked great dressed up with her hair down. To Jack's relief, the roll-out had been put away when Dan greeted them entering the suite.

Dan soon refilled Michelle's tumbler of Scotch. Slightly older than Patrice, she had been a nurse for over a year. After a rough four days in a local hospital emergency room, she was starting her three days off. Dan did most of the talking, rambling on about his "doctoral thesis" on existentialism. After Patrice told her in French that she and "Jacques" would meet them at the restaurant at 7:30, Michelle looked at Dan and said, "Let's go. You're not the kind of doctor I've been looking for, but you'll do for this evening."

When the bedroom phone rang, Patrice's and Jack's actions had spoken louder than their words for quite some time. It was 8:30 and Dan was calling from the restaurant. "We're going over to Michelle's place. Give us a call about a half hour before you're ready to meet us for breakfast." It would have to be at midnight when they met Michelle and Dan at the Ste Foy restaurant. Patrice still lived at home and couldn't spend the night, but that was a disappointment Jack could live with. Breakfast seemed to be over much too quickly. As he walked Patrice to Michelle's car, Jack asked her what the best dates were for him to return. "Labor Day," she responded. "It's a big celebration up here and less than three weeks away."

With $100 between them, Jack checked out of the Chateau at 9:00 AM. Their return trip went well for the first three hours. Radio news reported that Leonard Bernstein would be performing at the upcoming grand opening of the Kennedy Center for the Performing Arts; former Beatle John Lennon would be permanently relocating to New York, never to return to the United Kingdom; and Shamu the whale had just died at Sea World. "You were right Debre, this here Quebec City is all right." Dan replied, "I met my match. Michelle and I drank about 8 screw drivers before you showed up!"

Shortly after getting on I-95 in Maine, the TR3's compression began to fail. For the next six hours, the car would alternate between normal speeds going downhill, and then drop to an average of 10 to 15 miles per hour on flat stretches or inclines. It was almost four-thirty when they pulled into a garage in Quincy, Mass. After looking at the TR3, the owner offered Jack $150 for parts. Jack accepted on condition that they get a ride to I-95 South. They had good luck hitch hiking, arriving at the Providence apartment around 9:30PM. After picking up two 16 ounce six packs for the refrigerator, the two headed to Armando's on the motorcycle.

After finishing two pitchers they went to a night club called "the Jail" in a seedy section of Fox Point. That night Jack came closer to being killed in close combat than he ever had in Vietnam. It was not rare for Jack to become so obnoxiously drunk, that even if he was holding a wad of fifty dollar bills, a hooker would turn him down. Dan diplomatically attempted to disengage from five toughs who aggressively ordered them to leave, when Jack attempted to charm two of the regular bar queens. Jack however, wanted to talk tough, and then run like hell when after they made it out the door.

CHAPTER 8

Their exit wasn't fast enough. When they were outside a tough grabbed the back of Jack's shirt. Another one snatched his helmet and threw it over the fence. He then slipped on the pavement finding himself being stomped and kicked by the pack of five. He was able to do little more than curl up in a ball and shield his head and face. After attempting to stop the stomping, Dan soon joined Jack as a stompee. Fortunately a bar tender came outside and sprayed mace on the pack, telling them the cops had been called. They quickly retreated. After a drink on the house, the two retrieved their helmets outside with the bar tender and bouncer on the lookout, before leaving on the motorcycle.

The next morning Jack looked in the mirror at the knot between his eyes the size of a golf ball. His ribs were sore and bruised. "Perhaps I should matriculate at Laval" said Jack, as Debre emerged from his room, hung over and with two huge shiners. Dan was justifiably mad about the previous evening's avoidable near-disaster that Jack had triggered. With exaggerated mocking laugher he replied, "With your stellar college record you'll be lucky to get into RIC this January. What would Patrice think if she discovered her gallant Jacques' destination was to unemployment office before it closed on Friday? Next trip you should fly back while I hold down the fort at the Chateau."

Jack retorted "Hey Brown University doctoral candidate without even a B.A. after five years in three second tier colleges. At least my bullshit had a little more substance to it." Jack then left for his West Warwick apartment where he would shower and rest before heading to the beach for the weekend, after collecting his $75 unemployment payment. Dan would return to his second shift factory job. His shiners at least gave him some visible evidence to justify the four days he had called in not feeling well.

9. PIPE DREAMS

Jack mailed Patrice a post card from Westerly on his way back to West Warwick from the beach. Upon entering his apartment he noticed that the sofa was gone. His roommate Jim had left a note underneath a small cardboard box containing an ounce of grass. He apologized for the no-notice move, but "an opportunity in the Boston area had come up". Jack rolled and lit up a joint. Sitting in the now bare apartment Jack started to day dream. "No way will I give up an opportunity for an education and get a nothing job just to furnish this place so I can play house with Suzanne."

Jack's mind soon spawned a scheme for getting out of his lease. The next day he got an extension from the landlord after giving him a partial payment and a hard luck story. Five days later Jack threw a Labor Day party that began at one in the morning. Two rowdy couples, friends of Dan Debre who he had rounded up during last call at Armando's, honored Jack's request to "be very loud, just don't break anything." An hour of rebel yells, military parade command voice exercises, and female blood curdling screams produced the desired result.

Responding to the loud knock on the door, Jack gave his landlord and two police officers a cheerful greeting. As he held out a beer the landlord abruptly interrupted Jack with "You have 15 minutes to get your things out of here". The two young cops accompanying the landlord had been Jack's friends in high school. They could barely control their laughter while overseeing the eviction.

Dan didn't want a roommate but was fine with Jack remaining in his apartment until Columbus Day. That would

CHAPTER 9

give Jack time to carefully select a mechanically sound car that still left him about $3,500 from his Vietnam savings to resettle in Quebec. Jack went to a pay phone to arrange transferring the phone service at his former apartment to Dan's Providence address. Dan's had long been disconnected for nonpayment.

Jack's research in area libraries for Quebec relocation information was increasingly distracted by readings about current events. A mid-September riot at New York's Attica state prison resulted in 41 deaths. Investigative reporting later revealed that most of the fatalities would have been avoided had Governor Nelson Rockefeller managed the response more competently. A week later, the last My Lai Massacre Courts Martial rendered a not guilty verdict to Captain Ernest Medina, who had been Lieutenant Calley's company commander.

October arrived and Jack's motorcycle was still his only means of transportation. During his reserve drill, Jack's commander happily approved his transfer request to the National Guard. The following Friday evening of the Columbus Day weekend, found Jack drinking at Armando's with Dan and his friend Gordon Hofenmuller. Gordon was an untenured professor at Rhode Island College in his late twenties. Jack's incessant rambling about celebrating Prime Minister Trudeau's October 8th declaration of Canada as bilingual and multicultural persuaded Gordon to drive them up to Quebec early the next morning.

Gordon did all the driving. Jack nodded off in the back seat after several swigs from a fifth of Cognac that Dan had purchased in New Hampshire. Jack woke up when they were a half hour from Quebec City. After registering at the Chateau Frontenac, Jack immediately dialed Patrice's phone number, but got no answer. Dan had more luck when called Michelle. She was surprised, but spoke with him for several minutes.

PIPE DREAMS

Upon learning that Dan was in the City with Jack and Gordon, Michelle accepted his invitation to join them at the Bistro. She arrived at six o'clock, looking great in a skirt and sweater. The trio was mid-way through their second round of Cognacs. Michelle shook hands with Gordon, hugged Jack, and then gave Dan a long passionate kiss. When the next round was ordered, she gently explained to Jack that Patrice was in Montreal with a guy she had been seeing for several weeks. "It's a big ocean" responded Jack nonchalantly.

Michelle shifted her attention to Dan, asking about his doctoral thesis at Brown. After a dinner of hot sandwiches, they headed to a club in Ste. Foy, where Michelle thought a few of her friends might be that Saturday evening. "It's good to see Dan back to his old self" Gordon mused to Jack as they followed Michelle's Firebird to a restaurant-lounge.

The club was a well kept establishment with local patrons from their mid-twenties to early forties. After Dan and Michelle drifted into their own corner, Jack and Gordon got up and danced with several women. By about 10:30, Dan asked Jack to borrow $25. Ten minutes later Michelle said she would drop Dan off at the Chateau in the morning as the couple left.

Recognizing that Jack was becoming too radioactively drunk for any woman capable of standing to want to dance with, Gordon suggested they return to the Bistro. A couple of ladies initially shown some interest, but it wasn't long before Jack's negative charisma repelled them. After last call they returned to the Chateau and began pouring themselves Cognacs out of the bottle on the writing desk. It was still two thirds full.

Gordon diplomatically attempted explaining to Jack that acting interested in the local customs and culture would bring him far more success. Gordon, who taught Nitche, was both

CHAPTER 9

amazed and amused at the logic of Jack's rebuttals with words to the effect "Why should I appreciate a culture that hasn't won a war on its own since Napoleon?" and "Didn't I tell the girl at the club in Ste Foy that it was great that the Quebecois didn't keep all the habits of their Continental cousins and bathed regularly?"

Shortly after 5:00 A.M., Jack staggered into his room and passed out. At 1030 in the morning, Jack was awakened by animated conversation in the living room. Michelle was laughing after a story Gordon had just finished telling. Badly hung over but in good spirits, Jack emerged and joined the conversation. Michelle had to work that evening, so they would depart shortly and take the long way back through Montreal.

During their two hour drive, Dan recounted telling his rationalization to Michelle about how Jack's "post-Vietnam adjustment" was the reason he had failed to maintain contact with Patrice. Jack responded, "Michelle was very friendly to me this morning so she probably bought that hokum. Maybe she'll bring a girlfriend for me next time." Gordon added that if Jack had just made a few calls to Patrice, she might have even come down to visit him for a weekend. They all laughed when Jack asked if she would have been more impressed with his bare West Warwick apartment or Dan's palace in Providence. The trio only spent a couple of hours on a quick auto tour of Montreal. After dinner in a dingy restaurant, mostly patronized by clients who appeared to be from East Asian Commonwealth countries, they departed.

During the return trip Jack mused that "except for being bilingual, Montreal was not much different than any other North American center of cosmopolitan decadence." Gordon suggested that RIC would very likely admit Jack in January, but that he needed to make the Halloween application deadline. "Yea I'll do that," replied Jack, "right after I head

PIPE DREAMS

down to New York and watch the U.N. debate about letting the CHICOMS in."

Jack did follow up by completing the administrative details for the RIC application and making an appointment to speak with an admissions counselor on the 28th. With no absences or late arrivals during the week, Dan had accrued a healthy paycheck for the weekend. On Sunday afternoon, he decided to call in sick and drive down to New York in the 1964 Malibu Jack had just purchased for $200. After blowing through over $350 at the Back Fence Bar on Greenwich Village's version of Saigon Teas, they arrived at the U.N. parking lot at 3:30AM on Monday.

Black smoke billowed out of the Malibu's exhaust as they drove away when security ordered them out at daybreak. The red oil light glowed as they pulled into a gas station. After pouring in two overpriced quarts of oil, they had about $25 to get home on. They exited I-95 in White Plains when the oil light came back on to search for an auto supply store. After purchasing 8 quarts of oil and topping off at a gas station they were now down to $10.

On the Connecticut Turnpike, they listened to the WINS radio report that the Peoples Republic of China had secured enough votes from a coalition of communists and non-aligned U.N. members to displace Chiang Kai Shek's Nationalist regime. On January 1, 1950, the United Kingdom quickly recognized Mao's regime after they drove Chiang off the mainland onto the island of Formosa. Two decades later, the U.S. still officially recognized the Nationalists, who only controlled less than 10 percent of China's territory and population, as the legal government. Nixon's pending visit to Beijing however, signaled a major policy shift was imminent. Jack agreed with Senator Barry Goldwater's statement "Let the U.N. move to Jakarta or Beijing."

CHAPTER 9

The Malibu needed a quart of oil about every 25 miles, but was averaging about 18 miles per gallon of gas. The two travelers were hungry. Pulling into a Turnpike service area to add oil Jack said "We can't risk being broken down and flat broke." Dan laughed, entered Howard Johnsons, sat down at a booth and placed an order for French fries and a large cup of water. He told Jack "When the people in those booths leave we can snatch at least four uneaten pieces of fried chicken and some fried clams." Dan made the first grab while making a faux restroom trip, returning with his pockets filled with chicken wrapped in paper napkins. While exiting the restaurant via the men's room, Jack half-filled the paper cup with the clams.

The Malibu was down two quarts oil with an eighth of a tank gas when they arrived in Providence. Dan called his friend Bill, a yet to be employed recent engineering graduate, to provide some technical advice. Jack wanted to know the safest way to drive the Malibu into a river with sufficient thrust to make it submerge completely out of sight. He assured Bob that there was no fraud involved. Bill met them at Sal's Lounge, bringing a topographic map of northern Rhode Island. After two pitchers, Bill bought into Jack's ethical reasoning that he was merely avoiding a tow charge to a junk yard and not making a bogus insurance claim, so it wasn't a big deal.

The trio headed north on Rhode Island Route 146. After a 10 mile drive of unrestrained mayhem that entailed kicking out windows, slashing the seats, and tearing off the roof lining, the Malibu exited shortly after crossing into Massachusetts. With the radio blaring, Bill guided Jack for about 3 miles to a secluded bank with a steep grade along the Blackstone River. Under Bill's expert technical direction, the first real engineering task he had engaged in since graduating, the desired objective was accomplished. They then hiked on foot to link up with Bill's friend for the return trip. He was waiting at a diner near the Route 146 exit ramp. On their way back to Sal's, Dan remarked "If cops find a body in the trunk of the car in Attleboro, they know it was the Federal Hill mob. If they find it in Pawtucket, the East Boston mob did the hit."

Jack made it to his October 28th RIC interview, and was accepted as a transfer student for the January semester. That same day, Britain finally voted to join the European Economic Community. November began with the copper clad, oversized Eisenhower silver dollar being released into circulation. In Vietnam, General John Lavelle, the 7th U.S. Air Force commander, increased bombing raids against North Vietnam on his own authority. These triggered a Congressional investigation when they ended the following March, culminating in Lavelle's relief from command and losing a star in forced retirement.

The Day after Armistice Day, Nixon announced that 45,000 more troops would be withdrawn by February. On the evening before Thanksgiving, a passenger calling himself D.B. Cooper issued a bomb threat on a Northwest Airlines 727 over Oregon demanding $200,000 in cash and a parachute. Cooper released the passengers after the knapsack containing the cash and parachutes were delivered when the plane landed in Seattle. When the plane was airborne over Washington's Cascade Mountains he parachuted out the back door and was never seen again.

Jack rode his motorcycle to his National Guard unit's Christmas party at the Quonset Point Naval Air Station officers club. Although a typically cold December evening, it had not snowed so he looked the part in his Army dress blue uniform after brushing it off in the men's room. During the evening, Jack ended up negotiating the purchase of a new vehicle. Coincidentally, his commander was selling a 1965 Opel Cadet station wagon for $900. It was mechanically sound, but had been used on his farm for hauling. A final

CHAPTER 9

price of $750 was agreed upon, since Jack had to wait a week to pick it up.

As the year 1971 was quickly coming to an end, Jack had slightly less than $1,000 of his savings left. One evening Dan remarked "Good thing you listened to me and took advantage of the dollar when it was still worth something now that Nixon has devalued it." Technically only Congress could change the gold value of the dollar, but since Nixon had gone off the gold standard it had been effectively devalued by nearly 8 percent. Jack was always quick to recognize grand plans for quick earnings, whenever he heard Dan and his friend elaborate on them, for what they were – pipe dreams.

As Christmas Eve approached Jack felt relief that he would be leaving for a three week active duty tour right after New Years. That would enable him to replenish his cash reserve and find a decent apartment before the semester started. Feeling melancholy as Christmas approached he called Suzanne. She stayed on the phone for over an hour, so she obviously still cared for him. Since Jack had done nothing to demonstrate his seriousness about building their future, Suzanne was not going to abruptly drop the new guy she had been seeing. The year 1971 ended with Jack finally admitting that it was over with Suzanne, and with 158,000 U.S. troops remaining in Vietnam

10. A BLOWOUT YEAR

In 1971, Nixon's Defense Secretary Melvin Laird had launched the all volunteer force with a major pay raise. Junior enlisted troops now received pay and allowances competitive with private sector entry level wages. Strategically, this was intended to motivate enough enlistments to eliminate the draft. Included in the new strategy was a total force policy that relied heavily on reserve forces.

More funding was made available for reserve officers to attend schools and short active duty tours for professional development. This dovetailed perfectly with Jack's situation. On the morning after New Year's Day 1972, Jack boarded a flight for Columbus, Georgia. The active duty course he was attending would pay him a significant per diem allowance in addition to his regular pay. Jack's plan for financing his education was on track. However, his $5,500 Vietnam nest egg was gone, with only his 1965 Opel station wagon to show for it.

Shortly after arriving at Fort Benning, Jack ran into Captain Stolz, his last boss in Vietnam, and had lunch with. All of his off duty socializing however was spent with fellow student officers who lived by the golden rule "what happens on TDY (temporary duty) stays on TDY." A typical evening out involved hitting the night clubs in Columbus. At last call, Jack's group would then cross the Chattahoochee River to take advantage of the central time zone difference and later closing times in Phenix City, Alabama. Jack learned two major lessons on this TDY. The first was to always drive and never fly to future active duty tours. The second was to always meet, but never go out in the same car at night with married cohorts, because their "golden rule" appearance standards fell far short of the minimum.

CHAPTER 10

Since Mondays and Tuesdays were typically dead, Jack and his classmates spent those evenings in the officers' club lounge. They typically discussed current events while taking advantage of the inexpensive drinks. Much had changed besides beer in the barracks for the enlisted troops. New second lieutenants no longer had the option of volunteering for Vietnam out of the Basic Course to gain combat experience.

That January, President Nixon ordered the development of a space shuttle program. The Dallas Cowboys won Super Bowl VI, defeating the Miami Dolphins 24 to 3. General Creighton Abrams had requested authority to use additional air power over North Vietnam to respond to a communist force buildup. This indicated that another major offensive was eminent. Hanoi rejected President Nixon's 8 point peace plan after he also revealed that Kissinger had been secretly negotiating with the North Vietnamese. A Japanese soldier, who had hid in the jungles of Guam since World War II, finally emerged and surrendered to American forces - after 28 years!

Jack returned to Providence the second day of college registration week. His transfer credits made him a second semester freshman. This entitled him to a late Wednesday registration slot, only marginally better than the final ones on Thursday morning. The only remaining sections for required math and literature prerequisites met early in the morning. Jack selected a biology course that nursing students took which met at 10:00 A.M. twice weekly. He found afternoon sections for a history course in U.S. foreign policy, and a political science class in international relations.

Jack declared himself a History major with a Political Science minor. He would have to wait until late February for his GI Bill checks to start coming in, but still had close to 500 dollars left from his just-completed active duty tour. He needed little persuasion from Dan to join several of his RIC

A BLOWOUT YEAR

friends for a long weekend in Quebec celebrating the Winter Carnival. Jack and Dan left in the Opel Wednesday evening.

On mid-Thursday morning, they registered at the Chateau. Unlike the suites that served as their headquarters on past trips, they settled for a modest room with twin beds. Shortly after eight that evening, they met Dan's friends, who had taken the bus, at the Bistro. Jack understood that money was tight for students, but assumed that three and four years of college should have instilled in these faux intellectuals a desire for more local culture than McDonalds.

Dan had not thought about calling Michelle before leaving Providence, so he just now learned over a pay phone that she was seeing someone. He and Jack then broke away from the RIC group to hit their usual haunts. The sub-zero temperatures had frozen the St Lawrence and the entire City. Jack suddenly hit both elbows and knees to break a fall on a frozen downhill sidewalk. It took him five minutes to recover. However, remaining on foot in the old walled City, rather than driving the icy roads to St. Foy night spots was still the best decision. By the end of the evening funds were down to $20, so they would have to cut the trip short.

Departing Quebec at noon on Friday, they took the return route through St George. Heavy winds that had created eight foot snow banks buffeted the box-like Opel Cadet. After they pulled over to switch driving, the ignition would not kick in. In less than 10 minutes the severe wind chill factor aborted their attempt to hike to the nearest town. While stranded in the middle of no-where until shortly before dusk, only two cars had passed them going in the opposite direction. After three hours of sitting in the frozen Opel, a motorist finally stopped. It was dark and past 7:00 P.M. when the middle aged businessman drove them into the nearest village.

CHAPTER 10

The driver made a phone call from a diner after buying the two coffees, and then took them to a garage that resembled a converted barn. The proprietor, no older than 25, took Jack and Dan to the Opel and towed it back. The problem was soon discovered to be a $15 ignition coil. As the mechanic replaced it, Dan and Jack worked the pay phone attempting to poor mouth friends and relatives to wire money. Jack groveled on the phone to his dad, who agreed to wire $100 to the Chateau. Fortunately, the garage owner accepted five dollars in cash plus a $20 two-party check that Dan had in his wallet as payment, preempting the need to return.

Finishing off a six pack of Molson ale on the ride back to Quebec, they arrived shortly before midnight. After collecting the wired funds at the Chateau, they headed to the Bistro, finishing off the evening with the RIC group. The office at their friend Pete's low budget hotel was closed, so Dan nodded off in a stuffed chair in Pete's room, while Jack quickly passed out on the floor.

Wilson and Debre then met Pete and their other college friends for lunch at a McDonalds. Jack didn't mind playing student tourist, but was annoyed by their obsessive penny pinching. After finishing a case of La Bat, they hit the City's bars from ten until closing. Jack grudgingly shelled out $15 to one in the group who had earlier managed to score a dime bag. On Tuesday morning Jack was down to $10. Fortunately, a couple in the group was able to get a refund for their bus tickets, so the four completed a problem-free 400 mile return trip to Providence in the Opel.

Rhode Island College had long been a well respected teachers' college. During the sixties it had expanded to include a school of nursing and a liberal arts division. Since over 75 percent of the students were commuters, many sarcastically called RIC an extension of Mount Pleasant High School, which was located a block from its main entrance.

A BLOWOUT YEAR

In late 1971, the state lowered the drinking age, following up to the 26th Amendment's ratification which gave 18 year-olds the right to vote. Most evening social life for dorm students occurred in off campus establishments, either in North Providence, or on the East Side of Providence near Brown University. Jack was still living in Dan's Providence dive, which resembled Ratzo Rizzo's place in the movie "Midnight Cowboy." Sal's Lounge, a North Providence café with a mixed college and local blue collar crowd of patrons, became Jack's officers club. He felt too much like a duck out of water trying to mingle with the dorm students who dominated the club a few blocks from the campus.

Nixon's visit to the Peoples Republic of China from February 21st to the 28th, with historic meetings with Premier Chou En Lai and Communist Party Chairman Mao Tse Dung, greatly enhanced his stature. However, he was still a minority President and the Democrats overwhelmingly dominated Congress. Nixon's reelection was by no means guaranteed. In the Democratic nomination contest, the heavy favorite was Senator Edmund Muskie, who had been Humphrey's 1968 Vice Presidential running mate. He had the endorsements of most major leaders from all factions of the Party, including labor, and a commanding lead in the New Hampshire primary polls.

Senator George McGovern was the leading liberal challenger, running on a platform of a unilateral withdrawal from Vietnam. His base consisted mostly of liberal activists and the remnant of anti-war college students who had propelled Senator Eugene McCarthy's 1968 challenge to Lyndon Johnson. Still vocal and visible, but greatly diminished in size, they no longer had the draft as a tool for mobilizing students, who now were increasingly apathetic. U.S. troop levels in Vietnam would be under 69,000 by the end of April. Nixon might have had a "secret plan" to end the war after all.

CHAPTER 10

March began with the completion of the largest bas relief sculpture to date at Stone Mountain, Georgia. This Confederate memorial, with mounted figures of Jefferson Davis, Robert E. Lee and Stonewall Jackson, rivaled Mount Rushmore in scope. On the 7th, Senator Muskie, who had broken down in tears responding to an unflattering Manchester Union Leader article about his wife, won the New Hampshire primary, but with a disappointing 46 percent. McGovern's impressive second place finish with 37 percent provided him needed momentum. A week later in Florida, George Wallace muddied the waters with an unexpected and impressive 42 percent victory in a field of 11 candidates. Humphrey was a distant second with 18 percent followed by Muskie and McGovern. On the 22nd, Congress sent the ill-fated Equal Rights Amendment to the states for ratification.

Domestic and international events generated interesting discussion in Jack's advanced history of foreign policy and international relations classes. Both met in the afternoon. His classmates were mostly juniors or seniors closer to his of age of 22. Partying late into the evenings virtually every other night caused intermittent attendance in Jack's world literature, math and biology classes, which all met in the morning. Jack was behind but would use the upcoming Easter Break, which it was still called in majority- Catholic Rhode Island, to catch up. This plan however, was unexpectedly derailed on the weekend the vacation began. Bob Gerhard, their friend from high school and a Khe Sanh combat veteran, decided to end his troubled marriage and relocate to California. There he would continue pursuing his GI Bill goal of medical school.

After a Saturday night of heavy drinking, Jack joined Dan in his decision to help with the driving as far as Kansas City, where they arrived around midnight on Sunday. After they had rested at a motel on the Kansas side of the Mississippi, Bob wished the two luck as he dropped them off on a ramp to I-70 east. They began hitch-hiking back to Rhode Island that

A BLOWOUT YEAR

cold spring Monday morning with only the $20 that Bob had given them at breakfast. Having gone less than 50 miles after three hours, both realized this trip was one more half-assed drunken decision.

Jack suddenly uttered what was to become his refrain to every adversity of their homeward journey. "Fucking Gerhard! Fucking west coast Bobby!" Seven hours later they had finally made it through Missouri. During a long warm ride a driver shared a joint. Neither one noticed they had passed a critical junction and were no longer on I-70, until they had already traveled 50 miles north on I-55. Backtracking to I-70 would add another 100 miles to their trip. They decided to continue north to Chicago instead. Depending on luck catching rides, they could either continue east on I-80 and the Pennsylvania Turnpike, or I90 and the New York State Thruway.

As daylight disappeared and temperatures dropped near freezing their luck changed. Two students from Northern Illinois University not only gave them a ride, but also put them up for the night in a house near Springfield that they shared with two other students. Their generosity, which included dinner and breakfast, made the following cold morning, interrupted by several short rides, more bearable. After a lunch of canned Beefaroni and potato chips purchased from a Seven-Eleven, they were now down to $12.

Once more their fortunes improved when they caught a 200 mile ride that left them on I-90 in Indiana, 30 miles east of Gary. The new Cadillac was driven by a trucker who perfectly fit the stereotype of a northern blue collar George Wallace supporter. Jack tried to deflect the conversation to Vietnam after a bigoted analogy of blacks and the Chicago stockyards. Fortunately the driver didn't recognize the mocking nature of Dan's and Jack's stoned laughter at his bigoted utterances, or he would have abruptly dropped them off. By evening, two more rides had left them at an Ohio

CHAPTER 10

Turnpike exit near the Cleveland suburb where Jack's aunt and family lived. They were blessed again with another night of free room and board.

Their third day was another long cold one, with intermittent short rides through a 180 mile stretch of Ohio and northwest Pennsylvania. At dusk a well dressed salesman, who shared a joint through the final stretch of Pennsylvania, dropped them off at the New York Thruway entrance near Buffalo. The temperature had dropped to freezing. Dan, who had grown up with Gerhard, now joined in response to Jack's utterance. "Fucking Gehrard! Fucking west coast Bobby!"

Suddenly, the Lord again proved that He does indeed take care of drunks and fools. A driver, about 35 years old, stopped and told them that he was going though the Massachusetts Turnpike, and then south to I-495 where it interdicts I-95 about 20 miles north of Providence.

They arrived home shortly after 1:30 A.M. on Thursday, and dined on a sack of New York System hot dogs purchased with their remaining travel funds. Upset that no liquor stores were still open for Jack to cash his GI Bill check that was in the mailbox, they counted out pocket change for a pack of cigarettes. On the way to the Smith Street Dunkin Donuts they engaged in a spirited debate over who was entitled to being listed in the Social Register, and made bets on how long "Dr. Gerhard" would last in California.

In early April the Vietnamese communists launched a major offensive. American air power was still available, but advisors assigned to South Vietnamese units were the only remaining U.S. ground combat forces. Nixon's mining of Haiphong Harbor and stepped up bombing of the North gave significant press coverage to protests by anti-war Congressional Democrats. They did nothing however, to diminish Nixon's recently enhanced stature and favorable poll numbers.

Democratic Party reforms, enacted in the aftermath of 1968, were now finally in effect. These gave activists in the Party base far greater influence at the expense of party leaders, even in caucus states. The timing of the "Easter Offensive" did galvanize the McGovern Campaign's base of student and anti-war activists, enabling wins in a string of six caucus states in April and May.

With impressive second place finishes in Wisconsin, Pennsylvania, and Indiana, Wallace had demonstrated that he represented considerably more than reactionary forces in the South. On May 15th, after he had decisively won Tennessee and North Carolina, Wallace's campaign was abruptly derailed by an assassination attempt in Laurel, Maryland. Although the next day Wallace won Maryland and Michigan, recovery from his injuries, that left him wheel chair-bound for life, precluded further campaigning. Except in Illinois, where he had the backing of Mayor Richard Daly's Chicago machine, Muskie never recovered from his New Hampshire meltdown. This greatly benefited Humphrey, who won Pennsylvania, Indiana, Ohio and West Virginia.

Jack had renewed several friendships from his pre-draft college days. They had completed college the previous spring. Paul Baer, who had been commissioned through ROTC, was a fellow officer in Jack's National Guard unit and active in Cranston Democratic politics. Another one, Bill Freidel, was active in George McGovern's local campaign. During bar hopping trips to Coventry, Dan and Jack would run into their old friend Fred Shannon. Fred was supporting Muskie, and planning a comeback bid for his old state house seat following two defeats for the state senate.

McGovern's advocacy of more generous education and readjustment benefits attracted many campus veterans. Jack's military contemporaries certainly didn't support a communist victory. However, they believed it was time for the South

CHAPTER 10

Vietnamese to aggressively defend themselves. Retired Lt. General James Gavin's support of McGovern's defense program outweighed Jack's concerns over left wing elements in the latter's campaign.

Idealistic and naïve, but with an ego, Jack was easily manipulated by local McGovern people. He liked the attention he received speaking before student groups encouraging them to vote in the primary. By the middle of May, Jack had caught up in his three afternoon courses which were graded largely on the basis of essay exams and term papers. He was muddling through the math probability course but way behind in cellular biology. Jack had met a sorority girl from the University of Rhode Island which added to the distractions of the political activity and after parties. He took a "withdrew failing" grade in Biology, but still managed to finish the semester with a 2.5 GPA. Jack decided to enroll in the six week summer term at URI, and had also lined up five weeks of active duty with the Army.

McGovern won the remaining primaries, including a narrow victory in California's winner-take-all contest with 271 delegates. McGovern now needed to win over approximately 100 delegates who were either uncommitted, or pledged to other candidates who had withdrawn but not bound by state laws to still vote for them. Humphrey and McGovern had been the top Democratic performers in the primaries, with each polling approximately 25 percent of the popular vote. They were closely followed by George Wallace with 23 percent. Muskie was fourth at 11 percent. McGovern had the momentum however, with a solid lead of about 1,000 delegates, but still short of a majority. Humphrey, who had narrowly led him in overall popular votes cast in primaries, only controlled 354 delegates, behind Wallace's 367. These, combined with unpledged delegates and those scattered among the others totaled 1067.

A BLOWOUT YEAR

Many state laws only bound their delegates to the primary winner on the first ballot. Since most from those states were party regulars pledged to McGovern due to primary outcomes, they personally preferred another candidate. Therefore, blocking a McGovern first ballot nomination could very likely result in a brokered convention that selected a compromise candidate. A key element of that strategy was to successfully challenge winner-take-all primary rules in states like California, ironically, on the grounds that they violated the recent reforms designed to loosen control by the bosses.

McGovern's decisive Rhode Island victory came with an interesting fluke. That state's party regulars including the Governor, and Congressional delegation had backed either Muskie or Humphrey. The law establishing the primary was hastily enacted only weeks before the actual election, so the names of delegates for McGovern were not listed. The Party regulars controlled all the resources, and now were challenging the Elections Division pre-primary ruling that the winner could name the 22 delegates. This would effectively shut out the Governor, two U.S. Senators, both Congressman and virtually all other senior Democrats.

Rhode Island's Democratic establishment sought to avoid any state-wide fall primaries to preempt backlash against U.S. Senator Claiborne Pell that November. Popular former Governor and Navy Secretary John Chaffee would be the Republican Senate nominee. The Democratic establishment had not-so-subtly pushed incumbent Governor Frank Licht aside, after he had enacted an unpopular state income tax. They then coalesced around Warwick Mayor Philip Noel, passing over Lt. Governor Joseph Garrahy.

The McGovern Campaign had named Jack's before-the-draft friend, Bill Friedel, as a delegate. Bill and most of the 21 others McGovern appointed, had only limited resources to get to Miami for the Convention. They had no money for making their case in the media that Party regulars were not

CHAPTER 10

likely to stick with McGovern after the first ballot. Paul Baer, Jack's other political friend from his National Guard unit, was focusing on local races in the state's September Democratic primary. Several of Jack's fellow students at RIC had filed for local offices or the legislature. Jack would have liked to have run for state representative but was registered to vote in a machine-controlled Providence district where he had absolutely no roots.

On an early June evening, Dan Debre and Jack were smoking a joint while watching an evening news story about the local delegate dispute. A short story followed about Mayor Noel not having a challenger for the Democratic gubernatorial nomination. The wheels in Jack's mind began to turn. If a candidate did announce, media attention would be generated that could be used to focus on the issue of seating McGovern's Rhode Island delegates. Jack got on the phone and secured the endorsement of his old friend, ex-Representative Fred Shannon. This would at least give him sorr of a local favorite son status.

Dan and Jack both laughed after the later declared his intention to run. His subsequent announcement to the three Providence TV stations made the 11PM news. Jack spent the next several days visiting the TV studios and doing radio interviews over the phone and visiting local daily and weekly papers. To most of his friends' surprise, Jack came across very well, sounding very articulate when addressing issues.

Jack's status as an officer who had advised South Vietnamese units enhanced the main focus of his message which was seating the McGovern-appointed delegates. He even drew a polite round of applause from the Democratic State Committee the evening he addressed them before they endorsed Mayor Noel. Jack then "suspended his campaign" for the two weeks he went on active duty to teach at the state's National Guard officer candidate school.

A BLOWOUT YEAR

One evening, when Jack was out drinking with military associates after a field exercise, the local news ran one of his taped interviews. A major abruptly remarked "Hey look, a hippie with a clean shirt and a tie!" Later on, to Jack's surprise, he was confronted by several single issue nut cases who took his campaign seriously. He also found that unlike many campus volunteers, younger Party activists were kids of established politicians, maladjusted or both. On June 17th, a story about a break in of the Democratic National Committee headquarters in the Watergate complex in Washington, DC made the headlines. However, it never gained traction against President Nixon as a major campaign issue.

Wanting the good will of McGovern's activists, the Rhode Island Party regulars finally agreed to seat them as delegates. The regulars in turn, became alternates with full floor privileges. Jack started dating a graduate student he met at the URI summer session, which distracted him from efforts to organize a drive to collect 2,000 signatures to make the primary ballot. He did however, generate a little attention with telegrams to the RI delegation at the Miami Convention as "one of the State's Democratic gubernatorial candidates".

McGovern won the Democratic nomination on the first ballot. His acceptance speech at two o'clock in the morning however, revealed his campaign's ineptness to the entire Country. His post-convention "bump" was 37% McGovern to 52% for Nixon. This 15 percent shortfall would be the high-water mark of McGovern's campaign. Soon after the convention, Jack issued a gracious withdrawal statement from the Governor's race which made the back pages the paper. After dropping out of the URI summer session, he loafed around the beaches before leaving for Fort Benning at the end of July.

Jack's active duty tours were an immersion in the real world away from the pseudo intellectual banter of his college environment. Most military people associated McGovern

CHAPTER 10

with the extreme fringes of the anti-war movement. Jane Fonda's trip to Hanoi, where she was photographed sitting in the seat of an enemy anti-aircraft gun, was easily exploited by Republicans. This put many main stream Democratic incumbents on the defensive.

Making matters worse for Senator McGovern, two weeks after being nominated, was the revelation that his Vice Presidential running mate, Senator Thomas Eagleton, had received electro-shock therapy while being treated for depression many years earlier. Compounding the issue of McGovern's judgment in selecting him, was his backing off from his initial statement that he was "behind Eagleton 1,000 percent." When the later finally withdrew from the ticket, several leading Democrats rejected the number two spot on the ticket. McGovern finally settled on R. Sargent Shriver, a Kennedy in-law, former Peace Corps Director and Ambassador to France.

Watching the National news, it was readily apparent to Jack that McGovern was a lost cause. Nixon, while never popular, had scored an impressive list of foreign policy accomplishments. More recently he had signed a Strategic Arms Limitation Treaty with Leonid Brezhnev in Moscow. The residual troop levels in Vietnam continued to diminish. On June 28th Nixon had announced that no new draftees would be sent to Vietnam, affirming by policy what had been the de facto situation for well over a year. It was debatable whether McGovern could even carry the newly enfranchised youth vote. Jack however, kept his commitments, and from a practical standpoint realized that staying with McGovern would not hurt him in overwhelmingly Democratic Rhode Island.

When Jack returned from Fort Benning he devoted his activity to the final stretch of Fred Shannon's comeback primary. To the surprise of many, Fred defeated the incumbent for his old state house seat. McGovern's Rhode

A BLOWOUT YEAR

Island campaign had greatly changed from the spring primary. They wanted sensational tellers of atrocity stories from the Vietnam Veterans Against the War (VVAW). They had no interest in rational speakers focused on Vietnam strategy or policy changes. Of those Jack met in the VVAW, his gut told him that few had even stepped foot in Vietnam, let alone seen any combat. When the fall semester began he attended the student-focused McGovern rallies which inevitably sprang parties. Ambivalent about the abortion issue, Jack discovered during the spring primary that parroting feminist lines like "keep your laws off our bodies" could be a good ice breaker for bedding the "liberal little trollops".

Jack selected Fred Shannon's general election campaign however, for his serious political efforts and the project in his political science course on parties and elections. In Coventry, the entrenched local Democratic organization was not only bucking a strong anti-McGovern tide, but also weathering a major recent local scandal, that had been a major factor in Fred's primary win. On Election Day, Nixon scored a National popular and electoral vote landslide, even bigger than LBJ's in 1964. He narrowly won Rhode Island but carried Coventry by a landslide. Conservative Democrat Fred Shannon however, not only bucked the tide, but polled 60 percent of the vote.

Towards the end of November Jack began regularly attending classes. He salvaged the semester, but his overall GPA dropped to a 2.25. He completed all 15 semester hours he initially had registered for, but only earned one B. Jack always took it off the chin when his poor attendance caught up with him. However, he balked at the "C" he received in the parties and elections course. He had earned "Bs" on all his graded work, but received the lower grade based on a "class participation" requirement that the instructor added towards the end of the semester. On Christmas Eve, after the North Vietnamese reneged on the agreement they had made

CHAPTER 10

with Kissinger, Nixon launched Operation Linebacker 2, a massive series of B-52 raids over Hanoi and Haiphong.

11. ELUSIVE VICTORY

Continuing into the New Year of 1973, Operation Linebacker II had evolved into the largest massive heavy bombing campaign since World War II. The North Vietnamese communists had badly miscalculated. Nixon's recent landslide re-election made him unlikely to grant the North any further concessions. On December 30th, after the North agreed to resume "technical discussions", Nixon limited the B-52 raids to targets south of the 20th parallel. This spared further destruction to Hanoi and Haiphong, but continued to inflict major damage. On January 15th, five days before his second inauguration, Nixon suspended all offensive operations against the North. High level talks between Kissinger and Le Duc Tho would resume on the 23rd culminating in the Paris Peace Accords on the 27th.

When President Nixon and Vice President Agnew took their oaths of office they were at their high water mark. The Nixon-Agnew ticket had carried over 61 percent of the popular vote and had won everything on the map except Massachusetts and the District of Columbia. Agnew was now viewed as the man to beat for the 1976 GOP nomination. Nixon had negligible coat tails, however. The Democrats gained two seats in the Senate, now controlling it by 58 to 42 seats. Republicans did gain 14 House seats, but the Democrats remained solidly in control with a majority of 241 to 192.

In Rhode Island, with the exception of Nixon's win and Republicans gaining a handful of legislative seats, the Democrats easily won all state-wide races, both Congressional seats, and decisive majorities in both houses of the legislature. On January 22nd, former President Lyndon B. Johnson, whose presidency had been destroyed by Vietnam, died of a heart attack at the age of 64.

CHAPTER 11

At the beginning of the spring semester, Jack agreed to run on a slate vying for control of the Rhode Island Young Democrats or "YDs". It was led by Bill Friedel, his pre-draft friend who had been a McGovern delegate, and Tim Palastro, a union activist. Jack was easily flattered into being used both for his background, and ability to not only write press releases quickly, but to get them published. As the state YD convention approached Jack realized he had been played.

Jack had obtained his slate's only significant endorsement by Representative Fred Shannon. His running mates had revealed their desperate situation the afternoon before the balloting. While sharing a joint, Palastro suggested that Jack rough up the "machine's choice" for YD President. "We don't want you to hurt him, just corner him, and perhaps grab his lapels and tell him that Larry doesn't want you here." Jack looked at Friedel responding "You're kidding, right?" "You want to win don't you?" answered Bill. Both Tim and Bill released feigned laughter when Jack responded "You're on your own. Good Luck". "This is America" said Tim, laughing the whole thing off. The ticket lost the next day by more than 2 to 1.

Jack quickly distanced himself from Friedel and the local McGovern crowd. His main motivation for involving himself with that campaign the previous year was to make contacts for a future run. However, unlike respected National Democrats like General James Gavin and Henry Jackson who were seeking a realistic change in Vietnam policy that would protect U.S. interests, too many of these local loonies were borderline Marxists who wanted nothing short of a humiliating U.S. defeat. Personally, Jack got along well with Republicans. He was also coming under the influence of a RIC professor who had made a strong GOP Congressional run against an entrenched Democratic several years earlier.

Militarily, a major reorganization caused Jack's National Guard unit to lose positions, including his captain's slot, to units in other states. That was the official reason, but Jack correctly viewed that he was wearing out his welcome. Still a first lieutenant nearly two years after Vietnam, Jack opted against staying in the Guard in a non-promotable excess status, and found another captain's slot in an Army Reserve unit. This would also provide more summer active duty opportunities.

As a prerequisite to his plan for running for a seat in the legislature, Jack had also vacated the dive apartment in Providence and rented a place in Coventry. Jack did not desire a political career. He viewed a short stint in the state's part time legislature as great resume builder that would enhance his chances for admission to law school or a prestigious graduate program. Applying himself academically still remained very low on Jack's priority list, however.

On February 11th the Hanoi regime released the first American prisoners of war. Later that month, as a follow-up to Nixon's visit to the Peoples Republic of China, formal liaison offices were established between the two countries. By March 29th, the last remaining U.S. troops were withdrawn from Vietnam. It was starting to look like the U.S. might be heading for a 20th Century version of the 28-year post-Civil War era of GOP White House control. The Paris Accords had rendered the anti-war left an ideological debating society. On campuses Vietnam was now only a topic for academic debate.

On March 23rd, a major issue emerged that could at the very least prove embarrassing to the President. James W. McCord, a convicted defendant from the Watergate burglary the previous summer, had written a letter to Federal Judge John Sirica. McCord claimed that he and his co-defendants had been pressured to remain silent by Nixon's campaign organization, and that it was personally master-minded by the President's former Attorney General, John Mitchell.

CHAPTER 11

Rhode Island state senators and representatives were still only paid $5 per day, for a maximum of $300 per year. Jack's friend, Representative Shannon, appointed him as his legislative aide. It was a non-paying position, but gave Jack access to many of the state agencies and dovetailed well with his independent study project associated with a "Problems in State Government" course. Jack also became a regular contributor to college newspapers around the state, focusing on practical issues that were pending in the legislature.

Jack soon accepted an invitation to be the college newspaper's business manager. It was another non-paid position, but provided access to office space and equipment. Several years earlier, the state attorney general had ruled that student activity fees where a tax levied on students by their elected representatives and not subject to control by a state college's administration. The paper received approximately 25 percent of the $250,000 in student activity fees collected each year.

Most of Jack's fellow contributors to the paper were main stream liberals or lefties. As a civil libertarian, he had no problem smoking a joint with them however, especially if it was theirs. Many shamelessly prostituted themselves by writing favorable reviews of performing artists for "free stuff" such as record albums and tickets. Several thousand unread copies of the newspaper ended up in the trash every week. Jack therefore saw no harm taking advantage of this "free printing" by cutting out the pages with his columns and editorials for use as political handouts.

Besides keeping the books, Jack's main function as the business manager was as the liaison to the paper's faculty advisor, who was a World War II veteran. He had no role however, in editorial decisions over the predominantly left wing content. Since the paper even published Jack's items with an occasional conservative theme, it never occurred to him that he might be being used again to add a veneer of balance.

Jack rarely had issues with any of the academic faculty. However, a personality conflict soon developed with Al French, Jack's instructor in his Problems in State Government course. French, a doctoral candidate at Brown University, also ran the State Internship program whose participants came from all of the State's colleges. French resented having no control over Jack, who had access to the House floor and State House offices as Rep. Fred Shannon's legislative aide. The main resentment however, was based on Jeri, a girl in the program who Jack had started dating regularly. Jeri, had recently returned to college after dropping out for several years. She was mature, very intelligent and from out state, not your typical "second generation yokel ward heeler".

On February 7th, the U.S. Senate unanimously voted to establish the bi-partisan Select Committee on Presidential Campaign Activities. Democratic Senator Sam Ervin of North Carolina served as the Chairman. Ervin, a former state supreme court judge, was widely respected as a constitutional expert. Republican Senator Howard Baker of Tennessee was named the Vice Chairman. The hearings would not only be televised but broadcast live. Initially, President Nixon rebuffed Ervin's attempts to gain access to White House documents and staff, citing "executive privilege" and "separation of powers". Ervin responded that Nixon's constitutional arguments did not to extend to criminal behavior. The Senator even threatened to send the Senate's Sergeant-at-Arms to arrest White House staffers who refused to cooperate. Polls indicated that two thirds of Americans believed that Nixon was personally involved. Nixon finally acquiesced to public pressure and directed his staff to cooperate.

Shortly after April began, Martin Cooper made the first telephone call from a cell phone in New York City. The next

CHAPTER 11

day an official ribbon cutting ceremony officially opened the World Trade Center. On the 17th, Federal Express began its operations by launching 12 small aircraft out of Memphis International Airport. That evening this pioneer competitor to the U.S. Postal System delivered 186 packages to 25 cities, from Rochester to Miami.

On April 30th, the President announced the resignation of Attorney General Richard Kleindiest, and that he had fired White House Counsel John Dean and even his two closest aides, White House Chief of Staff H.R. Halderman and Domestic Policy advisor John Ehrlichman. General Alexander Haig, the Army's Vice Chief of Staff who had formerly been Kissinger's protégé at the National Security Council, was named as Halderman's replacement. The appointment of a professional military officer was intended as a symbol of a new start divorced from party politics.

On May 17th, the Senate Watergate Committee hearings began. Two days later Archibald Cox, a Harvard Law School professor, was appointed as the Special Prosecutor. The semester had ended before John Dean, the President's most damaging witness testified. Senator Howard Baker succinctly articulated the question that would determine Nixon's fate: ***"What did the President know, and when did he know it."***

Senior aides inside the White House itself had, at the very least, clearly been negligent in their management oversight responsibilities, if not directly involved themselves. Testimony before the Ervin Committee soon revealed that much more was involved than the break-in of Democratic headquarters by a few ex-White House staffers working as functionaries of Nixon's "Committee to Re-elect the President, or CREEP.

The semester, which Jack finished with two Cs, and three incompletes, including the Biology course he was repeating, ended prior to the most sensational Watergate testimony.

Even though all of his graded work averaged a borderline A/B, Al French justified knocking him down to a C for "insufficient class participation". Jack saved copies of all his papers and tests, plus the course syllabus that mentioned nothing about a class participation element. He had time until the end of the fall semester to submit an appeal.

Jack now looked forward to another summer he had filled up with active duty. From early June to mid-July he was scheduled for five weeks with his reserve unit. Jack would then spend August attending a "gentlemen's course" at Fort Benning. Down there he could date grown up women who "wore skirts, put on the war paint and had the decency to bathe regularly". With free weekends and evenings, Jack would have plenty of time to make up the two incompletes while he was in Georgia.

After 7 years as an undergraduate, Dan Debre finally received his B.A. in Philosophy, having accumulated nearly 160 semester hours while trying out three other majors. Along with three other students, Dan was now renting a large country house 10 miles north of the state line in Wrentham. It had become a popular post-last call party location for girls from the area who followed the bands around the local night spots. The final two weeks of the lease were nightly celebrations of Dan's crowning academic achievement. Jack was now free to show up almost every night. Feeling pressure to commit to a serious relationship, Jack had deliberately set himself up with a pattern of mildly obnoxious behavior so that his girlfriend Jeri eventually dumped him.

Before testifying before the Senate Watergate Committee, John Dean had told the Special Prosecutor's investigators that he had discussed the cover-up with Nixon at least 35 times. The President's defenders dismissed this as a desperate attempt by a functionary who had overstepped his authority to avoid prosecution. On July 13th however, Alexander Butterfield, an obscure former Presidential appointments

CHAPTER 11

secretary, revealed that Nixon had installed a system that recorded all of his meetings and phone calls since 1971. These tapes obviously included the critical meetings in which Nixon was alleged to have instructed his staff to involve the FBI and CIA in covering up the entire affair. Citing "executive privilege" Nixon categorically refused to turn over any of the tapes to either the Senate Committee or the Special Prosecutor. Over the next 12 months these tapes would be the focus of procedural battles in the federal courts.

During classroom breaks in Infantry Hall, at Fort Benning, Jack, his classmates, and student officers from other courses gathered around the TV monitors that broadcasted the live Watergate hearings. If the courts ultimately ruled in favor of the Special Prosecutor, and the tapes revealed any Nixon involvement, impeachment would certainly follow. Fascinating speculative dinner conversations ensued. If a partisan impeachment vote passed the Democratic controlled House, would two thirds of the U.S. Senate vote to remove him? If removed, could Nixon then be criminally prosecuted for illegal activities he had allegedly ordered his "White House Plumbers" unit to perform for gathering domestic intelligence?

The obvious never spoken military-related question was "What if he's guilty as hell and attempts to stay in office by force?" Jack had a vague concept for a Quebec exile under a martial law scenario, but never considered how he would resource it. Jack's "battle buddy" at Fort Benning was a captain named Mark Sheridan, a fellow Vietnam veteran who shared their BOQ apartment. The main focus of evening discussions over a six pack and a joint was the emerging "air land battle" doctrine to counter a Soviet invasion of West Germany though the Fulda Gap. These discussions typically ended when they reached their favorite Country-Western joints in Phenix City.

One late evening when a family crisis preempted two lady friends from meeting them, they decided to practice mechanized infantry tactics. Detouring from the route to their BOQ, they practiced mechanized bounding and overwatch techniques, substituting Jack's Carmen Gia and Mike's Volkswagen for a tank and armored personnel carrier, across an open parade field adjacent to the golf course on the main post.

The next morning Jack was unexpectedly called upon to present his tactical solution to a battalion active defense problem. Badly hung over, he had only scanned the handouts. However, with barely two minutes to look at the map, Jack got up and briefed a "bounding overwatch in reverse" concept to the cheers of his 200 class mates. Sheridan remarked over a joint on their way to Phenix City that evening "You know that 15 years from now if we're still around we'll at least be light colonels, and our spring butt class mates will be gossiping about us."

In September, Jack was back in Rhode Island for the Fall Semester, still taking advantage of the newspaper's offices and equipment as the business manager. He was now also on the student senate, a mal-apportioned rotten borough system that controlled a budget of over $250,000. Apathy reigned at the predominantly commuter college, so elections were rarely contested. The student senate was dominated by what Jack called "the second and third generation ward heelers and hacks, who hung around the State House and had to study to get Cs." His service was primarily motivated to ensure that the newspaper received its fair share of the budget, and because members received a stipend of $5 for each meeting.

The focus of the news suddenly shifted from Watergate. The top story on the front pages and evening TV news was that since early 1973, the U.S. Attorney for the District of Maryland had been investigating the Vice President. The criminal allegations were that Spiro Agnew had extorted and

CHAPTER 11

accepted bribes and committed tax fraud during his 1967-69 tenure as Governor of Maryland, and had even accepted residual payments as the Vice President.

Agnew immediately launched a counter-offensive dismissing the charges as "damned lies". On October 10th, however, Agnew resigned, accepting three years of probation in exchange for his no contest plea to an income tax evasion count. The more serious bribery and extortion charges were dropped. The personification of law and order to Nixon's "silent majority", who had been leading in the polls for the 1976 GOP nomination to succeed Nixon, was now gone!

Two days after Agnew's exit, the President nominated Congressman Gerald Ford of Grand Rapids, Michigan to replace him. Prior to the ratification of the 25th Amendment in 1967, a Vice Presidential vacancy remained vacant until the next election. Now, the President nominated a replacement for both houses of Congress to confirm. Jerry Ford, the moderately conservative House Minority Leader, was well liked in Congress where he had served since 1949. The nomination was well received by the press and both parties.

Political observers recognized that Ford's selection had involved considerable behind the scenes negotiations between the White House and Congressional leaders of both parties. An easy confirmation required someone respected for his integrity and viewed as a qualified potential caretaker; but nobody perceived as a leading 1976 Presidential contender. Coincidentally, Jack's father had a connection to Ford, who had attended a testimonial for him as the local Congressman after his father returned from 34 months as a prisoner of war in Korea. "Big Jack" had visited his D.C. Congressional office a few times, and his relatives in Grand Rapids still received "Jerry's" Christmas cards.

Within two weeks Nixon shattered any conciliatory feelings of bipartisanship from the Ford nomination. Archibald Cox, the Watergate Special Prosecutor, had repeatedly clashed with the White House over the release of tapes that had recorded 10 hours of meetings where the Watergate break in was discussed. Key witnesses testified under oath that the President had implicated himself during these meetings.

On Saturday evening, October 20, 1973, Nixon abruptly ordered the firing of Cox. After Attorney General Elliot Richardson and his Deputy William Ruckelshaus resigned in protest, Solicitor General Robert Bork reluctantly complied. Nixon then ordered FBI agents to close off the offices of the Special Prosecutor and Attorney General. The "Saturday Night Massacre" triggered over 50,000 telegrams sent in protest that weekend.

The press and public were outraged. An NBC poll showed a plurality of 44 to 43 percent of respondents favored impeachment resolutions that had been introduced by 21 U.S. House members. Nixon quickly recognized that disbanding the Special Prosecutors Office would trigger a full blown Constitutional crisis and a quick impeachment vote in the House. On November 1st, Leon Jaworski was appointed as the new Special Prosecutor. The Vice Presidential confirmation hearings had been expected to be relatively quick pro-forma events. The respective House and Senate committees were now closely examining Gerry Ford as a potential President. It would take until December 6th, almost two month after being nominated, for him to be confirmed and sworn in.

Mid-way into the semester the incomplete in Biology, that Jack never got around to making up from the spring, automatically became an F. That dropped his GPA low enough to place him on academic probation. This motivated Jack to begin turning assignments in on time and attend

CHAPTER 11

classes fairly regularly. During class discussions he enjoyed provoking paranoid ravings about how Al Haig was engineering a military coup for Nixon. All of his military friends, regardless of political persuasion, also recognized that as preposterous.

The final week of the semester Jack formally submitted an appeal of the C in the State Government course from the previous semester. Jack's partying every other night squashed any chances of a serious relationship developing with Julie, who he had been casually dating. In spite the D in his morning class however, he still finished the semester with a 3.0. This brought his overall GPA well out of the probation zone. With the support of the Department Chairman, Jack was postured well for his appeal, which would not be decided until the middle of the upcoming semester.

In Charleston, West Virginia, Carol Chenworth, who had graduated from Fairmont State University the previous Spring, was in the third month of a job working for the West Virginia Energy Department. Carol was refined, stunningly attractive, but very shy. She felt trapped in a lingering college relationship that was going nowhere. Upon returning to her apartment one evening, she received some unexpected good news. A letter from the National Governors Association was in Carol's mail box offering her an administrative assistant position she had applied for several months earlier.

She quickly accepted the job, with a starting date in early January. Carol's family had descendents who fought in the American Revolution, and a few who could even be traced to the Mayflower. Her father was one of the contractors who built the Jefferson Memorial's Tidal Basin walkway. Carol never had been interested in politics, but was looking forward to the cultural and historical experiences as much as the career opportunity. More importantly, this was a clean break from her college sweetheart, whose lack of ambition and academic achievement made Jack Wilson look like a Rhodes Scholar and prize catch.

12. OUT OF OPTIONS

By January of 1974, in spite of 8 months of White House Chief of Staff Al Haig's efforts, the President's political and legal problems continued to mount. Haig had risen to prominence as Henry Kissinger's protégé while attached to the National Security Council. After Kissinger became Secretary of State, Haig continued working closely with him to engineer more foreign policy achievements. Nixon had normalized relations with China, and his 1973 summit meetings with Soviet leader Leonid Brezhnev had produced an historic strategic arms limitation treaty.

Kissinger had negotiated disengagement agreements between Israel and its neighboring enemies Egypt and Syria. Israel's decisive victory during the three-week Yom Kipur War the previous October, was decisively influenced by Nixon's support with massive shipments of military materiel. Nixon had honorably ended the U.S. combat role in Vietnam, and the draft had been eliminated. The Saigon government's claims of gaining territory in contested areas where the Paris Accords had permitted communist forces to remain were probably exaggerated. However, for nearly a year without even U.S. air support, they had certainly held their own.

In his January 30th State of the Union message the President declared "one year of Watergate is enough", but it had not gone away. Earlier that day a jury convicted former White House aide G. Gordon Liddy, who had been arrested in the burglary. A top Nixon campaign aide, Herbert Porter, had pled guilty on a related offense two days earlier. Special Prosecutor Leon Jaworski continued aggressively pursuing grand jury indictments against former Attorney John Mitchell, H.R. Halderman, John Ehrlichman and four others. Even if Nixon survived, chances looked bleak for the GOP in the mid-terms, especially in Democratic Rhode Island.

Jack loathed Nixon, but viewed sentencing a President of the United States to prison as "bordering on banana-boatism". This was not the only issue that caused friction with his Democratic associates. Jack believed that second chances and assistance programs should be conditional. He made no effort to hide his contempt for gratuitous social programs like vocational rehabilitation scholarships for alcoholics and ex-offenders, and college financial aid programs with lax performance standards and vague repayment terms.

Jack was accepted into the State Internship Program for the spring semester. Al French was no longer involved, and Jack got along well with the new faculty advisor. His project focused on three bills that his internship sponsor, Rep. Fred Shannon, had introduced. One was a state bonus for Vietnam veterans. The other granted veterans up to 8 elective credits at state colleges. The third provided work release opportunities for minor offenders.

Jack registered for two late afternoon history courses, but had to show up twice each week for a mid-morning fencing class. In a knee-jerk reaction to the recent Arab oil embargo, Congress had lowered the national speed limit on interstate highways to 55 miles per hour. This generated multiple speed traps along the 20 mile stretch of I-95 and I-295 that Jack traveled daily. At $70 a ticket, they were an expensive nuisance.

While visiting his parents during the Christmas break, Jack became involved with Pauline, who he had met at a night club in the South Shore Boston suburb of Braintree. Pauline resembled Cybil Shepherd. At 23, she was a year younger and had worked intermittently as a model on the West Coast. She was divorced with a four year old boy. Pauline easily kept up with Jack, downing vodka and grapefruit juice, or even Johnny Walker Black on the rocks. He viewed this as a "quality of maturity lacking in sheltered college girls who

CHAPTER 12

still lived at home." Jack was still dating Julie back at the college and really liked her. Since Julie wasn't "giving him any" however, Jack frequently began using his "mother's health" as a cover for staying at his "duty girl's" Braintree apartment.

Over a year of hearings and investigations strongly indicated that a range of illegal activities by the Nixon Administration involved far more than burglarizing the opposition party's headquarters. Disturbing accounts surfaced revealing widespread abuse of power dating back to at least 1970. Top Nixon Aides had formed a special domestic intelligence gathering operation known as "the plumbers" to "stop leaks."

Under supervision of top White House aides, the plumbers not only gathered information to discredit Administration critics, but had even committed illegal acts themselves, like breaking into the office of Daniel Ellsberg's psychiatrist. A counterintelligence program (COINTPRO) had also apparently used the CIA illegally for domestic intelligence gathering. Military intelligence assets had also infiltrated anti-war activities. Nixon's political reelection committee had also widely engaged in sabotaging primary campaigns, most notably that of Senator Edmund Muskie in New Hampshire.

In early February the U.S. House authorized the Judiciary Committee to investigate whether grounds existed to impeach the President. On March 4th, a federal grand jury not only indicted seven of Nixon's closest associates, but even named the President himself as an unindicted co-conspirator. Testimony from recent trials had corroborated the testimony of John Dean and other key figures from the previous year's Senate Committee hearings. On March 15th, federal Judge John Sirica turned the sealed indictment over to the House Judiciary Committee.

OUT OF OPTIONS

Special Prosecutor Leon Jaworski continued to aggressively pursue a court order for releasing the tapes of the key 10 hours of Oval Office conversations. Testimony in the criminal trials overwhelmingly indicated that these tapes would prove that even if he did not actually direct a cover-up, Nixon had failed to aggressively prosecute the Watergate break-in. Polls were also indicating that a growing number of Americans believed that Nixon actually ordered the break-in. Paranoid lefties on college newspapers wrote alarmist editorials warning of the impending military coup Al Haig was orchestrating to keep Nixon in power.

Impressed by conservative GOP U.S. Senator James Buckley's reasoning in calling for Nixon's resignation, Jack changed his political registration to Republican. During his dabbling in Democratic politics Jack was never comfortable with the liberals. However, a rebuttal he made in a class to a taunting female classmate may very well have revealed his real motivation for converting: "I simply got tired of immature, braying liberal little she-asses who don't know how to use knives and forks, or even have the decency to bathe regularly."

Jack began interviewing to obtain a GOP nomination to make a spirited fight against an entrenched Democratic state senator that fall. Finding a new apartment would satisfy the state's lax law on voting residences. A credible campaign in a Democratic district would posture Jack well for a future political appointment. Jack was not surprised when the college newspaper's liberal editor tersely informed him that he had been "fired as the business manager for sloppy book-keeping."

By the end of March, things really began turning sour for Jack. He partied excessively with student veterans at other colleges, justifying it as "legislative work on his internship project." Jack continued his column on bills pending in the

CHAPTER 12

legislature that several other college newspapers still carried, but had fallen way behind on his course work.

Jack's personal life also caught up with him. After he broke it off with Pauline, she persistently called his parents' house, and also left messages at the campus newspaper. Not surprisingly, Julie summarily dumped Jack when one of the paper's "liberal little trollups" told her about his "duty girl." The academic affairs committee's turned down the appeal of his grade from the state government course the previous spring. Since his department chairman had supported him, Jack concluded that his reputation had taken root in the faculty grapevine.

Jack was now frequenting the bars in South County with Dan Debre. Dan had been leasing a beach house as a winter rental with three URI students, since returning from California several months earlier. It served as an all night party site after last call at the area pubs, similar to how the house in Wrentham had. On mornings after he had crashed on Dan's couch, Jack would read the newspaper before driving the half hour to his Coventry apartment. After showering and changing clothes, he then drove another 35 minutes to Providence.

On April 17th, Special Prosecutor Leon Jaworski issued a subpoena for 64 White House tapes. Nixon clung to his executive privilege and national security arguments against releasing them. However, he did attempt a compromise by releasing more than 1,200 pages of edited transcripts to the House Judiciary Committee. The Committee, which had begun impeachment hearings on May 9th however, insisted on the actual tapes.

One Thursday evening after a rare appearance for a late afternoon class, Jack and his friend Bob McKay, a fellow Vietnam veteran, upset some frat brothers in the campus pub. They were flirting with the brothers' favorite sorority queens who were definitely enjoying the attention. While Bob went to his car to retrieve a joint, Jack poured on the charm, embellished with superficial "cultural shit" he had picked up in European history courses. After he had ignored the frat brother telling him to "get lost", the situation escalated. Finally Jack answered their challenge to step outside.

After catching a sucker punch that cut the corner of his lower lip, Jack put on a display of hand-to-hand combat skills for several minutes. He tossed the three around without actually injuring any of them. Upon returning to the pub and discovering what had transpired, Bob McKay appeared outside. Setting the stage for Jack's graceful withdrawal, Bob shouted: "Be careful, that guy was a Montanyard advisor in Vietnam!" By that time security had been called, so Jack and Bob quickly withdrew to South County, where they laughed the episode off with Dan Debre's crowd.

As Jack exited a history class the following Monday afternoon, an assistant Dean greeted him with a letter summoning his appearance before the college disciplinary board. The pub incident had been a relatively minor bar room altercation where both sides could be blamed. During the actual altercation Jack had been outnumbered three to one, and also the only one even superficially injured. However, the powers that be had decided that Jack alone would be the example.

With two days notice, Jack appeared before the board. Dean Werme in the movie "Animal House" could not have assembled a better Kangaroo Court. Jack's attempt at challenging the impartially of two members he had criticized for wasteful spending on the student senate was rejected, as was his challenge of the only faculty member who he had ever had and issue with. Fortunately, Jack's mentor Dr. Ron Hoffman, the professor who had heavily influenced his GOP conversion, acted as his counsel. Otherwise, the outcome

CHAPTER 12

would probably have been far worse than the year of disciplinary probation Jack received.

Things were still going well for Jack in his reserve outfit, which had the mission of writing and conducting exercises for guard and reserve units throughout New England. Jack's boss, Colonel Bob Martov, arranged to put him on active duty for a week to write an exercise plan. Jack manipulated the situation into a conflict with finals and persuaded two professors to let him satisfy the exam requirements with research papers. When the semester ended he had an A for his internship project, a B in fencing, one "W" (withdrew passing), and two incompletes.

After finishing the week of reserve duty, Jack unexpectedly incurred a serious legal problem while visiting Debre and his roommates. They had decided to ride the state's 90 day eviction statute, rather than vacate on May 1st when rents on beach resort properties quadrupled. Two hours after Jack had arrived Dan rose to answer loud pounding at the front door. Suddenly, five local cops, led by one with a shot gun, entered the living room. Two went into the kitchen and emerged with a one pound bag of marijuana they had pulled from a pantry cabinet. The evictees and Jack were then arrested and taken to the local police station.

The detainees argued that they just finished smoking pot seeds and stems, so wasn't that convincing evidence that someone (probably the landlord) had set them up by planting the pot and phoning the cops? Jack probably would have been released fairly quickly, had he remained silent. However, drunken intellect won out over good judgment. He incessantly demanded that the police cease and desist from their "egregious violations of their civil liberties". Jack then uttered insulting epithets at them for several minutes resulting in his being taken into an interrogation room and roughed up. After about 8 hours in custody he was released and charged with frequenting a narcotics nuisance.

OUT OF OPTIONS

Jack had a free consultation with an ACLU attorney the following Monday. The frequenting charge was a real stretch, so getting it dropped would be easy. However, the lawyer would not pursue a civil rights violation or civil suit against the police department. Jack subsequently filed a complaint with the local FBI office for the physical abuse. A brief story about the incident in the paper abruptly ended Jack's negotiations for a GOP leaders nomination, even for a hopeless state senate race.

In early June, Jack drove to Fort Drum, located in northern New York next to the depressed city of Watertown. Colonel Martov had arranged for Jack to be on the advance and stay behind details, which provided him an additional 5 days' pay to the 15 he would earn with his unit. The support of Martov, a maverick among his 11 peers in the top heavy unit, shielded Jack from direct fallout due to his recent misadventures with the police. Nearly broke, Jack benefited from spending all but three of the 21 days in the field. His only expenses were a modest BOQ charge and paying back the $50 Martov had loaned him.

Upon returning to Coventry, Jack had another two weeks to kill before his next month of reserve duty at Fort Benning. He vacated his apartment, farmed out his furniture to several friends, and stored the rest of his things at his parents' house. A few days before leaving, Jack attended a farewell bash for Dan Debre, who was temporarily living in a friend's cottage on Johnson's Pond in Coventry.

Rather than face charges of possession with intent to sell, Dan had decided to jump bail for points west. Dan final legal act in Rhode Island was to dictate a telegram over the phone responding to the license suspension notice he had just received from the Registry of Motor Vehicles. "I do not recognize your agency's authority on this matter, and shall

CHAPTER 12

continue to operate on public roadways within the State of Rhode Island and Providence Plantations."

The next week while out prowling the Columbus, Georgia night clubs, Jack met Stephanie. She was an attractive full figured blonde, about five feet six. A psychology major at Auburn University, "Stephie" shared Jack's vices. The two immediately clicked. At 22, she was entering her fifth undergraduate year. They spent their first night together on the floor of the apartment of an Army aviator who Stephie's girl friend had hooked up with. Since Jack shared his BOQ with a roommate, he began commuting the hour-long ride to Auburn, Alabama almost every evening.

The impeachment hearings dominated TV, which Jack would watch with his class mates during breaks on the monitors in Infantry Hall. Despite Nixon's June visits to Israel, and reinforcing President Anwar Sadat's transition from a Soviet client to a U.S. ally with a visit to Egypt, his poll numbers remained at rock bottom. In the South however, Nixon retained considerable popularity. As they shared a joint and a bottle of Chablis, Stephie's admiration of the President stimulated spirited debate about the merits of the case.

On July 8th, Nixon's attorney James Sinclair, and Special Prosecutor Leon Jaworski made their oral arguments before the U.S. Supreme Court. Both had directly appealed to the Court to decide the relevance of the White House tapes to a Watergate-related criminal trial. On July 23rd, Chief Justice Warren Berger, President's Nixon's own appointee, issued the Court's unanimous ruling that Jaworski had proven a "sufficient likelihood that each of the tapes contained conversations relevant to the offenses charged in the indictment."

The Court also addressed the issue of executive privilege by rejecting Nixon's claim to an "absolute, unqualified

OUT OF OPTIONS

Presidential privilege of immunity from judicial process under all circumstances." It further ruled that "a claim of Presidential privilege as to materials subpoenaed for use in a criminal trial cannot override the needs of the judicial process, if that claim is based, not on the ground that military or diplomatic secrets are implicated, but merely on the ground of a generalized interest in confidentiality." On July 27th Nixon was ordered to deliver the subpoenaed materials to Judge John Sirica's District Court.

On July 24th, the House Judiciary Committee began debating five articles of an impeachment resolution. Two spurious articles relating to the bombing of Cambodia and Nixon's taxes were defeated by a vote of 26-12. However, 7 Republicans joined the 21 Democrats on the Committee in voting to impeach the President on at least one of the two articles of obstructing the investigation of the Watergate break-in; and misusing his powers and violating his oath of office. However only two GOP members voted on the "contempt of Congress" article related to non-compliance with House subpoenas.

There was no doubt that the full House would vote to impeach Nixon. However, Nixon still clung to the hope that a coalition of Republicans and conservative Democrats would provide him the 34 votes needed to survive a Senate trial. As Nixon faced conviction from the Senate, Stephanie informed Jack that the university housing office warned her against continued overnight guests. At the end of July, the couple rented a trailer together on Wire Road on the outskirts of Auburn. They furnished it with items from various yard sales that regularly ran on Saturday mornings in the sprawling university town. Stephie assured Jack that she would pay her half when she received a check from her parents. They continued watching the impeachment drama play out on the news every evening.

CHAPTER 12

On August 5th, Nixon released the tape of the June 22, 1972 meeting with Halderman that recorded his participation in a plan to cover-up the Watergate break-in investigation. The President refused to resign however, announcing his intent to fight conviction and removal in a Senate trial. In an August 6th White House meeting with GOP Senators Hugh Scott and Barry Goldwater, and House GOP Leader James Rhodes, Nixon was informed that he could count on no more than 15 votes for acquittal in the Senate. After the meeting, Goldwater was reported to have said "This is just one damn lie too many. Nixon needs to get his ass out of the White House now!"

On the following evening, August 7, 1974, Nixon announced that he was resigning effective the next day. After a dramatic farewell ceremony late the next morning, Nixon was gone. Within minutes after his predecessor lifted off in his final flight in the Presidential helicopter, Gerald R. Ford was sworn in as the 38th President. On August 20th, the new President nominated former New York Governor Nelson Rockefeller, whose immense wealth made him one of the most powerful men in the country, for the Vice Presidency.

In mid-August when his course at Fort Benning ended, Jack remained in Auburn. His plan was to find a guard or reserve unit to transfer into, and transfer to Auburn University for the winter quarter in January. Since the cost of living was much cheaper than in the northeast, he and Stephanie could easily upgrade to an apartment. Although a sound concept, Jack never checked out the details. Even if he made up the incompletes from the RIC spring semester, Jack discovered that he would barely be a sophomore, if the University even admitted him.

Stephanie's parents, who were from Mobile and had been paying the University directly for her dorm, refused to increase her $100 monthly allowance to live off campus. Even if Jack enrolled for the fall quarter as a nonmatriculating student, it would take at least two months for his GI Bill checks to start coming in. He did find a reserve unit where he could perform equivalent training drills for up to a year while remaining assigned to his current one in Rhode Island. However, just about all the units in the South, where the military was still highly regarded, had waiting lists for captain's positions.

On September 8th, Ford announced a full and unconditional pardon of Nixon on the grounds that it was in the best interest of the country. Democratic partisans however, immediately charged a corrupt deal had been struck. Thus, the period of bi-partisan good will towards Jerry Ford abruptly ended, exactly a month after he assumed office. This also assured that the Rockefeller nomination for Vice President would be subjected to lengthy House and Senate Committee hearings.

Back in Auburn Jack received more financial bad news. His assigned reserve unit's full time staff cited a non-existent regulation that required him to transfer out in two months. When Jack responded that he would appeal to Colonel Martov, they informed him that Martov was no longer with the unit. Friction continued growing between Jack and Stephie. Her pot head friends were constantly hanging around their trailer and frequently spending the night.

Finally, Jack and Stephie recognized that setting up house together had been a mistake. Stephie moved back into the dorm. Down to $300, Jack called his friend Mike Fitzgerald, a fellow veteran from RIC who had transferred to UMass-Boston. Mike Welch agreed to put him up for several weeks at his place in Quincy. On October 7th Jack was back in New England working in a warehouse in Norwood, Massachusetts.

Mike had mid-level ties to Massachusetts' liberal GOP Governor Frank Sargent's reelection campaign. The Nixon pardon, on top of Watergate had all but assured a wave

CHAPTER 12

election for the Democrats in the November mid-terms. Sargent however, had supported many liberal programs. After succeeding John Volpe in 1969, he had easily won the office in his own right against Boston Mayor Kevin White the following year. Sargent's handling of the mass demonstrations against a federal court order mandating bussing to desegregate Boston's schools, was largely credited for avoiding widespread violence.

Jack viewed the Sargent campaign as a worthwhile effort. It could also posture him well after he transferred into the Massachusetts National Guard after his pending reserve promotion. Jack immersed himself in campaign events and the many after parties they spawned. When Election Day came however, the Nixon albatross could not even be shaken off by moderately liberal Frank Sargent, who decisively lost to Michael Dukakis.

An executive level reorganization over the summer had replaced Colonel Martov with Bill Abate, who Jack had previously clashed with. Even worse, Abate was close to the full time unit administrators. They were Jack's military peers but controlled administrative and personnel actions. They also resented Jack because Martov had frequently reversed their decisions in his favor.

At his November drill, Jack discovered that the unit administrators had never submitted the payroll for his August and September drills. Jack had performed them with an Alabama unit after receiving Martov's prior approval. He also discussed it over the phone with the administrators, but they claimed that" he never followed up with a written request." Colonel Abate only approved amending the unit records to record Jack's absences as authorized, but refused to overrule the administrators' decision not to pay him.

The real blow came when he discovered a promotion board had passed him over for captain. Jack's evaluation reports in the captain's position he had held for two years should have assured his selection, but had probably been omitted from his record. Correcting a material error was just a matter of submitting a well written memorandum with supporting documents to a standby board. Jack decided to transfer out of his unit into an unpaid individual ready reserve status.

Transferring enabled him to correct the errors in his records directly with the Army Reserve Personnel Center, and avoid bureaucratic manipulation by his unit administrators. It also preempted a likely mediocre evaluation by Abate that could have assured a second pass-over, terminating his commissioned status. The significant income he was temporarily forfeiting was far less than the cost of litigation, which could drag out for several years.

At the National Governors Association a news story about little-known, outgoing Georgia Governor Jimmy Carter, who had started campaigning for President in New Hampshire, caught Carol Chenworth's attention. Carol wondered if this meant she would be seeing more of Russ Melton, a Carter staffer from Atlanta who she had been casually dating since the summer. Socially she had found the Georgia boys to be a lot smoother than the Louisiana crew, whose events in their hotel suites coworkers warned her to avoid when Governor "Fast Eddie" Edwards was in town.

Jack was now a college dropout, working in a warehouse. His two incompletes had automatically become Fs when he missed the suspense for turning in the work he owed. That dropped his grade point average to a 2.07. However, that average still met the minimum Rhode Island College criteria for automatic readmission under the category of "a former student who had left in good standing." Jack's only remaining option for elevating his status was to reenroll at RIC in January.

CHAPTER 12

On December 10th the Senate finally voted 90 to 7 for Nelson Rockefeller's confirmation. On the 19th the new Vice President was sworn in immediately after the subsequent House vote of 287 to 128.

13. LAST MAN STANDING

January of 1975 marked the beginning of Jack's fourth spring semester at the college. President Ford seemed decent enough, but the economy continued to decline in spite of his WIN, or "Whip Inflation Now" campaign. The Republicans had been decimated in the previous November mid- term. In Congress they were down to barely one third of the House members and 38 seats in the Senate. Most of Ford vetoes could be easily overridden. Events in Southeast Asia were going badly for U.S. supported governments in Laos and Cambodia.

The class on U.S. Foreign Policy in Asia that Jack and his three fellow Vietnam veterans had signed up for should be very interesting. Jack was on a total sabbatical from the military, and chose Indonesia for the topic of his semester paper, not Vietnam. Nearly two years after U.S. troops had withdrawn, the only people with bigger problems than Jack Wilson's seemed to be Lon Nol, and Nguyen Van Thieu.

Now 25, Jack Wilson was still on disciplinary probation for the incident in the campus pub the previous school year. His major challenge however, was a recent college curriculum change. Jack now needed to complete 45 more semester hours to graduate in January, or spend almost another year there. One course he had to pass was cellular biology, which he was repeating for the second time. Jack had enrolled in it three years earlier assuming it would be fun and games because it was a prerequisite for nursing students. To Jack's dismay, that course not only required regular attendance, but weekly labs as well. The second time around, an incomplete automatically turned into an F. due to his inaction. This type of course was impossible for Jack to write his way out of with his standard B minus paper, written

CHAPTER 13

during an all-nighter the last week of a semester over a couple bottles of Beaujolais.

Jack went to see his old friend Paul Baer who had recently started a job in the new Congressman Edward P. Beard's office. "Eddie" had pulled a major upset over the four-term incumbent in the September Democratic primary, before easily winning a landslide in November. A house painter, Beard had been a one term state representative from Cranston, who gained prominence by taking on Governor Philip Noel over the squalid conditions at the state hospitals. He also had benefited from his predecessor's well publicized drunk driving arrest in New Hampshire, and a split within the Providence Democratic organization.

Paul gave Jack a VIP-style welcome introducing him to all the Providence staff before taking him into his office. Jack then asked him if he could find out if there was anything in his military records bad enough to cause a second promotion pass over. A shrewd operator, Baer would not send a typical Congressional inquiry on Jack's behalf. That would only generate a vague pro forma response. Instead Paul would use a tactic of calling a contact in the Army's Congressional liaison office, implying that he was considering Jack for a job.

About a week later, Jack received the information he needed. One of Paul's probing questions noted that Jack still held the same rank in which he had served in Vietnam four years earlier, and asked if this could be a red flag. The response indicated that nothing adverse was in his file, but that the most current evaluation report the board that had passed him over had seen dated back to November, 1972. This confirmed Jack's earlier assumption that two strong evaluations he had since received in the captain's slot he held in his former unit had been omitted from his promotion file. If he finished his degree, pursuing a military career could still be an option.

When Jack had transferred to the individual ready reserve in December, he had also given up a well paying part time job. His cash reserve was nearly exhausted and his course overload made a part time job that semester unfeasible, Jack's regular income was now limited to monthly GI Bill checks. Jack calculated that he could sustain the "Credit Moblier circular flow system" that Dan Debre had taught him for about a year without damaging his credit. However, that would require disciplining himself to using one open credit card for making payments on the other three, and on very few personal indulgences. His GI bill was enough for paying the rent on his apartment, food, and gas for his clunker, but where would the Johnny Walker Black, Beaujolais, Moet Chandon and Strasbourg goose liver pate come from? By default Jack put his nose to the academic grind stone.

By early March as mid-semester approached, he was holding his own carrying a 6 course, 20 semester hour load. He was even doing well in the biology course. Jack was surprised how courses he had a mental block against taking really weren't that difficult if you attended regularly and did the assignments on time. Jack now felt comfortable enough to go through a couple of cases of beer with friends on the weekends. He even got himself "in shape" applying the protein synthesis theory he learned in biology. Jack resumed doing isometrics and followed a dietary regimen of eating a can of tuna for each six pack, which got rid of his beer belly and kept the weigh off. Jack was still smoking three packs a day but this diet and the isometrics sure made him look fit.

Jack had noticed an announcement in a recent Army Reserve Personnel Center bulletin. President Thieu had awarded the Vietnamese Cross of Gallantry to every U.S. veteran who had ever served there. Jack correctly saw this as a part of public relations strategy to generate U.S. public support for more military aid. Cambodia was under a major

CHAPTER 13

communist assault. This was a bad omen for the Republic of Vietnam.

In the mornings, Jack and fellow Vietnam veterans in his class closely followed the unfolding Southeast Asia events in the papers. The communists in Laos had staged a virtually bloodless coup against the neutralist government. For a brief period afterwards, Laos even had the unique status of a communist monarchy. President Ford was no fool, and recognized that any military action to save the Lon Nol regime in Cambodia from the Khmer Rouge would guarantee impeachment.

The absence of any military response in Cambodia and rapid evacuation of the U.S. presence emboldened the North Vietnamese and their Viet Cong allies. Communist forces were no longer just conducting limited attacks in areas adjacent to those where the 1973 Paris Peace Accords had permitted them to remain. Coordinated full scale attacks were now underway, not only around major provincial capitals in the north like Da Nang and Hue, but in three of the four military regions.

The fall of Ban Me Thut on March 13th, was followed by President Thieu's disastrous decision to withdraw the ARVN forces from the western highlands to the east. His intent was to hold the population centers along the coast. Poorly planned and incompetently executed however, it soon turned into a rout. Panicked civilians intermingled with military convoys as the NVA pounded the retreating ARVN with artillery, when they weren't attacking. Every day newspapers showed a map of South Vietnam with ever increasing numbers of provinces that had fallen colored in black.

U.S. Ambassador Graham Martin steadfastly insisted that the South Vietnamese government could hold out. He refused to authorize U.S. entry visas for their nationals except for family members of U.S. citizens. Want ads appeared in major daily papers that caught Jack's interest. Wealthy Vietnamese were offering huge dowries for Americans who would marry their daughters and get the families out. A dowry of several hundred thousand dollars would enable him to live the lifestyle of the aristocrat Jack styled himself. Jack thought Vietnamese women were attractive enough, and besides he probably wouldn't have to remain married on paper for more than a year if he wanted to walk away.

In Washington Carol Chenworth was taking notes at a meeting between a dozen staff members from the Governors Association and the White House. When President Ford unexpectedly dropped in for a few minutes she had the opportunity to shake his hand. Carol was seeing more of Russ Melton, who had been kept as the Georgia liaison to the Association by George Busbee when he succeeded Jimmy Carter. Russ had hoped to join Carter's Presidential campaign but was blocked by Hamilton Jordan. That seemed fine with Carol, who was focused on getting married and starting a family. She knew very little about politics so to her Russ's Georgia job seemed more stable than the long shot Carter campaign. They made plans to spend a week of Carol's vacation in Atlanta that summer.

Jack and his cohort Bob McKay began to do the research to determine how to obtain the necessary visas and to verify their prospective new in-laws' net worth. Jack remarked jokingly to Bob, an ex-enlisted man, "Being an officer and former advisor entitles me to be the son-in-law of not less than a deputy cabinet minister, or least a major general. You'll have to settle for entering the family of a colonel, but one who was a corrupt chief of a province with a thriving black market." That would take time. This was 20 years before the age of the internet or even fax machines, so most research would have to be done manually, by phone and through the mail. The research section of the Brown University library was a good place to start. Costly cables

CHAPTER 13

could be paid for by their future in-laws once a connection with the prominent family was made.

Jack estimated that establishing the contacts and obtaining the required documentation to enter Vietnam could be completed by mid-May. By then he would have completed his heavy course load and boosted his impressive 2.07 grade point average by at least a half point, even if he didn't make the Dean's list. They could even fly to Saigon and return with their wealthy new families by the time summer school began in June. If Jack's family didn't want to live in Rhode Island with him, that was OK. Never being vulgarly materialistic, he would only ask for a modest house on the East Side of Providence as a wedding present.

By April, Da Nang and Hue had fallen, and the last remaining Central Highlands enclave around Cam Ranh was being evacuated. Jack and his veteran cohorts in the foreign policy course could not believe how quickly the ARVN was disintegrating. Jack's old province had surrendered without firing a shot. Commanders were flying out in helicopters abandoning their units. Billions of dollars in vehicles, helicopters, tanks and artillery pieces were abandoned intact. It looked like the 1971 prediction that Colonel David Hackworth had made that the NVA flag would fly over Saigon by the summer of 1975 might have been on target.

The remaining U.S. military presence was a 200 man Marine detachment that guarded the embassy and consulates, and the small 50 member U.S. Defense Attaché's Office on Tan Son Nhut. The DAO's main function was coordinating the delivery of military aid. Jack had no contacts in either of those. Jack always had avoided associating with the American contractors who he viewed as sleazy and corrupt. His only option for initiating contact was a well written letter he mailed to the DAO during the second week of "Operation Baby Lift." In typical fashion, Jack's letter expressed concern about the welfare of four junior ARVN generals by-name. He implied but did not outright claim a personal association with those "gallant officers whose leadership had inspired the forces I had the honor to serve with as an advisor". Jack concluded by asking that the DAO relay his concerns and to inform them of his willingness to assist their families. Jack already had his passport and hoped to make contact with his "new in-laws" by the end of the April.

Jack's main focus however, remained on getting his papers done and studying for finals. He also had a new girlfriend whom he had met on an evening out during a weekend visit to his parents' house. Jack had learned years earlier that if you stayed sober in the higher end clubs, the gorgeous ones were just as easy to hook up with as last call material. Denise was a stunning blonde who resembled a young Meryl Streep. She was a year younger, but already had two masters' degrees. Denise was a cost accountant and adjunct professor at a major university in Boston, who lived with her mother in one of the South Shore Boston suburbs. A Republican, she seemed impressed with Jack's military background and by his comparisons of themes in articles from her editions of Business Week, with those he had read in National Review.

Denise wasn't turned off by Jack's shabby apartment either. That proved his theory that the only things the ladies cared about were that the clothes were hung up; dishes weren't overflowing in the kitchen sink, and that the bathroom didn't look like a Texaco station. Denise's do-gooder Methodist background sure beat his duplicitous Catholic upbringing. They quickly became friends with benefits.

Denise caught Jack's attention on several occasions by mentioning she could not stand underachievers. That was OK because his pending humanitarian capitalism venture to Saigon would generate a quarter of a million dollars by the time he graduated in January. Hopefully she would understand the humanitarian motives for his marriage on paper, especially one that wouldn't even last a year. How

CHAPTER 13

would he tell her? Jack had filed his tax return early, and so received a healthy refund just before the April 15th filing deadline. It would be enough to take Denise out in style for a month, and to zero out the Visa card that kept the other three current.

The rapidly deteriorating situation in Vietnam continued. All that remained of the Republic of Vietnam were a few provinces surrounding Saigon and the Mekong Delta region, where the late John Paul Vann's strategy was apparently succeeding. The few thousand remaining American civilians were mostly businessmen and contractors. Hundreds of them were now leaving daily on outbound flights from Tan Son Nhut, Saigon's main airport.

The U.S. embassy and consulate offices were glutted with Vietnamese seeking entry visas. The only Vietnamese who could obtain a U.S. visa were those with American relatives. Hundreds of thousands of South Vietnamese allies, including many average citizens who had loyally assisted U.S. military and intelligence operations, were at risk of severe retaliation if the communists succeeded. Ambassador Graham Martin stubbornly insisted that the GVN would prevail and prohibited all U.S. assistance to Vietnamese trying to leave.

The NVA were now within striking distance of Saigon, but the 18th ARVN Division was stubbornly holding on to Xuan Loc. On April 19th, the ARVN commander, Brigadier General Le Minh Dao was ordered to withdraw, but the stubborn and gallant stand at Xuan Loc indicated he could continue to mount a viable defense. "Wouldn't mind having him as a father-in-law" mused Jack. Bringing their new Vietnamese relatives back to the States for the wedding could now possibly have to be done under fire. Jack and Bob McKay raised their "Vietnamese son-in-law adoption fee" to $350,000. Bob would insist on a new Mercedes, but Jack would only expect some kind of prestigious ARVN neck decoration for valor.

On April 21st President Thieu finally resigned, flying to Taiwan with several suit cases full of gold bullion. Dong Van Minh, a neutralist, who had served briefly as President after ousting Diem in 1963, seemed to be the only non-communist potentially acceptable to Hanoi as the leader of a coalition government. However, the President was now Tran Van Houng, a seventy-two year old weak and pliable politician, who Thieu had replaced Nguyen Cao Ky with as Vice President. Houng showed no willingness to resign, however.

Earlier that month Congress gave a resounding no to President Ford's request. There would be no U.S. air strikes limited to the South or even an emergency military aid package. U.S. Ambassador Martin finally authorized initiating the evacuation of U.S. government agency employees. As senior commanders and members of the high command deserted their posts, President Houng stubbornly resisted pressure to resign until April 28th. The National Assembly then elected Dong Van Minh as President. By then the NVA divisions were in Saigon's suburbs. Damage from communist artillery attacks made Tan Son Nhut unusable to inbound and outbound commercial airline flights.

Helicopters or ships at the Newport docks were now the only ways out. Jack continued diligently finishing his four term papers that even reflected some genuine scholarly research. He only had time to keep up with events by listening to radio news reports on study breaks, or looking at newspapers in between classes. In a desperate last grasp at a negotiated settlement with the communists, President Minh demanded that all Americans leave country. If it worked, a coalition government might at least be able to last several months and Jack and Bob might still be able to pull off their humanitarian venture. Jack however, was fantasizing about the upcoming Saturday with Denise.

CHAPTER 13

For the first time Jack turned all his papers in on time. Another first would be completing a semester with every course he had initially registered for, and without even one incomplete! On the evening of the 29th, Jack got together with his cronies from the Southeast Asia Foreign Policy class at Sal's Lounge. They entered about nine o'clock that evening, which was the morning of the 30th in Saigon. The owner greeted Jack, telling him "Minh has just surrendered." Jack looked at Bob and shrugged his shoulders before ordering a pitcher of beer. Both were stunned but also in denial, talking more about their new girlfriends.

Jack breathed a big sigh of relief that he had not told Denise about his planned humanitarian capitalism venture. The next morning's front page picture on the newspapers featured former South Vietnamese Premier and Vice President Nguyen Cao Ky standing on the deck of the U.S. aircraft carrier Blue Ridge. During the week prior to the collapse, Ky had emerged from the virtual house arrest Thieu had put him under, in attempting to rally a final stand. Jack believed that Ky was a far more effective leader than Thieu, and that LBJ had made a major mistake abandoning him in 1967.

Over the next week Jack completed the semester. Roger Whittaker's song "The Last Farewell" was rising in the charts. For the next several months, whenever Jack heard it, thoughts filled his mind of fellow soldiers who didn't return alive and the decent average Vietnamese he had known who probably had been abandoned. "What a perfidiously disgusting betrayal!" His $350,000 dowry and house on the East Side may have just gone up in smoke, but it was a grand scheme none the less. Lon Nol and Nguyen Van Thieu were both gone, but Jack Wilson was still standing.

14. LEAVING ON A HIGH NOTE

Less than two weeks after the humiliating defeat of America's South Vietnamese ally, the new Khmer Rouge agrarian communist regime in Cambodia boldly challenged the United States. On May 12, 1975 they forcefully seized the Mayaguez, a U.S. commercial ship in international waters. The ship's distress message was picked up by an Australian vessel and relayed to the U.S. Pacific Fleet. President Ford convened the National Security Council, immediately ordered a reconnaissance mission to locate the ship, and declared the seizure an act of piracy.

After the Chinese refused to relay a diplomatic message to the Cambodian regime to immediately release the ship, Ford initiated military operations. On May 14th, a battalion task force of Marines assaulted Ko Tang Island and bombing of the Cambodian mainland commenced. By the 16th, the Marines had overcome heavily armed resistance and successfully rescued the Mayaguez crew. Although 16 U.S. servicemen were killed and three helicopters were shot down, Ford's decisive response very likely preempted a replay of the Pueblo seven years earlier, when the North Koreans held that illegally seized vessel's crew for a year.

The President's handling of the Mayaguez gave him an eleven point bump in the polls. Jerry Ford however, still had a major political problem developing within his own Republican base. Conservatives were urging former California Governor Ronald Reagan to seek the 1976 GOP nomination. Ford, a consistent mid-west fiscal conservative during his 25 years in Congress, could only be considered liberal on civil rights. Reagan however, was doing nothing to discourage his supporters.

On the speaking circuit Reagan was becoming increasingly critical of major Nixon policies that Ford had permitted to

CHAPTER 14

continue. These included increasingly uneven treaties and trade deals with the Soviet Union under détente, and going along to get along with the Democratic-controlled Congress on domestic spending. Henry Kissinger remained the architect of U.S. foreign policy, and had recently initiated negotiations with the Panamanian government to eventually turn over the Canal. Ford had also upset the GOP's conservative wing by naming Nelson Rockefeller as Vice President.

"Rocky" was the GOP's Eastern Establishment leader since his first election as Governor of New York in 1958. He won wide acclaim by liberals for his strong advocacy of civil rights, support of more permissive state abortion laws, voluntary rehabilitation of drug offenders in lieu of prosecution, and big spending on massive state construction projects. Rockefeller's star had faded however, especially after his botched handling of the 1971 Attica prison riot in which 29 inmates and 10 hostages were killed. A Congressional investigation followed an attempted coverup that claimed the 10 hostages were killed by inmates cutting their throats. Autopsies revealed that all fatalities were from gunshot wounds from a hail of over 3,000 rounds fired by prison guards and police storming the prison through hazy tear gas. In December, 1973, Rockefeller resigned after 15 years in office, to head a self-funded "Commission on Critical Choices" hoping to remain politically viable.

The Vice President had been Kissinger's patron before he became Nixon's National Security Advisor in 1969. Many conservatives believed that Rockefeller was actually pulling Ford's strings. The President's refusal to meet with Alexander Solzhenitsyn, the most prominent exiled dissident from the Soviet Union, after the later had spoken to an AFL-CIO dinner in Washington on June 30, reinforced that perception. In his speeches, Solzhenitsyn not only attacked the Soviet Union, but also any efforts to accommodate it. Four days earlier, Indira Gandi, neutralist Prime Minister of

LEAVING ON A HIGH NOTE

India, hailed as the world's largest democracy, declared a state of emergency. She cited a "deep and widespread conspiracy" against her government to justify suspensions of civil liberties through 1977. Internationally Gandi had sometimes sided with the Soviet Union. These events fueled rumors by conspiracy theorists that Rockefeller and Kissinger, both détente supporters, were engineering a backdoor coup to gain the Presidency that Rocky had failed three times to win. Ford supporters cited the subsequent orbital docking of an American Apollo with a Soviet Soyuz spacecraft on July 17th, as a major milestone in detente.

On July 10 the President formally announced that he would be a candidate in 1976. Having switched to the GOP only two years earlier, Jack Wilson had already decided that he would support Ford over Reagan in a nomination contest between the two. He viewed Solzhenitsyn's speeches as a nostalgic longing to return to the idyllic spiritual roots of the Tsars, rather than advocacy for a modern constitutional democracy. To Jack, a foreign policy of maintaining a strong nuclear deterrent to avoid a nuclear confrontation, and playing China and the Soviets against each other made sense.

Jack loved Reagan's jingoistic rhetoric but viewed him as unelectable because he was too close to the John Birchers and other "primitives" like Goldwater had been. Jack found the right wing conspiracy kooks entertaining, at best. The previous fall, Governor Malcom Wilson, Rocky's successor after 15 years as his lieutenant governor and four-time running mate, lost to Hugh Carey by over 800,000 votes. Jack viewed that as a clear indicator that Rocky had little remaining political capital, despite his immense wealth and influence. Jack also saw Rocky's gubernatorial blunders as evidence that he was in politics because his father saw him as too dumb to trust with important family businesses like brothers David and Lawrence.

CHAPTER 14

Obtaining his B.A. in January was now Jack's main priority. He had just completed the spring semester on the dean's list. The "C" he received in a public administration course that met at 8:00 AM, lowered his average to a 3.65. His graduation objective was definitely realistic, but would require another course overload of 10 semester hours during the seven-week summer session, and 20 hours during the fall. Summer school preempted a 90 day active duty tour that the Army was seeking volunteers for, to run a refugee center for recent Vietnamese evacuees at Fort Chafee Arkansas. Jack would have to pick up some money on a construction job in August.

Jack's summer courses were Civil Liberties, Modern Latin America and Urban American History. While studying Juan Peron, Jack admired Peron's leadership style, in spite of his fascist politics. The Argentine oligarchs and military establishment had always loathed Peron. However, Peron's "personalismo" style endeared him with the troops by building up the prestige and authority of the sergeants, and inspirationally haranguing the troops after engaging in physical tasks with them. Jack easily related to it it since he had always ensured that he got dirtier than the troops during extended time in the field.

Denise started a two week European vacation during the second part of the summer term. Before she left they went to see "Jaws" when it was released. The movie ultimately hauled in $123.1 million by the end of its initial run, making it the first modern blockbuster. Jack used the evenings Denise was gone for solid research for his school papers. However, he still found time to Tom-cat around the clubs with Bob McKay, who was also in summer school after missing June graduation by six credits. The fall of Saigon had aborted their humanitarian capitalism venture, but Bob's adventuresome spirit was undeterred. He would be off to Buenos Aires on an arms peddling scheme to Peronistas when he received his degree in August.

In mid-July the college conducted several orientations for the incoming freshman class. They seemed very focused on preparing for post-college careers and were mostly apathetic politically. Wilson and McKay were surprised that the freshmen coeds seemed as impressed with their military backgrounds as their status as seniors. Jack went on a date with one from Newport named Mary Lou, to see the movie "The Wind and the Lion". The positive Hollywood depiction of Teddy Roosevelt's tacit approval of an armed incursion into Morocco to rescue an American missionary hostage, and the Arab brigand portrayed by Sean Connery, pleasantly surprised Jack. Was this a sign of a positive shift in the national mood? After dropping Mary Lou off at the dorm where she would catch a bus back home in the morning, Jack, who was 7 years older, wondered how her parents would react if he showed up for a date at their house.

Jack had received four post cards from Denise before she returned from Europe the last week in July. Although she didn't smoke, she brought him a pack of cigarettes from France, Belgium, Germany and Italy. Denise had never expressed interest in Jack's tales about his off-duty military escapades. On several occasions she had also reiterated her dislike of "underachievers." These signals were enough to limit Jack's drinking when he was with Denise to no more than a few glasses of wine. She seemed impressed however, that he had "Aced" all his courses and started a construction job putting in footings for houses. The pay was good, but the work involved hard manual labor under hot and dirty conditions.

In the mid-seventies, semi-skilled construction jobs still paid well enough to provide an way for an ambitious student at a state school to earn a good share of their expenses. Within three decades, substandard wages paid to illegal immigrants would make those opportunities vanish. Over dinner one evening, Denise agreed with Jack that Ford's

CHAPTER 14

August 5th pardon of Robert E. Lee, restoring his full citizenship rights, was a gesture to the GOP's right wing base. They also discusscd July's recent events, including Arthur Ashe defeating Jimmy Connors to become the first black man to win the Wimbledon singles title; and the disappearance of former Teamsters Union President Jimmy Hoffa near Detroit.

Because Denise lived at home with her widowed mother, she always insisted on leaving Jack's North Providence apartment in time to be home before 2:00 A.M. However, she always followed-up by suggesting they take a trip together. With Labor Day on the horizon, Jack planned on asking her to go to Quebec with him for the long weekend. One evening, after seeing the movie "The Eiger Sanction", they went dancing at a Braintree club. As Jack was coming back from the men's room, Colleen, a girl he had a one night stand with just before he had met Denise, was sitting at the bar. She gave him an enthusiastic greeting, grabbing his hand and pressing it closely to her breast while aimlessly chit-chatting for about a minute.

When he returned to their table, Jack explained to Denise that Colleen was a political person he had met a while back. Jack rationalized that since Colleen did have a politically-related job as an investigator for the Massachusetts Attorney General's Office, that he wasn't really telling a bold-faced lie. However, he never could master the political art of looking someone in the eyes while being less than fully truthful. Denise held Jack close as they danced over the next hour. However, when he sprung the question about Quebec while driving her home, she not only declined, but told him she would be too busy to see him until "maybe early October."

Jack rolled the dice and called Colleen late the following morning hoping she might be up for Quebec. Her voice reflected a cross between annoyed and hung over as she responded "I'm really tired and not feeling good right now." She then abruptly hung up. Since he had never called Colleen after their one night affair, this confirmed Jack's gut feeling, that she had seen him with Denise the night before, and that her enthusiastic greeting was merely contrived to screw things up for him.

Alone on a Friday night, Jack hit the downtown Providence night spots. Under the young Republican Mayor Vincent "Buddy" Cianci, the district not far from the courthouse was undergoing a major renovation and had become a popular evening spot. Jack met Cathy, an attractive student at Providence College. As the two had breakfast after Jack had followed her new 2 + 2 Mustang to an East Side diner, he learned that Cathy was just out of high school and only starting college. Never-the-less, he showed up at her parents' house for a Saturday night date. While walking back to his car from her door after their brief good night kiss, Jack laughed to himself while thinking how well he got along with Cathy's father, but had nothing in common with her.

Jack spent the final week of August preparing a documented appeal to the Army's standby promotion board. It included the two evaluation reports that had been omitted from his file when the reserve captain's board met the previous October. He also completed over a hundred hours of correspondence courses which credited him with a good reserve year. Fall registration at the college would start the Tuesday after Labor Day, which fell on September 1st. Rather than taking a trip, Jack decided to pay down his Visa cards with most of the $1,200 he had just made on the construction job.

Jack hit the clubs in the Boston suburbs while visiting his parents over the long weekend. That Friday evening he met Penny, a beautiful brunette in her mid-20s. She told him she wasn't sure she could go out the following evening but to call her around mid-afternoon. Over dinner Saturday evening, Penny shyly told Jack she was afraid that telling him she was divorced and needed to find a sitter for her three and four year

CHAPTER 14

old boys might scare him off. He smiled, assuring her that it wasn't a problem. The two engaged in deep conversation and heavy petting until one in the morning and went out again the next two evenings.

On September 5th, the first Friday of the fall semester, Lynnette "Squeaky" Fromme, a groupie of Charles Manson's murderous cult, attempted to kill President Ford in Sacramento. Fortunately the .45 caliber pistol she pointed directly at him while standing a few feet away, failed to fire. As the Secret Service attempted to skirt Ford out of the area, he ordered them to put him down, and continued walking to the California statehouse. He didn't tell Governor Jerry Brown what had just happened until after their 30 minute meeting. He then delivered a speech on crime to the California legislature.

Saturday evening, while having dinner with Peggy at the home of a married couple, Jack learned that she was a Jehovah's Witness. He was vaguely familiar with their pacifist, anti-secular, anti-government beliefs, but that didn't dampen his desire to continue their budding relationship. The following week, the FBI captured heiress Patty Hearst, who after initially being kidnapped by a criminal gang styling themselves the Symbianese Liberation Army, had actually participated in several bank robberies with them. This news was soon eclipsed by a second assassination attempt on President Ford on September 22nd, as he was leaving the St. Francis Hotel in San Francisco. This time, the would-be assassin, Sarah Jane Moore, actually got off a shot, but it was deflected by Oliver Simple, a bystander.

Jack and Penny continued seeing each other Wednesday evenings and on weekends, but her repeated requests for him to study with one of her Jehovah's Witness congregation's leaders made him uncomfortable. Jack's strong feelings for her were somewhat deflected by the attention he was receiving from the East Side girls at the college who were

English Lit and Art majors. They had taken a liking to him over the past year after he had proved himself quite successful in leveraging superficial knowledge about Dostoyevsky, Monet, Faberge, Diego Rivera, and other European artists he had picked up in history courses. Jack held court with them daily in the Student Union. He also enjoyed flirting with Mary Lou and several other freshman coeds he had met during the summer session. This eased the pain when the relationship with Penny ended exactly a month after it began.

"What a bunch of control freaks" thought Jack while driving back into Providence at eleven o'clock that first Saturday night of October. Wearing his signature frontier style suede jacket, Jack dropped into Spatz, an East Side pub and restaurant near Brown University. Spotting Mary Lou sitting with three girlfriends, he approached their table. Monique, who was the most stylish and attractive of them, but very extroverted and obnoxiously tipsy, shouted "Hey, John Wayne's alone on a Saturday night. One of his duty girls must have given him the clap!" The girls giggled after Jack responded "I'm really impressed! I didn't think you were old enough to know any words stronger than pee-pee and ca-ca yet."

Feeling a jab in his back, Jack turned around and was face-to-face with Paul Baer, his old pre-draft friend. They had later served in the Rhode Island Guard together before they both wore out their welcome. Paul was making the rounds with his boss, Congressman Eddie Beard, whose blunt outspokenness during his first year in office made him very popular among students and even many professors. Besides Fred Shannon, Beard was the only established Rhode Island politician who still had anything to do with Jack since his legal misadventure the previous year.

After Eddie shook hands with the girls Paul pulled Jack over near the waiter's station at the bar where they huddled.

CHAPTER 14

As one of only two of the State's Congressman, Beard was now a major rival and real threat to Governor Philip Noel. Their animosity continued to swell, and an inevitable showdown was looming on the 1976 horizon. Jack assured them that his recent switch to the GOP would not preclude his ghost writing supporting editorials again.

Mary Lou asked Jack to join them when he returned to their table. At last call they all eagerly accepted Jack's invitation to join him at the restaurant across a block away. Mary Lou shyly kissed Jack on the cheek when he dropped her at her dorm on the way back to his apartment. On their date the following Saturday, she insisted on leaving Jack's apartment to return to her dorm at 11, but invited him to watch the premiere of Saturday Night Live with her friends in the TV lounge. Jack enjoyed Chevy Chase's portrayal of Ford, but became increasingly annoyed by Monique's constant interruption whenever he and Mary Lou were conversing.

President Ford's calm reaction to the two assassination attempts enhanced his stature. Other events soon occurred that indicated he was indeed his own man. In mid-October, his outright refusal to New York City Mayor Abe Beam's request for a bailout, after years of fiscal mismanagement coupled with the stagnant national economy had brought the City to the verge of bankruptcy. On November 3, Vice President Rockefeller used this as an opportune time to withdraw his name from consideration from the 1976 GOP ticket. Rocky cited "avoidance of inter-party bickering" as the reason.

Rocky had accepted the Vice Presidency with the understanding that he would be a full partner. However, Donald Rumsfeld, Ford's Chief of Staff soon began to frequently omit him from the loop, even on domestic policy, for which Rocky was supposed to have overall responsibility. Jack viewed the timing of Rocky's announcement as self-serving, because it postured him as the noble Vice President who sacrificed his position by opposing his own President to advocate for a Congressional bail-out of his beloved City.

Jack completed his mid-terms with an A, two B's, a C plus and a D minus. His senior seminar grade would be based on a thesis paper that argued a conservative resurgence in the United States was far more likely than an evolution into democratic socialism. His 8:00 A.M. macroeconomics course was developing into a major hurdle however, even though he was taking it under the pass/fail option. Jack needed to spend at least 8 extra hours during each of the six remaining weeks of the semester to catch up.

If Jack didn't pass macroeconomics, he would miss graduation by four credits. In January, new curriculum requirements would go into effect that would require 19 more credits for his degree. All would have to be in science, math and foreign language courses that he would have to regularly attend. Suddenly, Jack remembered Dan Debre's precedent from two years earlier. When Dan had found himself six credits short of a degree, he picked them up after a reevaluation of the transcript from the college in Connecticut he had transferred from.

Jack had been admitted as a transfer student four years earlier. The college had since added several new programs. Chances were good that several courses might now be offered that were equivalent to at least two of the subjects for which he had earned 30 credits through CLEP exams. Jack met with his academic advisor who quickly set up an appointment for a reevaluation of his transcripts.

Expecting an ordeal, Jack humbly entered the office of the attractive female admissions officer. "How many credits do you need, Jack?" Looking at his open file on her desk he replied "Four, but do you think you might be able to find six just to be safe?" She picked up a pen and quickly wrote and

CHAPTER 14

circled 18 hours on a form destined for the records office. He looked her in the eyes smiling as they shook hands. Out of character, Jack refrained from a come-on attempt as he sincerely thanked her.

A college policy gave graduating seniors the option of accepting a mid-term grade of B or higher in lieu of taking the final. Jack met the criteria in three of his courses. Since the transcript review had just awarded Jack 18 more semester hours, he was now a de- facto graduate, except for his thesis paper. Jack also had recently received official notification from the Army of his pending reserve promotion to captain.

Since the Army was still going through major reductions, all paths to active duty were through repetitive extensions of short active duty tours. For officers with Jack's background, those opportunities would not be available until early summer. He still had done absolutely nothing tangible to plan for life after graduation. Jack had burned all his bridges to any type of politically-appointed job in Rhode Island, and had not even registered to take admissions exams for graduate or law school.

On Thursday the week before Thanksgiving, Jack watched the news while sitting at the bar eating dinner at Sal Lounge. Ronald Reagan had just announced that he would seek the GOP nomination. Ford's frequent vetoes of spending bills and shedding the Rockefeller albatross had not been enough to prevent it. This prompted a knee-jerk decision by Jack to volunteer on Ford's primary campaign in New Hampshire in January. Since the ski industry was backing Ford, the lodges might even give discounts to campaign volunteers.

Jack returned to the college library, where earlier that day he had just begun research for his senior seminar thesis. Mary Lou joined him at his table. Two hours later, when the public address system gave the 15 minute closing announcement she declined to go to Spatz with him. Since

Mary Lou didn't have any important classes on Monday or Tuesday, she was going home early for Thanksgiving and had to pack.

Of Greek ancestry, with brown eyes and hair darker than mahogany, Mary Lou fit Jack's aesthetic ideal of a Mediterranean beauty. She was serious student, but definitely liked and admired Jack. She had also spent a lot of time with him on campus. The several times they went out together, Mary Lou always protested "this isn't a date" beforehand. Although Jack never kissed and told, his politically active female adversaries typically smeared girls on campus who dated him as "Jack's duty girls." Mary Lou was still a virgin and definitely didn't want that moniker for the next three and a half years.

As Jack was checking out several books, he felt finger nails gently stroking his "lats" from behind. It was Monique. He accepted her invitation to do a joint outside. Monique then accompanied Jack to Spatz. She looked cultured and sophisticated but had always been borderline obnoxious during their interactions around Mary Lou. Jack therefore had no inhibitions about letting his "power drinking" out of the closet. Monique eagerly kept up with him while provoking his most base animal urges.

At daybreak, Monique passionately kissed Jack goodbye when he dropped her off at the dorm. Later that morning he met with his senior seminar faculty mentor, but avoided the student union. That evening in the library Monique found him working on his paper. She had no difficulty breaking him away for a weekend of power drinking and passion. The following weekend Jack spent an uneventful Thanksgiving with his parents.

The ride continued to be bumpy during his final weeks at the college. One morning Jack's shallow knowledge of the arts was exposed as he pontificated about Monet with the East

CHAPTER 14

Side girls. He looked like a deer-in-the headlights as a little witch, who was one of their wannabes, deliberately asked him a staccato of focused questions about several of Monet's works. Judy, with whom he had a real connection, gently grabbed his hand saying "It's OK Jack, we always knew, but that was one of the things we loved about you." Marge, the married member of the group, chimed in "What really amazed us is that you seem to sincerely believe that living the life of a rue somehow makes you enlightened and compensates for your horrible politics!" It was all good natured. Deep down though, Jack realized he was nothing more than a superficial intellectual starting to believe his own bullshit.

Days later, Jack's land lady informed him that she would not honor the discount that her soon-to-be ex-husband had given him that summer in exchange for advances on the rent. Jack felt sorry for her, but didn't have the money for the retroactive rent she demanded. The college's attorney even sent a letter on Jack's behalf advising his land lady that legally, her husband was her agent and that Jack had acted in good faith. In Mafia-controlled North Providence however, other resolution methods for payment due disputes were frequently used. Jack soon made a midnight exit and began couch surfing at several friends' places and staying at his parent's house on the weekend.

On December 8th the President reversed himself and grudgingly signed the $6.8 billion New York City bail out. On the 17th, John Paul Stevens, renowned for his expertise on anti-trust law, was sworn in to replace William O. Douglas on the Supreme Court. As Ford's appointee, Stevens was assumed to be a conservative because Ford had been a leading Congressional advocate for impeaching Douglas, the Court's leading liberal for 36 years. During Stevens' 34 year tenure, conservatives would be sadly disappointed.

LEAVING ON A HIGH NOTE

On December 23rd, Congress enacted the Metric Conversion Act and established the Metric Board for the purpose of encouraging, but did not mandate eventual conversion. Three days later, the Soviet Unit inaugurated the first supersonic transport service with its Tupolev-144 airliner from Moscow to Alma-Ata. On the 28th, the "Hail Mary" play was born during a Divisional playoff game. With 32 seconds left, the Cowboys' quarterback Roger Staubach threw a desperate 50-yard winning touchdown pass to Drew Pearson to defeat the Vikings. The following day, a terrorist bomb explosion at New York's La Guardia Airport killed 11 and injured 75 people. On New Year's Eve, Jack attended a friend's low-key party in Cranston by himself thinking, "Why didn't I call Denise back, in October?"

Back on campus in early January, Jack knew that it was definitely time to move on. By the fourth night that Monique put him up in her dorm, she had him sleeping on the floor. He found it bizarre when she encouraged him to resume his relationship with Mary Lou! He received a B minus for the thesis paper that he finished in the student union a half hour before it was due. In spite of his modest 2.86 overall GPA, the 3.5 average in 36 hours of history courses he had taken qualified Jack for the Phi Alpha Theta honor society. At the induction dinner in the Faculty Lounge, he basked in the glory of being served by the sorority queen waitresses who mostly loathed him. He engaged in animated conversation with the college President while consuming nearly a fifth of Johnny Walker Black over the evening.

Jack frequently used most of the funds from his monthly VA checks and other income to pay down the balances of his Visa cards, which increased his credit limit. Jack's discipline in keeping one card open to be able make payments on the other three during lean periods, resulted in two more being issued to him since the summer. Jack still had three months of eligibility remaining on the GI Bill. The VA only had a requirement for satisfactory progress, not attendance. He

CHAPTER 14

therefore quietly registered for three graduate courses in January, which he only sporadically attended, and then dropped them all shortly after the benefits ran out in April. His debt on the VISA cards totaled around $7,500, but he still had $5,000 in unused credit left. Compared to Wall Street, and banking and mortgage company standards that spawned the 2008 financial meltdown, this was a noteworthy achievement in financial management.

Jack picked up his degree at the records office without attending the graduation ceremony that was scheduled the following hour. While cutting through the Student Center on the way to the parking lot, he was surprised to see Judy and Marge, two of the East Side girls sitting at a table. They had been waiting there hoping to catch Jack so they could say good bye. Touched, Jack had a cup of coffee with them for old times' sake.

There had always been a strong mutual attraction between Jack and Judy. She had been available in September, but he was seeing Penny. Judy was now in a serious relationship with someone she began seeing in October. Jack got up and briefly hugged Marge. After about a minute into their mutually strong embrace, Jack gently broke away from Judy. Hiding his emotions, he smiled saying "Got to run. Being late on a second date with a new duty girl would be so unseemly." In the four yearbooks covering Jack's time at the college, a drawing of a rolled diploma above his printed name surrounded by pictures of his fellow graduates is the only evidence he was ever there.

15. THE LONG COUNT

President Ford began 1976 with a modest lead over Reagan in polls among GOP voters. With hawkish conservatives however, firing James Schlesinger and replacing him with Donald Rumsfeld as Defense Secretary, following the former's critical comments about the Helsinki summit with Brezhnev, negated any benefit Ford gained from the Vice President's withdrawal. The inflation rate had been reduced to 5 ½ percent, but with the 1974 recession still lingering, unemployment had risen to nearly 9 percent. On January 19th, Ford prevailed over Reagan in the Iowa caucuses by less than three per cent. On the Democratic side Jimmy Carter gained momentum with his surprise win. Reagan was also closing in on Ford in New Hampshire, the first-in-the-nation primary.

Congressman James Cleveland chaired the President's New Hampshire campaign. Reagan had the support of Governor Meldrim Thompson and William Loeb, The New Hampshire Union Leader's publisher. Loeb had referred to the President as "Jerry the jerk" in an editorial. Ford deliberately avoided visits to that state following a "Rose Garden" strategy that adopted recommendations from a confidential memorandum. It candidly addressed how the President's informal style fueled perceptions that he was an inept and weak leader not up to the job. To overcome this, Ford enhanced his Presidential image by maximizing highly publicized official White House events, while minimizing off the cuff campaign remarks.

A family man known for his warmth, friendliness and integrity, 10 years earlier President Ford would have been the boy from Middle America who made good. He was the adopted son of Gerald Ford, Sr., a salesman for a family-owned paint business, who his divorced mother had married when he was two-and-a-half years old. Raised in Grand Rapids, Michigan, Ford attended public schools, achieved the

CHAPTER 15

rank of Eagle Scout and had been the captain of his high school football team. He graduated from the University of Michigan, where he played center and linebacker, while also working part time. After coaching boxing and football at Yale for several years, he earned his LL.B. there in 1941.

Ford briefly practiced law in Grand Rapids before he volunteered for the Navy soon after Pearl Harbor. He saw combat in the Pacific as a navigator on the aircraft carrier USS Monterey, before separating as a lieutenant commander in February, 1946. Ford's critics however, portrayed him as an accidental unelected President. Television cameras had also captured the President in minor stumbles, most notably while exiting Air Force One on an Austrian state visit. Soon afterwards, Chevy Chase, a young comedian, would persistently satirize the President over his perceived clumsiness and bumbling in skits on the new TV pop culture weekly "Saturday Night Live".

Jack drove the 100 miles to Concord from his recently rented apartment in Holbrook, Massachusetts to make contact with the Ford Committee's New Hampshire headquarters. It was staffed mostly by volunteers who were local Republicans. They were in the process of organizing phone banks and distributing campaign material to the local GOP committees around the state. The all-volunteer operation gladly accepted Jack's offer to help. "He sure liked getting rip roaring drunk" thought Jack, walking past President Franklin Pierce's statute, after quickly touring the capitol building.

On his drive back that Friday Jack briefly stopped into the Massachusetts Ford headquarters in Belmont. He learned that State Representative Andy Card, a key Ford supporter, was from Holbrook, his new voting residence. Card was in his late twenties and a rising star as one of two dozen Republicans in an overwhelmingly Democratic-dominated legislature.

Jack ended up at the Newport Naval Base officers club that evening to catch up with his old friend Paul Baer over dinner. The two had a close bond from their military association that transcended politics. Baer was waiting on the sidelines, prepared to file for Rhode Island's June Presidential primary as a delegate for Governor Jerry Brown, who he expected to announce. Paul had no plans for New Hampshire, but apprised Jack of good night spots for hanging out during overnight stays up there.

Jack was a registered Republican in Massachusetts, but had no problem ghost writing on behalf of Baer's boss, Edward P. Beard, one of Rhode Island's two Congressmen. "Eddie" had decided to seek another term instead of going head-to-head against Governor Noel for retiring Senator John O. Pastore's seat in the September primary. This did nothing to diffuse the conflict between the two. Noel was engineering an endorsement of Warwick's Mayor, Eugene McCaffery, over Beard, by the Democratic State Committee that he controlled.

Paul told Jack he would probably need his help "organizing a few political things" later in the spring. After dinner, Paul introduced him to the "Datum' Club", a nightclub on the base for junior officers that was very popular with younger professional women from the surrounding area. When they parted company Paul pulled a document out of the briefcase in his Mercedes. "When I saw this I thought of you" he said handing it to Jack. It was a schedule of longer active duty tours, not widely publicized, that the Army had programmed for the summer.

The protracted recession had prompted a record number of Democratic candidates. Well qualified, nationally known contenders like Senators Henry Jackson, Birch Bayh, and later Frank Church, would have done well under the old system dominated by party leaders. The strategy of little

CHAPTER 15

known ex-Governor Jimmy Carter however, recognized how multiple wins in primaries that most states now held, would decisively influence the outcome. Carter was a 1946 Annapolis graduate who had served in the embryonic nuclear navy. He projected a populist "New South" image with potential to win in the North. The most likely threat that fellow populist Fred Harris, a former Oklahoma U.S. Senator, posed was as a spoiler.

Carter's most potentially lethal populist rival was on the right, however. Alabama Governor George Wallace, formerly an arch segregationist, had a proven track record in primaries going back to 1964. He had to be eliminated early, ideally in Southern primaries. The 1969 Chappaquiddick incident still lingered in too many memories for Senator Ted Kennedy to be a serious contender. Carter repeatedly proclaiming his born again Christian faith disturbed many liberals, who were urging Jerry Brown, California's young new Governor, to run. On January 27th, the Ford Administration vetoed a U.N. resolution favoring the establishment of an independent Palestinian state.

Jack spent the next evening with Denise. They had resumed seeing each other a week earlier. She seemed comfortable with Jack's current endeavors and accepted his shabby apartment with an entrance at the top of an exterior staircase that resembled a Dodge City movie set. It made sense not to lease a better place since he would be spending many nights in New Hampshire, hoping a paid opportunity on Ford's campaign might develop. Denise finally agreed to spend an overnighter with Jack. They enjoyed each other's company as Jack drove around that cold February Saturday, dropping off campaign literature to Republican activists in a dozen small New Hampshire towns.

The "Granite State" primary epitomized retail politics, as it still does today. Driving through Nashua on the way to their hotel early that evening, Denise and Jack saw Fred Harris

THE LONG COUNT

shaking hands on Main Street. Late Sunday morning, they noticed Birch Bayh and his entourage in their hotel lobby as they checked out. Driving back Denise caught Jack's attention when she gently made the remark "People like you never grow up." He was totally clueless that it was prompted by his not recognizing professional obligations she had to her cost accountant's job and the university courses she taught two evenings during the week.

As he began a three day stint of volunteering the following weekend, Jack found the ski lodge near Henniker his friend Paul had recommended. The only time he had been on skis in his life was a clumsy attempt at water skiing in Georgia when he was 20. That Friday evening however, Jack used a pickup line on a cute nurse from Concord named Sandy, about how his "combat-wounded knee prevented him from resuming that beloved sport." It was successful for a future date, but not enough to show her the old Augusta auto accident knee scar that night, to reinforce his bullshit.

Sandy worked nights and was only able to see Jack for a few lunch dates. He still wanted to develop his relationship with Denise however, so he limited the remainder of his overnight stints to weekdays. Jack's campaign activities mostly involved phone banking or recruiting volunteers for them, and delivering campaign materials. A few of his ghost written letters did appear under signatures of local Republicans in The Union Leader, however.

Denise's job had made here unavailable, and Sally was back with her old boyfriend. Jack therefore, had decided to drive up for the final two days with Judy, a girl from Norwood he had met while clubbing over the Christmas holidays. On the evening of February 24th, Jack only recognized Congressman Cleveland, former Governor Water Peterson, and a deputy national campaign manager in the crowd of 200 at the Ford victory party. When they left for their room a half hour after midnight, Ford held a slim 1,000

CHAPTER 15

vote lead. On the Democratic side, Carter clearly won with 28 percent. Congressman Morris Udall gained momentum as the runner up with 22 percent. Birch Bayh's 15 percent third place finish could keep him viable for another month.

Judy was still asleep as Jack watched the Today Show news report that Ford had barely defeated Reagan by 1.5 percent. During a local news break, a tall, impressive young School Board member and Reagan supporter named Bob Smith, caught Jack's attention. In an interview Smith noted that "Governor Reagan clearly gained the momentum by winning nearly half the State's delegates against a sitting President last night."

Before dropping Judy off in Norwood early Wednesday evening, Jack continued weaving a bodacious lie about how he had to spend the evening calling Florida campaign contacts before flying down there for a month on Thursday. Friday evening, to prevent any encounters like he had before the Labor Day weekend, Jack took Denise to Plymouth for dinner and a movie, and on Saturday to Newport.

Narrow as it was, the President's New Hampshire win positioned him well for the following week's Massachusetts primary. Volunteering in the Ford headquarters in the tony suburb of Belmont, Jack noticed a distinct difference from the down-to-earth New Hampshire Republicans he had just been with. Dominant Massachusetts party moderates like Senator Ed Brooke, former Governor John Volpe, and his successor Frank Sergeant, whose positions would make a liberal Democrat blush, backed the President. So did the conservative GOP Chairman, Gordon Nelson.

The GOP preppies in his age range, who dominated the Massachusetts Ford grass roots leadership, reminded Jack of several of his former military peers. He was impressed however, by an attractive professional woman in her early thirties named Janet. She was a full time State GOP functionary who was frequently in Belmont as the state party liaison to the Ford Campaign. Denise had informed Jack however, that she would be available to attend a Ford rally the following Saturday afternoon, and also to meet him Tuesday, at the Ford victory party after her class.

The networks all called the primary for the President before 9:30 P.M. on Tuesday, but Reagan would still receive a third of the Massachusetts delegates. Jack met George Donovan, a Reagan supporter who showed up at the Boston hotel to solicit support as a delegate. Any GOP voter could participate in the upcoming Congressional district caucuses, and vote for two delegates for Ford, and one for Reagan. A fellow Benning OCS graduate, George was a decorated Vietnam veteran who had previously run a very strong campaign for state representative in a Democratic district. They were engaging in an animated conversation with Janet who was obviously enjoying their attention. A preppy functionary in a bow tie named Richie, abruptly interrupted them.

Without bothering to excuse himself, Richie began rambling on about his sister's recent vacation. George, an Irish-Catholic business owner and Stonehill College graduate, suddenly said to Jack in a voice loud enough for Richie to hear "Ever notice how entitled these lisping preppie swishes are? That is until someone grabs them by their neckties and teaches them manners." Suddenly Jack saw Denise enter the ball room. Forcing himself to stop laughing, Jack directed George's attention toward her saying "I need to introduce you to one of your lovelier constituents." After George charmed Denise, he spotted Andy Card, who he introduced them to. A half hour later as they were all leaving, George, also a Captain in the National Guard, gave Jack some contacts who could expedite the details if Jack later applied for an appointment.

Reagan supporters could easily explain away Ford's March 2nd Massachusetts and Vermont victories from two

CHAPTER 15

liberal states as not unexpected. Ford's convincing primary win in Florida on March 9th, followed by an even bigger 9 point win in Illinois a week later however, cleared indicated that Reagan's campaign could be in trouble. It was almost broke too!

On the Democratic side, Massachusetts gave Senator Scoop Jackson hope and kept Mo Udall in the game as viable contenders, but Carter had won liberal Vermont with 45 percent, 20 points more than Sargent Shriver, a Kennedy in-law and the 1972 Vice Presidential nominee. Carter went on to edge out Wallace in Florida, with Jackson finishing a respectable third. The March 23rd North Carolina primary gave Carter a decisive 20 point victory, eliminating Wallace. In that state's GOP contest, Reagan finally won an impressive 7 point victory over Ford. By mid-March with hawkish Senator Jackson and Udall gaining little traction as alternatives, Idaho's Senator Frank Church and Jerry Brown, both liberals, finally entered the race.

In April, the President rebounded with big wins in Wisconsin and Pennsylvania. Reagan however, continued to win delegates in caucus states. Most primary states awarded delegates proportionally, so Reagan was gaining significant delegates as a strong runner-up in primary states that Ford had won. Although never a segregationist, Carter's opponents raised his failure to publicly support civil rights legislation as a State Senator from 1962-66, and during his unsuccessful 1966 run for Governor. He had defeated former Governor Carl Sanders running as a George Wallace Democrat in the primary. He did however reject segregation in his 1971 inaugural address.

On April 6th, defense hawk Scoop Jackson's sweep of most of the New York State delegation blunted Carter's narrow win over Congressman Mo Udall in Wisconsin. Two weeks later in Pennsylvania however, he effectively finished off Jackson with a 20 point win. Carter's base of a little more than 35 percent was enough to continue the winning streak over scattered opposition.

On a mid-April Saturday afternoon, Andy Card chaired the GOP caucus in Jack's Congressional District that fewer than 100 Republican voters attended. He had showed up with Denise, in response to George Donovan's invitation. In addition to Card and a lady running for the other Ford delegate's seat, they also voted for George, who was elected as a Reagan alternate. While briefly socializing with George, Jack mentioned that he was starting a three month active duty tour at Fort Drum the end of May. Laughing, George turned to Denise saying "You won't have to worry about Jack fooling around in that desolate place. Next to those Watertown women, our Brockton queens are classy!"

One Sunday morning at the end of April, Jack was awoken by a 6:00 A.M. phone call. It was Paul Baer. "I have a critical mission that could help Eddie, and you're the ideal person to pull it off. Are you free next Saturday?" "Sure" said Jack. Paul went on to explain that the Rhode Island Young Democrats (RIYDs) were holding their annual state convention in Smithfield. The keynote speaker would be Mayor Gene McCaffery who had just received the Noel-controlled Democratic State Committee's endorsement against Congressman Ed Beard. "Do you think you could round up some Rhode Island College students to show up for a spontaneous demonstration and to vote our guy in as RIYD President? I'll meet you there with the signs." Jack replied that it would be a cakewalk.

Jack spent Thursday and Friday on the RIC campus recruiting and training his "old disciples." As a known Republican, Jack would attend as Paul's guest but could not speak or vote. Jack called Mark Lawson, an eloquent English major and recruited him as Baer's floor manager. The tall, bombastic Navy veteran and biker, finishing his junior year, had made Jack look tame at RIC Student Senate meetings.

CHAPTER 15

Mark asked Jack if he'd mind if he brought Monique, one of Jack's former duty girls. "Not at all" replied Jack, "That will be a REAL marriage made in heaven."

An hour before show time, Jack and Mark met Paul in Smithfield outside the Knights of Columbus hall that the RIYDs had rented. Over the next hour four dozen students, that they had recruited from nearby RIC and Providence College, showed up. Mary Lou even came with her new sophomore boyfriend. Paul paid most of their membership dues at the door from a wad of ten dollar bills in his pocket.

The outgoing RIYD President, Susan McGrail, opened the meeting. Mark immediately made a motion demanding that Paul Baer be given equal time to speak as Congressman Beard's surrogate. When she ruled it out of order a "spontaneous" floor demonstration began. Later on, loud boos drowned out McCaffery's applause, before, during and after his remarks. Susan McGrail, no doubt fearful that Beard's candidate could succeed her, recessed the convention for the day. Members who attended would be notified when and where to reconvene to elect new officers after their eligibility had been verified.

Jack returned to Massachusetts. Over dinner that evening, Denise rolled her eyes as he explained with great animation how the plan he had told her about the night before had gone off so successfully. Jack felt kind of sorry for Susan McGrail when he saw her picture under the headline "Pandemonium at Young Democrats Convention" on the front page of the Providence Sunday Journal. A serious student three years younger than Jack, Susan was now in law school. She had been in several of his courses at RIC. Jack always thought she was kind of cute, but too goody-two-shoes for him. Susan was also very intelligent. Her undergraduate research papers could have easily been used as enclosures to legal briefs in any court, unlike Jack's spurious drivel fresh off the typewriter. She had to deliberately be wearing blinders not to

THE LONG COUNT

see how bogus and sleazy Noel's ham-handed attempt to dump Eddie Beard was.

On May 11th, Senator Church narrowly won Nebraska. Carter soon received heavier blows however, when Jerry Brown beat him by 10 points in Maryland on the 18th, and a week later in Nevada. Although Carter continued winning more primaries, his only big victories came in states where neither Brown nor Church appeared on the ballots, and the only alternatives listed were favorite sons, or candidates who were effectively finished. During those first two weeks in May, Governor Reagan gave the President major body blows with four big wins in Texas, Georgia, Indiana and Nebraska. Besides picking up a major block of delegates, Reagan had demonstrated broadening national appeal. Texas shut out U.S. Senator John Tower, a Ford convention floor manager, as a delegate.

Since the President lost his birth state of Nebraska, he had to win big in Michigan, which he represented in Congress for 25 years. Jack had been staying at his parents' house since giving up his Holbrook apartment the end of April. He was still seeing Denise exclusively, but friction developed the weekend before Jack left for Michigan to volunteer on the campaign the final week before the May 18th primary. Denise had insisted on going home rather than staying overnight at the motel Jack rented.

Ford won big in Michigan with 65 percent of the vote, and also decisively by 16 points on the same day in Maryland. Jack's trip was also an opportunity to visit his two widowed grandmothers and several other relatives still living in Grand Rapids, who he had not seen since high school. Jack appreciated his paternal grandmother's stories about life under the Tsar, and his younger uncle's stories about his grandfather's bootlegging activities during Prohibition.

CHAPTER 15

On May 25th, Jack reported for duty at Camp Drum after driving through the depressed upper New York region around Watertown. Trips to see Denise would be worth the 14 hours of driving and motel charges, even if she didn't stay overnight. Jack's active duty pay and allowances through Labor Day would also ease the pressure of nearly reaching the $20,000 debt limit from his multiple credit cards.

When the primaries ended on June 8th, Ford had won 17 states polling 5.2 million GOP votes to Reagan's 11 states with 4.7 million. In the critical count of delegates who would actually choose the nominee, both had over 1,000. Ford had a slight edge but short of the 1,130 needed to win. For the next two months they would engage in a bitter struggle for over 100 still uncommitted delegates. Ford, as a sitting President, was reduced to personally calling these local GOP grass roots leaders seeking their support.

On the Democratic side, Carter had an overwhelming delegate lead. He had won 30 state contests, and polled nearly 4 million more votes than his closest rival Jerry Brown. Ohio had locked in the nomination for him. Brown refused to withdraw and his name would still be place in nomination, but stopping Carter was now a pipe dream. Paul Baer would attend the July 15th Convention as a Brown delegate.

For the President, his 4th of July Bicentennial addresses at Valley Forge and Philadelphia could not come soon enough. Several follow-up premiere events that week would dovetail perfectly with his "Rose Garden" strategy. Queen Elizabeth II was making a U.S. tour that would include a White House state dinner on the 7th, followed by visits to several northeast cities. The heavy media exposure on the Queen's events would deflect media attention from recent national issues that Reagan cited as evidence of a weakened America caused by eight years of Nixon-Ford policies.

THE LONG COUNT

On June 20th, the President had ordered the evacuation of Americans from Lebanon following the assassination of Francis E. Meloy, Jr., the U.S. Ambassador to Lebanon, in Beirut. Reagan had great appeal to many veteran leaders who opposed the amnesty Ford gave to draft dodgers shortly after he assumed office, even though it was conditional. They were also not enthused over the admission of women to Annapolis on July 8, a year after West Point and the Air Force Academy had done so. Fiscal conservatives felt betrayed when Ford signed the Railroad Reform Act that February. It enabled the formation of Conrail from 13 failed Northeast railroads that had filed for bankruptcy protection, and would be run by the government until 1986, when it would be sold to the public.

On the Saturday before the 4th of July, Jack looked up from a safety control plan for a live-fire attack problem he was reviewing. Paul Baer stood in front of his desk smiling. "How can I help you sir" said Jack rapidly rising to an exaggerated position of attention. Paul, who had once been his junior, was now wearing captain's bars. Jack had to wait until September, because his recent selection occurred on a second consideration after a pass over. Paul was now in a Reserve Special Forces unit, and would be at Camp Drum until the 14th directing opposing forces against some Connecticut National Guard units on their annual training. "Meet me at the officer's club at 6." "Yes sir" responded Jack.

Upon greeting Jack at the bar Paul asked "How would you like to go meet the Queen with me in Newport next weekend?" "If my 1968 Volkswagen engine doesn't seize up on the way" replied Jack. Paul had already lined up transportation on a National Guard aircraft that was flying a Connecticut Congressman up for a visit. His girlfriend Jeannie would meet and drive them to their BOQ rooms that were already reserved at the Newport Naval Base. Paul then

CHAPTER 15

asked Jack if he could help "churn out some hokum" for a Providence Journal editorial.

On the 10th, the Queen would be dedicating the Trinity Church Square in Newport. She would then embark the royal yacht Britannia with the President for dinner while the craft navigated across the channel to the naval base. The arch political enemy of Paul's boss, Governor Noel, controlled the itinerary in the City of Newport, and would try manipulating access to the best areas for press exposure to favor Beard's primary opponent, Mayor Gene McCaffery.

Noel would not however, control events on the Naval base, where the President would fly in from Otis Air Force Base, and before departing, would disembark the Britannia after it docked at the base. "We'll be going to these non-partisan patriotic events in uniform on guest passes from my boss who will greet and see Ford off with the rest of the state's Congressional delegation. We need to upstage Noel by rounding up an entourage of Navy and Marine Corps officers at the Datum Club Friday evening." "It will be my honor" responded Jack, who viewed the Governor as a jumped-up grease ball.

Carol Chenworth was in Hershey, Pennsylvania that Independence Day weekend with the National Governors' Association. Her boyfriend Russ from Atlanta was also there with Governor Busbee's Georgia entourage. For Carol it was a combined weekend get-away. Hamilton Jordan still was blocking Russ from joining Carter's campaign, but he would still attend the Democratic Convention as a delegate. Carol accepted an invitation from her good friend, who was a Rhode Island liaison to the Association to attend the Queen's Trinity Square dedication in Newport the following weekend. Russ, immediately seeing the opportunity for networking with New England delegates and for spending another weekend with Carol, subtly included himself in the invitation.

THE LONG COUNT

Denise accepted when Jack called the next day, inviting her to meet him in Newport that Friday evening. Two days later when Jack called Denise back, responding to a message she had left him, she apologized for having to cancel their plans. Her uncle, who had put her through college, was visiting that weekend. Paul Baer's girlfriend could probably fix him up with a date. It was going to be a long summer in depressed Watertown however, so Jack wanted to be sure he could satisfy lustful urges on the trip. Thinking if any old duty girls were from that area, he remembered the flashy, stylish freshman he had engaged in power drinking passion with during his final weeks RIC.

Monique was from Middleton, a few miles from Newport's Easton's Beach. "Jack, how have you been?" asked Monique enthusiastically after being called to the phone by her father. Jack responded "I'm flying into Newport from New York Friday to support the Queen's visit. I need a cultured and sophisticated date to accompany me to some of the events." "How did you ever get to do that?" Jack explained that Paul Baer, who she had met at Spatz one evening, had passed on the Congressman's invitation to join him in the Presidential greeting party. When he asked how she had been doing, Monique told him that she made it through her freshman year on the dean's list and was transferring into the Rhode Island School of Design in the fall.

Jack asked Monique if staying overnight with him would be a problem. She laughingly told him not to rent a car because they could get around in the 1973 Firebird convertible her father had just given her. "My divorced Dad's like a 45 year old version of your friend Bob McKay." Jack then gave her details about their Friday and Saturday activities so she would know what clothes to bring.

Captain Baer and Lieutenant Wilson disembarked the Connecticut National Guard helicopter in Newport shortly

CHAPTER 15

after 4:30 P.M., wearing their summer tropical worsted (TW) uniforms. Paul looked sharp in his jump boots and green beret. Jack just wore low quarters and his garrison cap, but looked impressive enough with his badges and Vietnam ribbons, or "runner up awards" as they were now being sarcastically called.

Paul's girlfriend Jeannie, who was also a staffer in Ed Beard's Providence office, drove them over to the officers club. Her Mercedes, a lighter blue color than Paul's, was embellished with Congressional staff tags. Jack called Monique from the club to give her directions. From there they went to register for their BOQ rooms and drop off their bags. On their way to the main gate to meet Monique, they drove by Destroyer Peer, where the Queen's yacht Britannia would dock.

Monique pulled into a parking area outside the main gate. The top down was down, and "The Bitch Is Back" by Elton John was blaring from the 8-track tape system. Wearing shorts and a halter top she jumped out of the car and threw her arms around Jack. After turning down the sound system, Jack drove to the entrance gate, returned the Marine guard's salute and then signed for a two-day temporary vehicle pass. Monique had never seen Jack in uniform and seemed turned on after Jack received a second salute.

They went to Jack's BOQ room, which resembled a Ramada Inn, for Monique to change. In 45 minutes, they had to meet Paul and Jeannie for dinner. Then they would go out dancing. Within five minutes they had regressed to their previous passion but with only half the power drinking. Jack declined a screwdriver when she fixed herself one while unpacking. He wasn't on the wagon, but had to play the professional that evening.

They were only 10 minutes late arriving at the club. Jack was still wearing his TWs, considered proper dress for a formal dining room in July. The uniforms were for effect because Jack and Paul would be recruiting the next day's entourage throughout the evening. Baer, was standing at the bar talking to two Navy lieutenant commanders. Jeannie sat on a stool next to Paul. She politely interrupted to introduce Jack and Monique as they approached. Monique looked fantastic dressed like a flapper out of "The Great Gatsby" movie, and asked Jack to get her a "Cape Codder."

Jeannie knew of Jack by reputation, but had only briefly met him once, a year earlier. It was also a novelty for her to be socializing with a crony of Paul's who was a real live Republican. While Jeannie asked him a lot of probing questions over dinner, Jack began having a déjà-vu feeling as Monique began interrupting at every third sentence. Monique seemed pleased when Jack shifted the discussion to Monique's artistic creativity and the Rhode Island School of Design.

Most patrons in the dining room were senior officers except for a few lieutenants who appeared to be dining with their wives. Paul suggested spending a half hour in the lounge after dinner recruiting a few more senior officers for Eddie's entourage, before moving on to the Dat-um Club. Monique didn't have much to say to Jeannie. She finished off another Cape Codder while their two escorts buttonholed three Navy commanders and two Marine Corps majors.

When discussing the next day's events, Jack mentioned to the senior officers that former Navy Secretary John Chaffee was expected to join the President's party after greeting him, without mentioning that the former Republican Governor was now a U.S. Senate candidate. Likewise, Paul said nothing about partisan politics, only "Jeannie's boss' role" in greeting the President as a member of Rhode Island's Congressional delegation. They would follow this script with the junior officers who were expected to be at the Dat-um Club.

CHAPTER 15

Jack pulled over three times, responding to Monique's constant fondling, while driving the four miles to the popular night spot. Unlike the patrons who typically wore civilian clothes that late in the evening, Baer and Wilson remained in their uniforms to prompt two lead-in questions. "Why are you still in uniform so late?" and "What is the Army doing here?" Penny was actually there as a staffer, but they were just there on a pass from another duty station. They merely responded that they were helping out Paul's girlfriend, a Congressman's staff member, by "distributing passes to encourage military participation in the next day's historic patriotic events."

Things went very well from the time they arrived shortly before 9, until around 10:30. Three more Cape Codders brought out Monique's attention craving self-centeredness. To avoid a scene, Jack had to spend virtually the remainder of the evening either dancing with or catering to her. In addition to the drinks, insecurity prompted her behavior since they were encountering a good number of attractive, well educated female student officers in stylish civilian attire. Around 11:30 Jack begged off from Paul and Jeannie as he left with Monique.

Monique complained about being hungry. While driving to an off-base restaurant Jack thought "Hope she doesn't start off with Bloody Marys before breakfast!" To his great relief, Monica became gently affectionate during the drive back to their room. That evening, after driving in from T.F. Green Airport in Warwick, Russ Melton and Carol Chenworth check into the downtown Newport hotel where the Rhode Island Governor's party was staying.

The next morning nearly two dozen Navy and Marine Corps officers showed up in their dress whites, some with guests, at the officers club to meet Congressional staffer Penny for breakfast. Her two Army friends, Paul and Jack, were wearing their dress blues. They boarded a chartered bus that would take Eddie's entourage over to greet the President, on to Newport, and then, back to their cars at the officers' club parking lot later that afternoon.

Monique looking stunning as always, was pleasant enough. Jack had been taking a shower however, and didn't see Monique pour herself two Bloody Marys earlier in their room. At breakfast, she poured vodka into her tomato juice from a flask in her purse it didn't seem like a big deal to him. A good sized crowd greeted the President when he touched down at the base. Except for elected officials from the region most people were military and their dependents assigned to the base. The story about the disbarment of former President Nixon by New York, a reminder the pardon, received scant news coverage.

Congressman Beard rode the bus with his military guests to Trinity Church Square. He was accompanied by millionaire auto dealer Richard Lorber, who was challenging Noel in the primary. Seeing Eddie surrounded by his Naval escort, former Navy Secretary John Chafee, broke away from the area that had been roped off for the President's party to come over and shake hands with them. Gracious as always, the former Governor not only invited Eddie, but also Lorber, who potentially could be his November Democratic opponent, to join him so they could personally meet the Queen. The plan had more than succeeded!

Jack noticed that Monique suddenly seemed pale and woozy, so he discreetly walked her back to the bus. She nodded off on the bus while he went out to buy some 7 Up and a bag of potato chips for her. They spent nearly two hours on the bus until the Queen and President left to dine together privately on the Britannia. Ed Beard said good bye to the Naval officers before being driven away with Lorber by his aide, who had followed the bus over.

Paul, grinning broadly, walked to the back seat where Jack sat with Monique resting her head on his shoulder. Penny

CHAPTER 15

mentioned meeting Russ and Carol, a nice couple from Georgia that Tim Kennedy had introduced to them. Captain Kennedy was part of Noel's National Guard entourage and knew Paul and Jack from previous service together. He had invited the Georgia couple to go to the Dat-um club with him and his wife later that evening.

Jack passed on seeing the Presidential departure and brought Monique back to their room. Jack felt relieved. He stroked her hair gently as she stretched out under the covers on the bed after undressing. "You need to take a nap for a little while." Monique responded with a smile then and nodded off. Jack changed into a pair of shorts and a T-shirt and left for a walk. Jack could not deny that only Divine intervention had preempted an embarrassing scene. The highest level people who noticed anything unusual were Paul and Penny.

By the time Jack returned to their room an hour later, Monique had caught her second wind. After an hour of power drinking passion, they left for dinner at a small restaurant off the base. Both wore casual but tasteful clothes. She jabbed Jack playfully after he said "promise me we won't make tomorrow's front pages." Monique poured the shot of vodka that remained in her flask into the half glass of orange juice she drank while eating her cheeseburger.

They spotted Paul and Penny at a large table as soon as they walked in to the on-base night club. About eight of the junior officers from the day's events sat with them. Jack recognized and quickly shook hands with Tim Kennedy, who was sitting at the table next to theirs. They had never been close and had lost contact over three years ago. When Monique returned from the ladies room, her expression turned sour when she saw Jack engaging innocently in conversation with two of the female officers. He stood up and asked her to dance.

THE LONG COUNT

    Within an hour, Monique was sloppy drunk. Jack was interested in listening to the young ensigns describe the intelligence work, for which their school was preparing them. He smiled at a refined elegantly dressed young woman who was sitting with a guy at Tim's table. Carol Chenworth returned the smile but quickly looked away. Monique went to the ladies room after a childish attempt to make Jack jealous by dancing excessively close with a young ensign she had dragged onto the dance floor.

    Ten minutes later, Jack heard Monique's voice utter in a loud slurring rage "Don't talk that way to me bitch! I'm with Congressman Beard's party." After slithering quickly over to Monique, Jack discovered that the bartender had refused to serve her. He put his arm around Monique and began whispering flattering bullshit into her ear as he gently escorted her to the door. While driving away, Jack cringed behind the steering as she screamed her final obscenities.

    In the morning, as Jack carried their luggage to the car, he noticed the empty vodka bottle in the trash. It had been a full fifth when Monique unpacked Friday afternoon. "She was must have had a few Bloody Marys when I was in the shower yesterday morning," thought Jack. He then drove to the restaurant they were at the evening before. Over breakfast Monique said she was sorry for behaving so badly the previous night. She then gave a self-pitying rationalization "I know I'm just another duty girl to you and felt sad that we won't be seeing each other again."

    Jack gently responded "Monique, you're well on your way to becoming a successful commercial artist or fashion designer. You're way out of my league and don't need to be wasting your time with someone whose life is a crap shoot." She broke into a big smile after Jack said when she dropped him off "Sitting on a bus with the sexiest girl on Aquidnick Island was a bigger thrill than seeing some dumpy queen.

CHAPTER 15

Maybe someday I'll catch the brass ring and you'll hire me as your chauffer."

Ten minutes later, Paul pulled up in the Mercedes. "You weren't just smooth this weekend Jack, you were actually gallant!" said Jeannie, as he got into the back seat. For over an hour they shared some good laughs over coffee at the main club before Jeannie dropped them off to catch their helicopter back to Fort Drum. That evening Paul told Jack what a big deal it was for Jeannie to give anyone such a compliment. "Never thought I'd see the day when Jack Wilson wasn't the one getting the bums rush but doing the rushing!" On Tuesday evening Jack saw Paul off at the Watertown airport, where he caught his flight to La Guardia. The Democratic National Convention was starting Thursday at Madison Square Gardens.

16. HOLLOW FORCES AND LUSTING HEARTS

The Democrats were well postured when Congresswoman Barbara Jordan, an African American from Texas, delivered the keynote address to the convention delegates on July 12th. The country was still in a recession. Only two years earlier, the Watergate scandal had ended with the resignation of President Nixon in disgrace. Only President Ford's pardon had preempted certain indictment and criminal prosecution. Since 1953, the Democrats had only controlled the Presidency for 8 years. However, for over two decades they had dominated both house of Congress.

The primaries had already decided that Governor Jimmy Carter was the presumptive Democratic nominee. The main point of contention was over the 1976 rules themselves, which made it harder for women and blacks to challenge delegations where they felt under represented. Desiring to avoid a public debate over a minority report to change delegate selection rules, Carter forces met with representatives of a women's caucus. The Democratic Woman's Caucus agreed to avoid a floor fight by accepting a compromise. Party Rules for future conventions now mandated that state delegations would have an equal number of men and women.

Unlike the conventions of 1968 and 1972, divisive and dragged out credentials challenges and floor fights were thus avoided. During the roll call Carter was easily nominated by over two thirds of the delegates. Governor Jerry Brown and Congressman Morris Udall each received over 10 percent. The remaining five percent scattered among candidates who had withdrawn or favorite sons.

CHAPTER 16

On July 15th, Jimmy Carter gave a folksy upbeat acceptance speech during prime for millions of Americans to watch. The next night Carter's choice for Vice President, Senator Walter Mondale of Minnesota and a long time Humphrey protégé, received over 94 percent of the delegates. The Democrats then adjourned having achieved their objective of a unified front for a huge post-convention bump. Their nominee, Jimmy Carter, departed Madison Square Garden with a 33 point lead over President Ford.

The following week Jack listened as his mother read a copy of Army correspondence over the phone that had been forwarded from his previous address. "By direction of the President, Captain John P. Wilson, Infantry, is advanced, promoted and commissioned as a reserve officer of the Army under Title 10, U.S. Code". Jack said good bye on a cheerful note, assuming that the stand-by board had granted his appeal of the previous year's Passover, and promoted him retroactively. Jack anticipated a ceremony Thursday afternoon, followed by a long weekend in Massachusetts with Denise.

Jack opened the Federal Express envelope when it arrived at mid-morning on Wednesday. He took it in stride upon discovering that the promotion order from the Army's Adjutant General would not be effective until September 19th, two weeks after his tour ended. The real letdown occurred during Jack's call to Denise, who had made plans to go to Cape Cod with a girlfriend and would not be available until early Sunday afternoon. Thinking back to January, when they had started seeing each other again, and when Denise said "I've gotten rusty," Jack began feeling remorseful about Newport.

Jack decided to spend his remaining five weeks at Fort Drum without any more weekends back to New England. Although he had gotten to know some of the local girls who were regulars at the Watertown night spots, he hadn't dated any of them. There were no opportunities for any follow-on tours in September, so he needed to save money to tide himself over with until he found a job.

Jack kept up on current events by watching the evening news and reading the papers. On July 27th, an unexpected public health scare erupted. Four veterans who had attended an American Legion convention in Philadelphia from the 21st through the 24th died suddenly. By the first of August, six more had died. All of the veterans, ranging in ages from 39 through 82, had complained of tiredness, chest pains, lung congestion, and fever. The Center for Disease Control was baffled by this strange "Legionnaires' Disease" which ultimately caused 29 fatalities. It would take a year for the CDC to discover that it was a bacterium. Both the Reagan and Carter campaigns attempted to exploit this, even though the only connection to President Ford was that it had happened on his watch.

On August 4th the Soviets conducted a nuclear test. That Saturday afternoon, Jack ran into his friend from Massachusetts, Captain George Donovan, while watching the news at the officers club. The U.S. Viking 2 had just gone into Martian orbit after an 11 month flight. Scientists in Pasadena also announced that Viking 1 had found the strongest indications of possible life on Mars to date. George was looking forward to going to the GOP convention as a Reagan alternate on the 15th. After leaving to meet some officers from his unit, he gave Jack the number of his Kansas City hotel, and some contacts to pursue for joining the Massachusetts Guard in September.

The following week Jack found it odd that George never contacted him again, and that even his unit wouldn't provide information about his status. Jack resigned himself to having to rely exclusively on the TV networks and daily papers to keep up on GOP convention events. On August 12th, the Christian militia operating in the Golan Heights defeated a

CHAPTER 16

Palestinian base camp at al-Za'tar, killing 2,000. The following day the South African apartheid government pledged support for a negotiated settlement in white-ruled Rhodesia.

When the Republican National Convention delegates convened on August 16th, those still uncommitted were estimated at between 93 and 115. Although the President had won more primaries and over 800,000 more popular votes cast than Governor Reagan, the nomination could still go to either one. Prior to arriving at the convention, Reagan made a bold unprecedented move. He announced that if he was nominated, Pennsylvania's moderately liberal U.S. Senator, Richard Schweiker, would be his selection as Vice President.

Rather than drawing moderates and centrists as Reagan had intended however, the move backfired. Reagan's staunch conservative supporters were infuriated by his choice of the "liberal Schweiker." North Carolina's U.S. Senator Jesse Helms even initiated a movement to draft New York's GOP U.S. Senator James L. Buckley, who had originally been elected running as New York's Conservative third party nominee, as an alternative to Reagan. The Schweiker announcement did, however, generate a vote to test each candidate's relative delegate strengths.

During the first evening of the convention, Reagan's floor managers offered a rules change that would have required all candidates to name their Vice Presidential choices prior to the balloting for the Presidential nominee. Their objective was to draw additional delegates to Reagan from one of the GOP factions disgruntled by Ford's choice. The President's convention operatives succeeded in defeating the proposed rules change by a vote of 1,180 to 1,069, after sarcastically dubbing it the "misery loves company" resolution. The next evening, Ford was nominated on the first ballot by a vote of 1187 to 1070. Former Attorney General Elliot Richardson received one vote. In his acceptance speech Ford confidently challenged Carter to a series of debates. These would be the first TV debates since 1960, and the first ever with a sitting President against a challenger.

The following evening, nearly 95 percent of the delegates approved the President's choice of Kansas Senator Robert Dole as his running mate. The selection of Dole, a solid midwestern establishment conservative, who had survived the '74 Democratic mid-term landslide, reflected considerable deliberation by Ford. Dole, a highly decorated combat wounded World War II veteran, was known for his acerbic wit. However, five percent of the hard core Reagan delegates scattered their votes among 30 people, including Senator Jesse Helms. Reagan delivered a brief, eloquent and gracious address prior to the President's acceptance, which included a debate challenge to Jimmy Carter.

Historians will always debate whether the Schweiker gambit cost Reagan the nomination. Nonetheless, he had electrified the convention. Coming within 70 votes of capturing the nomination from a sitting President, he had made it one hell of a race. More importantly, Reagan had inspired a generation of younger conservatives to become active in politics. These included Bob Smith, a New Hampshire History teacher, and Duncan Hunter, who had recently started to practice law in Southern California. Both were to become leading Congressional defense hawks in the 80s and 90s.

It had been three years since the draft had ended with the advent of the all volunteer force. One mid-afternoon Jack Wilson was performing duties as an observer-controller of a live fire platoon attack exercise. The parent company was from the New York National Guard's 1st Battalion of the 69th Infantry of the 42nd "Rainbow" Division. During World War I the Division was made famous by luminaries like Brigadier General Douglas MacArthur, its chief of staff and later a brigade commander, and by Lt. Colonel William

CHAPTER 16

"Wild Bill" Donovan and Father Francis Duffy, the battalion commander and the chaplain respectively, of the "Fighting 69th."

Historically, the "Fighting 69th" had been comprised predominantly of Irish Americans. However, Jack noticed several distinct changes since his last contact with that organization just two years earlier. The ranks which had been predominantly white, now seemed to reflect the diversity of New York City with significant numbers of Puerto Rican and African American troops. "A good thing" thought Jack, since during the sixties Guard and Reserve units had received attention for lagging decades behind the fully integrated active forces.

A company commander got Jack's attention after he had asked when his other two rifle platoons would conduct the exercise. "That's all I've got. Out of 150 authorized, my strength is 70. I have 10 new people away at basic and advanced individual training, so only 60 are here, counting me. The mortar platoon is a matrix unit assembled from elements of all three of the battalion's rifle companies." This response made Jack recall Reagan's allusion to a "hollow force" in his criticisms of Ford's military policies, especially under Defense Secretary Donald Rumsfeld.

The term "hollow force" characterized military forces that appeared on the surface to be mission capable. However, closer examination indicated major shortages in personnel, equipment, and maintenance. Cuts in funding also resulted in major training deficiencies. Without the draft as a motivator, all of the services were experiencing problems meeting their recruiting objectives, even with the major pay and benefits increases for entry level personnel. Attracting the best and the brightest to fill officer training programs and highly skilled technical specialties became an exceptionally difficult challenge.

Personnel challenges were compounded within units of the reserve forces. During the sixties, they had enjoyed ranks filled with large numbers of part time soldiers who were college educated or highly skilled and predominantly white. Many of their families also had connections that enabled them to jump the long waiting lists from which units filled their vacancies. During the Vietnam force buildup, the Johnson Administration made the deliberate decision not to mobilize guard and reserve units for that conflict.

Reserve component units had instead been designated as a strategic reserve for reinforcing forward deployed forces in Europe in the event of a Soviet invasion. Consequently, well educated and skilled youth viewed service in the guard or reserve as a far better option than being drafted or enlisting for two to three years. They completed their service obligations with 6 months of active duty for training, followed by five and a half years of training with their reserve or guard units one weekend each month and two weeks every summer.

When the draft-motivated enlistments started expiring in 1973, units were fortunate if they could replace three or four separations with one new enlistment. Because minorities had just begun entering the reserve components in large numbers, senior ranks were mostly held by whites. This created a false perception of disparate treatment to an outsider. Most of the officers and seasoned senior sergeants in the battalion Jack was evaluating were white, with many coming from the ranks of New York City's police and municipal employees. The captain who commanded the company Jack was observing, was a Vietnam veteran of Puerto Rican ancestry. Recruiting combat experienced minorities, and encouraging applications of new minority enlistees for officer and non-commissioned officer training programs, would eventually resolve the imbalance.

CHAPTER 16

The day following Ford's nomination, an incident occurred in Korea with real potential for triggering a major armed conflict. The Korean War had ended with an armed truce in July, 1953. Since then, senior military representatives of the United States, Peoples Republic of China, North and South Korea met regularly at the truce village of Panmunjom, designated as a Joint Security Area (JSA). They typically discussed and resolved incidents and armistice compliance issues. The JSA straddles the North and South Korean border in the center of the five kilometer wide demilitarized zone. Under terms of the armistice, the North Koreans and United Nations forces led by the United States and South Korea, maintained small units there.

On the afternoon of August 18th, an American and South Korean work detail was trimming branches from a poplar tree that blocked observation. Captain Arthur Bonifas, the American commander, ignored a North Korean lieutenant's harassing threats which were routine within the JSA. Suddenly the North Koreans attacked, wielding crowbars, pipes, clubs and axes. Knowing that American troops required orders from their officers to fire their weapons, they quickly beat Captain Bonifas and his deputy, 1st Lieutenant Mark Barrett, to death. In less than 10 minutes it was over, and the North Koreans gone.

Within hours, an appropriate response was being developed and debated at the highest levels of the United States and South Korean governments. On August 21st, three days after the murders, "Operation Paul Bunyan" was launched as show of force, deliberately calculated not to escalate into an all out war. Three B-52 bombers and 27 heavily armed helicopters flew over the JSA as a convoy of 23 vehicles carrying 110 American and South Korean troops entered and then stopped at the site where Captain Bonifas and Lieutenant Barrett had been killed.

HOLLOW FORCES AND LUSTING HEARTS

The entire poplar tree was cut down and hauled away as 150 North Korean troops observed for 42 minutes doing nothing. The intimidation tactic worked, backing down the North Koreans. Jimmy Carter essentially deferred to the Administration. "At least the readiness of America's land power hasn't deteriorated to the point of not being able to beat a third rate power" thought Jack, "at least not yet. Wonder what the outcome of the GOP convention would have been if this had happened two weeks sooner?" On August 28th the Soviets performed another nuclear test.

Jack had returned to Massachusetts after finishing his active duty tour. The engine of his 1968 Volkswagen seized up near Syracuse. Fortunately he was towed to a garage that worked on used VWs. The owner agreed to swap Jack even for a 1966. It was mechanically sound, but had electrical problems and front fenders attached to the frame by coat hanger splices.

By Labor Day the President had somewhat recovered, but was still 15 points behind Carter in the polls. Vice President Rockefeller gained some notoriety while on a campaign swing with Bob Dole through upstate New York on Sept 16th. In an almost instantaneous response to someone in a group of heckling leftie State University of New York at Binghamton students, Rocky gave the obscene middle finger gesture right back. The photo that made most major newspapers showed an obviously pleased Dole in the background. According to the William Norton Smith biography of Rockefeller, he was giving out autographed pictures of that picture until he was finally persuaded it was beneath the dignity of the Vice Presidential office to do so.

In Rhode Island, Congressman Ed Beard trounced his establishment challenger in the Democratic primary. The bigger surprise was watching Governor Noel acknowledge his defeat by Richard Lorber, Beard's primary running mate. "John Chafee will blow him away like last year's leaves" uttered Noel bitterly during a TV press conference.

CHAPTER 16

Several days before the effective date of his reserve promotion, Jack called Denise even though he had made no effort to contact her since late July. She congratulated him, but was not available to celebrate. He then called Paul Baer who met him at the Dat-um club in Newport the following Saturday evening. The student officers who had participated with them in the July Presidential visit had all moved on.

With both wearing civilian clothes, Paul pinned on Jack's railroad tracks in an impromptu ceremony. For the benefit of three cute female ensigns sitting at a nearby table, Baer boisterously read the promotion orders signed by a brigadier general. After several hours of rowdy drinking, the bartender shut them off. The girls declined their invitation for a midnight breakfast, so Paul drove Jack back to his car in Providence. After a 2:00 A.M. breakfast the two parted company.

Shortly before leaving for a second shift foreman's job in an auto parts warehouse he had recently started, Jack received a call from a Massachusetts National Guard infantry brigade two weeks after he had called the contacts George Donavan had provided. Two days later, he arrived at the Lexington armory for an interview, wearing civilian clothes as directed. Two majors, who were considerably older than their active duty counterparts, introduced themselves as Jack entered the conference room.

Neither one of the two majors reacted when Jack mentioned Captain Donovan's referral. Neither did Jack react when both frequently predicated their remarks with "if you're accepted" when they described, but considerably understated, some of the challenges units were experiencing. Jack by now had mastered reserve component officer personnel policies better than many human resources types. Even though by statute, the Commonwealth had to appoint him as a captain if they accepted him, the states controlled the

HOLLOW FORCES AND LUSTING HEARTS

Guard and were free to reject him. "Thank you Captain, you'll be hearing from us" said one of the majors as the interview ended. With October approaching, Jack began submitting substitute teaching applications to the surrounding school systems.

Carter continued projecting himself in the general election, as he had in the primaries, as a reform minded former Governor and Washington outsider. His core leadership group dubbed the "Peanut Brigade" received heavy media attention as it crisscrossed the country. Leading members was his mother "Miss Lillian" and his colorful younger brother Billy, who came across as a beer drinking good ol' boy. The Carter Campaign was also aided by concerts hosted by the popular Allman Brothers and Marshall Tucker bands.

Carter's green colored media background portrayed the image of a simple, hard working peanut farmer. Carter's TV ads reminded Jack of a 1970 rebuttal ad that his gubernatorial primary opponent former Governor Carl Sanders had run. It convincingly exposed the Carter myth that he had pulled himself up by the bootstraps after coming from a poor farmer's family.

On September 23rd, the President finally rebounded. During their first televised Presidential debate in Philadelphia, watched by an estimated audience of 69 million, Ford demonstrated a mastery of the issues. Carter's vagueness underscored Ford's charges that he lacked the background and experience needed by an effective national leader. By the first week of October, the President was no longer on the ropes and polling only two points behind Carter.

The Ford surge was soon halted however, during the second televised debate in San Francisco on October 6th. The President stumbled badly when he declared that "There is no Soviet domination of Eastern Europe," an assertion he

CHAPTER 16

elaborated upon when moderators, assuming he had misspoken, questioned him again. On October 13th, the U.S. Civil Rights Commission released a report indicating that the Puerto Rican poverty rate in the Continental United States was, at 33 percent, the highest of all racial and ethnic groups in the country.

The Republican ticket took another blow the following week during the first ever Vice Presidential debate. Senator Robert Dole asserted that needless casualties roughly equal to the population of Detroit in "Democrat wars from World War I to Vietnam" had been caused by the unpreparedness of Democratic Presidents. The media immediately seized upon Senator Walter Mondale's response that he had earned his "hatchet man moniker" to portray Dole as mean and heartless. Carter's lead had increased by 7 points.

Governor Carter's moderate image masked the platform the Democratic Convention had adopted that advocated very liberal progressive social initiatives. His sincere evangelical Christianity, expressed as "born again" at that time, made many secular elements uneasy. Defections to former Senator Eugene McCarthy's third party candidacy could very easily tip closely contested states to Ford. To ease their concerns, Carter gave an interview to Playboy Magazine. He assured readers that they need not fear an initiative to legislate Carter's religious views on sexual conduct. He then attempted to find common ground by explaining the Christian position that all sin is equally offensive to God. Specifically addressing sexual sin, Carter admitted that he had often sinned by "lusting in his heart" for women besides his wife, and so was therefore in no position to judge anybody who "screws a lot of women."

The November issue of Playboy, which was not scheduled for release until the end of October, hit the newsstands almost immediately. Moderately conservative voters and especially women, who had been leaning to Carter, began defecting.

HOLLOW FORCES AND LUSTING HEARTS

Less than two weeks before Election Day, the race was too close to call.

At the same time the public learned that Jimmy "lusted in his heart," Ronald Reagan ramped up his activities, actively mobilizing the GOP conservative base for Ford. Reagan's TV ads contrasting the Ford and Carter national security positions were highly effective. Carter countered with his endorsement by hawkish former Defense Secretary James Schlesinger, who Ford had fired and replaced with Donald Rumsfeld. On October 21st, the Cincinnati Reds won the World Series over the New York Yankees in four games. The President seized upon the opportunity to tap into sports fans with a series of joint appearances and TV ads with retired baseball star catcher Joe Garagiola, that ran through election eve.

The Constitutionally prescribed "first Tuesday after the first Monday of November" fell on the 2nd. Although Carter maintained his early lead in the national popular vote throughout the evening, the results in the states that would determine the decisive Electoral College majority were not decided until 3:30 in the morning on the east coast. When the networks called Mississippi, Jimmy Carter had secured the majority of electoral votes needed to become the first President elected from the Deep South since 1848.

President-elect Carter, surrounded by his family and supporters in Plains, Georgia, gave a brief and gracious victory statement. The White House reported that Ford had already gone to bed shortly after 1:00 A.M. When all the votes were tallied Carter had won 297 electoral votes to Ford's 241. Carter also had won a bare 50.08 percent majority of the popular vote, polling 1.7 million more votes than Ford, whose percentage was 48.2. Slightly less than two percent scattered among minor party candidates. One unfaithful Republican elector from Washington eventually cast his vote for Reagan.

CHAPTER 16

A 4:30 AM phone call woke up Carol Chenworth in her DuPont Circle apartment in D.C. "Did you see me on NBC news during President Carter's victory speech?" Russ Melton asked her. He would be coming up for the inauguration, most likely with his parents. Russ still had not penetrated the inner circle of Hamilton Jordan and Jody Powell so he didn't speculate about a possible Administration job. Too tired to start thinking about a dress for the Inaugural Ball, Carol quickly fell back to sleep after the call ended.

At mid-morning, First Lady Betty Ford read the concession telegram while standing next to the President, who had worn out his voice making campaign speeches. Nobody could really fault him for the delayed concession. A shift to Ford of 5,559 votes in Ohio, and 3,687 in Hawaii, would have been enough to keep him in office with 270 electoral votes. In spite of the overwhelming odds against him, Jerry Ford had nearly pulled off a miracle. He had carried 27 states, including California largely through Reagan's efforts. Ford's strong finish was even more remarkable because it occurred with the Democrats simultaneously retaining their lopsided House and Senate majorities. The headline of a Time Magazine election edition editorial "In the end, decency wasn't enough" was a fitting political epitaph.

Ten days after the election a Congressional scandal broke. Over 90 members were implicated in a scandal involving illegal gifts they had accepted from Tong sun Park, a businessman and agent of the South Korean government. The roots of the scandal were in Nixon's decision to make substantial cuts to the U.S. military troops stationed in the Republic of Korea (ROK). The incumbent ROK President at the time was Park Chung Hee, the first of a series of military strongmen who governed the country from Syng-man Rhee's overthrow in 1961 until the mid 1980s. Park's objectives, by working the Congress controlled by the opposition party, were to preserve the remaining U.S. military presence, secure substantial U.S. funding for the ROK's military modernization program, and to counter increasing criticism of Park's crack down on political and civil liberties.

During the Cold War, it was common policy for U.S. Administrations of both parties to supported non-communist friendly autocrats as a more desirable alternative. Typical examples were the Shah of Iran, the Franco regime in Spain, King Faisal of Saudi Arabia and military regimes in Turkey, Greece, and numerous Latin American countries. The scandalous aspect of "Koreagate" was that commissions from American rice sales to the ROK were being shared with those facilitating favorable decisions.

Just prior to Thanksgiving, Jack received an unexpected package in the mail. It was a commission signed by Governor Michael S. Dukakis, appointing him as a captain in the Organized Militia of the Commonwealth of Massachusetts. Also enclosed was a copy of orders in standard military language announcing his National Guard appointment and assignment as the air operations officer of the 26th Infantry Division's mechanized infantry battalion. The extra money would enable him to upgrade to a better apartment and make some much needed repairs on his 1966 Volkswagen.

Jack's December training assembly was a real eye opener for him. He learned that a little more than a year earlier, the battalion had undergone a major reorganization. The headquarters and two of the rifle companies had previously been a Corps-level engineer organization. The heavy weapons company had been a heavy truck company. The next day during a staff visit to the only rifle company that had always been an infantry unit, he met Don Levy, the unit commander. Don had previously been the company executive officer under Captain George Donovan. He then described George's recent misadventures to Jack.

CHAPTER 16

One early morning the previous summer, when George was leaving a diner in Watertown with some fellow brigade staff officers, a truck had been left running that blocked their car. When George couldn't find the driver inside, he got into the truck intending to move it a few spaces so they could get out. Suddenly a man came running towards him waving a club in his hand. As George drove the truck around the block the police stopped and arrested him for grand theft auto, but the charges were eventually dropped.

The local Watertown newspaper that owned the truck however, discovered that George was a local Massachusetts elected official and sent a release to his hometown paper. A member of George's unit, who didn't like him, saw the article and mailed it to the commanding general. The general was outraged and began relentlessly pursuing his elimination. After receiving a totally baseless career-killing evaluation, Captain Donovan demanded a Court of Honor under a little known state military statute. George successfully argued his case and was subsequently reassigned to the state headquarters training directorate.

Understanding now why George had never gotten back to him at Camp Drum, Jack called him later that evening. George explained how his Watertown court appearance had caused him to miss the GOP convention. He then went on to candidly describe Jack's new military command. George explained that probably 85 percent of the 26th Infantry Division's infantry officers above the rank of major had never served on active duty other than for training. Fewer than half had even gone through resident courses at Fort Benning. They had re-qualified as infantry officers on paper by completing correspondence courses, "probably after copying the answers from someone else."

George then described how the two star division commander, although a highly decorated World War II combat veteran, made no secret of his hostility to Vietnam experienced officers. "He much prefers pliable graduates of the state's OCS program." Donovan went on to describe how almost to a man, the senior officers and commander of his former brigade fabricated non-existent incidents to justify a career-killing efficiency report on him. George laughingly described how the colonel broke down under oath during his Court of Honor, admitting that he had succumbed to pressure from the general after the Watertown charges had been dismissed. Donovan's take on the reorganization was "The incompetent trough-swilling Massachusetts swine bureaucrats in uniform gave up the engineering and transportation units because naturally, there were more senior officer positions in the division they're attempting to save."

The two then caught up on political developments that had transpired since August. Although George had been a Reagan supporter, he too was sorry to see Ford go. After the Playboy interview neither one was really worried about President-elect Carter establishing a morality police. James Schlesinger was returning to the cabinet, but as the Secretary of Energy, not Defense as Jack had hoped. They were both disappointed by the appointment of Cyrus Vance as Secretary of State. "We can kiss the Panama Canal good bye" said Jack. George elaborated on his memories of Vance as a lack luster Deputy Secretary of Defense and a weak special envoy for LBJ during the 1968 Pueblo crisis. George concurred with Jack's view of Harold Brown's appointment as Secretary of Defense as potentially laying the groundwork for a second wave of "McNamara's whiz kids." Brown, a former Secretary of the Air Force, was an arms control expert who had earned a PhD in physics at the age of 21 and had been a protégé of Edward Teller.

Most of the media attention now focused on Jimmy Carter, who established the Blair House as the President-elect's official transit residence by operating out of there during his visits to Washington. The outgoing Ford Administration was

CHAPTER 16

still functioning, however. One year earlier, the President had signed an omnibus energy bill. It was a compromise that accepted a 12-percent reduction in domestic oil prices in return for authority to end price controls on oil over a forty-month period. The U.S. economy remained dependent upon 35 percent of its oil from foreign sources, making it extremely vulnerable to embargos like OPEC's after the 1973 Yom Kippur War.

On December 15th, the Ford Energy Department announced plans to store up to 500 million barrels of crude oil in the salt dunes on the Gulf Coast. On New Year's Eve, the President proposed statehood for the U.S. Commonwealth of Puerto Rico. This was widely viewed as a desperate attempt by Ford to remain relevant as he had not consulted Congress before hand. Other critics contended that statehood was an issue for the Puerto Rican people to decide. On that same day, mixed economic news indicated that inflation was holding steady at 4.8 percent, but that unemployment remained high at 7.8 percent.

On January 9th at the Rose Bowl in Pasadena, the Oakland Raiders won Super Bowl XI, beating the Minnesota Vikings 31 to 14. On the 12th, President Ford delivered an upbeat final state of the union address to Congress. He expressed optimism for an eventual peace settlement between Israel and its Arab neighbors in the Middle East, and emphasized the imperative for maintaining an edge in the strategic balance between the United States and its allies and the Soviet bloc. On the 17th, convicted murderer Gary Gilmore, who had rejected further appeals, was executed by a Utah state prison firing squad. This ended a 10 year hiatus on capital punishment in the country.

The uneasy peace of the bi-polar standoff between the two superpowers continued. The Soviet Army Group headquarters in Wittenberg, East Germany, had 22 heavily armored divisions available, with supporting air power and tactical nuclear weapons, to invade the West through the "Fulda Gap." Although massive Red Army formations were no longer stationed within other Eastern European countries, the Soviet Union still dominated them. Within hours, forces could quickly be projected from nearby border regions of the USSR to suppress any movements resembling the Prague Spring of 1968.

At noon, on a cold, icy January 20th, Russ Melton, his parents and Carol Chenworth watched from a good vantage point within the roped off area on the Capitol lawn less than 100 feet from the platform where James Earl Carter took the oath of office as the 39th President on the family Bible. The new President graciously began his inaugural address with "For myself and for our Nation, I want to thank my predecessor for all he has done to heal our land." This drew extended applause. To symbolize a new era of a Presidency accessible to the people, the President, First Lady Rosalynn Carter and their 8 year old daughter Amy, walked the mile and a half from the Capitol to the White House.

After an excessively long time catching a cab, Russ and Carol arrived at the D.C. Armory for the first of two inaugural balls they would attend. The traditional location was mobbed as they looked at the President's mother, Miss Lillian, waving to the crowd from a balcony. They had an easier time hailing a taxi to the second Ball at the Shoreham, where they met Russ' parents. Carol half expected the President's brief exchange with Russ, since the two had visited the Governor's Association together. She was surprised however, that Billy Carter seemed to know Russ quite well, during their conversation that lasted nearly ten minutes.

Jack watched the inaugural events on TV through Ford's departure from the Capitol by helicopter. Jack had accepted the results and of the election. As he drove to work from his new apartment in Weymouth, his thoughts were that the new

CHAPTER 16

President indeed deserved a fair chance. Jack's primary political interests had always been foreign policy and national security. The worst Jack expected from the Democratic victory was that they would likely spend money like drunken sailors on domestic programs. "How bad could it be with an Annapolis graduate in charge?" The next day, Jack felt like he had taken a punch to the solar plexus. "Looks like Bob Dole was right" thought Jack, "this guy really is a Southern fried McGovern."

On President Carter's first full day in office, he announced a full and unconditional pardon for up to two thousand men who had avoided the draft, by fleeing to Canada and other foreign countries. It excluded only those who had deserted while serving in the Armed forces, and civilians who had engaged in acts of violence. True, a majority of younger Vietnam veterans had never wanted to serve there. However, few felt ashamed for doing their duty, and all still mourned for their comrades who did not come home alive. Ford's conditional "work your way back amnesty" was more than fair. It didn't place this small minority on a pedestal above the millions who answered their nation's call, but more importantly, it didn't dishonor the memories of those who made the ultimate sacrifice.

ABOUT THE AUTHOR

Chuck Winn, a retired Army Colonel, is a native of Grand Rapids, Michigan. He graduated from high school in Coventry, Rhode Island and attended college for a year before being drafted in 1968. After serving briefly as an acting sergeant, he was commissioned from OCS at Fort Benning in 1969, and then served in Vietnam as an advisor to South Vietnamese irregular units. He left active duty and remained in the National Guard while attending Rhode Island College on the GI Bill. Chuck was also a legislative aide and politically active while earning a B.A. in Political Science and History. He subsequently served with the Massachusetts National Guard's full time force for six years before reentering active duty. Chuck held numerous infantry company command and battalion intelligence and operational staff assignments, and was the Commandant of Cadets at Tuskegee University during the 1980s. His assignments as a strategic planner in the Pentagon included Headquarters, Department of the Army and the Office of the Secretary of Defense. For two and a half years he served with the U.S. Forces Korea Headquarters in Seoul. He holds a Masters Degree from Troy University and is a graduate of the U.S. Army War College. Chuck is a member of the U.S. Army Officer Candidate School Hall of Fame and the Phi Alpha Theta Historical Honor Society. Chuck lives with his wife, the former Lynn Carol Scott, in Stuart. They met in Washington, DC, where Lynn had a career as an association executive. Since the military, Chuck has been a member of the political organizations of several state-wide federal and Congressional campaigns in Florida.

Made in the USA
Lexington, KY
12 August 2019